W9-AXS-895

Just like that, Vivian knew.

She could give her heart to a cowboy like Josh Sloan, if she let her heart jump first. If she let her heart take the lead. But the risk wasn't worth the inevitable hurt. Because when it came to love, there was no ribbon for a second-place finish. Nothing to celebrate. And Vivian needed wins now more than ever.

And something about her cowboy told her she didn't have enough grit to recover from his kind of heartbreak.

It was all a pretense anyway.

That perfect fit of their hands. *Pretend.*

That hit of awareness. *Pretend.*

Even that hint of a connection. *Pretend, too.*

Vivian loosened her hold and let her fingers slip free from her cowboy's. After all, Vivian certainly had enough grit to keep from falling for a fantasy, didn't she?

Dear Reader,

I have a big family that's spread from coast to coast. Despite the distance, we are very close-knit. One of my favorite things is when our entire family gets together. It's a week of eating too much, laughing too hard and enjoying each other's company. When we gather for the holidays, well, that just levels up the fun and reminds us how blessed we are to have each other.

In *His Christmas Cowgirl*, professional barrel racer Vivian Bryant has been doing things on her own for years. And horse trainer Josh Sloan is the same. But thanks to their families, this strong-minded cowgirl and this stubborn cowboy just might find that standing together is much better than standing alone.

It's Christmas in Three Springs, Texas, where the hot chocolate is served sweet, the Christmas carols are set on repeat and there's always room around the Christmas tree. So, slip on your favorite holiday sweater and join the fun.

I love to connect with readers. Check out my website carilynnwebb.com or chat with me on Facebook (carilynnwebb) or Twitter (@carilynnwebb).

Happy reading!

Cari Lynn Webb

HEARTWARMING

His Christmas Cowgirl

Cari Lynn Webb

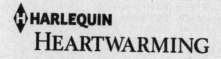

HARLEQUIN
HEARTWARMING

If you purchased this book without a cover you should be aware that this book is stolen property. It was reported as "unsold and destroyed" to the publisher, and neither the author nor the publisher has received any payment for this "stripped book."

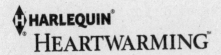

**HARLEQUIN®
HEARTWARMING™**

ISBN-13: 978-1-335-47551-0

Recycling programs
for this product may
not exist in your area.

His Christmas Cowgirl

Copyright © 2023 by Cari Lynn Webb

All rights reserved. No part of this book may be used or reproduced in any manner whatsoever without written permission except in the case of brief quotations embodied in critical articles and reviews.

This is a work of fiction. Names, characters, places and incidents are either the product of the author's imagination or are used fictitiously. Any resemblance to actual persons, living or dead, businesses, companies, events or locales is entirely coincidental.

For questions and comments about the quality of this book, please contact us at CustomerService@Harlequin.com.

Harlequin Enterprises ULC
22 Adelaide St. West, 41st Floor
Toronto, Ontario M5H 4E3, Canada
www.Harlequin.com

Printed in U.S.A.

Cari Lynn Webb lives in South Carolina with her husband, daughters and assorted four-legged family members. She's been blessed to see the power of true love in her grandparents' seventy-year marriage and her parents' marriage of over fifty years. She knows love isn't always sweet and perfect—it can be challenging, complicated and risky. But she believes happily-ever-afters are worth fighting for. She loves to connect with readers.

Books by Cari Lynn Webb

Harlequin Heartwarming

Three Springs, Texas

The Texas SEAL's Surprise
Trusting the Rancher with Christmas
Her Cowboy Wedding Date
Falling for the Cowboy Doc

Return of the Blackwell Brothers

The Rancher's Rescue

The Blackwell Sisters

Montana Wedding

The Blackwells of Eagle Springs

Her Favorite Wyoming Sheriff

Visit the Author Profile page
at Harlequin.com for more titles.

To friends past and present.
You all made an impact on my life. I'm better for your friendship. Thank you for the memories.

Special thanks to my writing group for their advice and steady support. To my husband and family for listening to every plot problem and character detail and continuously cheering me on through all of it.

CHAPTER ONE

"THIS IS AN appropriate time to discuss retirement," Dr. Caslin said.

Retirement. Vivian Bryant wanted to cover her quarter horse's ears and yell "blasphemy!" at the on-site veterinarian for the Oklahoma City Rodeo Roundup. Instead, Vivian smoothed her fingers through her competition horse's light brown mane, silently assuring him that she had his back, then she worked to set the veterinarian straight. "Dusty is only fourteen years old. He's in his equestrian prime."

Not to mention Dusty still had the desire to race. And a drive to win in the arena, which often outmatched Vivian's. Dusty loved competing. At least, he always had, until this weekend when he'd started favoring his leg. Vivian curved her arm around Dusty's neck and whispered words meant to comfort them both.

"Unfortunately, his arthritis is aging him and putting him at risk for serious injuries. And now he has a definite ligament problem."

Dr. Caslin continued examining Dusty's right foreleg. "I know this is hard to hear, Vivian."

It was impossible to hear. Dusty was more than Vivian's competition horse. He was her teammate. Her barrel racing partner for the past ten years. At times, on the road, her only companion. A high school graduation present from Vivian's grandmother, Dusty was now Vivian's last link to her late relative. Thanks to her beloved horse, Vivian had found the courage to keep chasing her dream like she'd promised her grandmother she would always do. And that dream was finally within her grasp.

"Sure, we had a few slow starts these past weeks. But that was on me and my nerves. Dusty is always steady. Always ready." And always the first one to calm Vivian, in the arena and out. Dusty nudged her shoulder as if sensing Vivian's growing unease.

"How were your runs this weekend specifically?" Dr. Caslin shifted to examine Dusty's left foreleg before glancing up at Vivian. Her gaze clear and direct. "Did he take the first barrel too wide? Decrease his speed?"

Yes. And yes. Vivian hugged Dusty tighter. Her fingers tangled in his mane. Had she pushed him too hard? Let down her teammate who never dropped her in the arena. No matter the conditions, Dusty always kept his legs under him and protected Vivian in the saddle. In return, she was supposed to protect him when she was out of it. She'd noted his subtle changes for a while. Nothing obvious. Nothing she could pinpoint on the ground. *Oh man.* She'd failed him. All in her quest to be better. Faster. Sooner. All in her bid to make her own selfish dream come true. Vivian inhaled a shaky breath and pulled herself together.

"His hooves are bruised too." Dr. Caslin stood and ran her hand over Dusty's muscular hindquarters.

"What are his best treatment options?" Vivian asked. Beside her, Dusty's ears twitched backward, and he stomped his back leg as if he wanted to prove he was more than fine. More than ready to compete.

Or perhaps that was Vivian and her own wishful thinking. *Please. He's all I've got.*

"Dusty needs rest and ice baths for his bruised hooves. Therapy for his current ligament injury." Dr. Caslin stepped closer to Vivian. Her stiff, clinical approach softened along with her words. "Then we need to discuss long-term plans for his arthritis and his retirement options."

There was that word again. *Retire. Dusty?* That was like asking Vivian to set aside a part of herself. One of the best parts of herself. More than that, Dusty was the better half of their barrel racing team. During their practice sessions, Vivian would right each tipped barrel and find Dusty already back at the start. Ready to run again. His determination spurred Vivian not to give up, despite the losses and frustrations that came with the sport.

Even more, Dusty liked the challenge. And he liked to win. Vivian was counting on his fighting spirit and confidence for the last rodeo of the year. Where winning would prove to her family that the rodeo was exactly where Vivian and Dusty were meant to be. Where they truly belonged.

"You know Dusty would make an ideal stablemate for a young gelding." Dr. Caslin snapped her portable medical bag closed and stroked her hand over Dusty's neck. "He could travel with you to keep your new competition horse calm and you'd still be together."

Again, Vivian wanted to cover Dusty's ears and assure her horse she wasn't replacing him. Not turning him into a companion horse, along for the ride and not allowed into the real show. Never mind that Vivian lacked the funds to simply purchase a new competition horse, not to mention cover the costs of caring for two horses on the road. Vivian cleared her throat.

"We were supposed to ride in the Silk and Steel Cowgirl Stampede in two weeks."

"I know this is difficult, but we can't risk injuring him further." Dr. Caslin touched Vivian's arm. Compassion curved across her face. "You can compete in the stampede, but not with Dusty."

But how was she supposed to do that? Vivian had learned to barrel race on Dusty in college. Vivian and Dusty had moved from practice arenas to amateur competitions and finally to the professional circuit. They'd run every single race as a team. They'd crossed state lines, county lines and finish lines together. Vivian didn't know *how* to compete without her trusted horse leading her. Dusty nuzzled her hand until her fingers relaxed. The same as he'd been doing for years whenever Vivian was too tense and needed reassurance.

"I'd like Dusty to board at my place here in town for the next week," Dr. Caslin said. Her words were resolute. "That way I can oversee his therapy myself. Then we can reassess."

Now Vivian needed to leave him too. What if he needed her? What if she needed…? Vivian leaned into Dusty's side and wanted to hang on. But the experienced veterinarian had one of the top equestrian rehab facilities in the area. His care would be above anything Vivian could provide at her campsite. Her horse—her teammate—and his care came first. No matter how much it hurt. Finally, Vivian managed a small nod.

It took almost an hour to get Dusty loaded into Dr. Caslin's trailer. Not because of the horse's injury. But rather Vivian's lengthy instructions from the shavings Dusty preferred in his stall to his favorite feed blend. Then she had to explain if he pawed the trailer, he wasn't being contrary. He just wanted a drink, and that led to even more insider tips. Twice Vivian wanted to concede and tell the patient veterinarian it would be best for everyone if Vivian simply came along and slept in the stall with Dusty. After several assurances that it would all be fine and more than a dozen pats of understanding on her arm from Dr. Caslin, Vivian finally stepped away from the trailer and allowed Dr. Caslin to leave.

Vivian was numb by the time she returned to her camper at the rodeo campgrounds. And out of sorts. Miserable too. This being one of those times when doing the right thing didn't feel so good.

She picked up Dusty's favorite horse blanket she'd left draped over the portable corral fence, then collapsed on the compact sofa inside her camper. She was supposed to be brushing down Dusty, running over her race mistakes and describing their next destination. She was supposed to be looking after her horse. Beyond running cloverleaf patterns in the arena, that was her job. Beyond the racing adrenaline rush, she found her center in the quiet moments with her horse. Her joy too.

She truly was simply a girl with a horse she adored and a dream. Now she didn't have her horse. And she felt completely lost. Worse, Vivian feared Dusty's career might not be the only thing coming to an end. Vivian hugged Dusty's blanket, finding comfort in the horsehair and the familiar smell, and let her tears finally fall.

A while later, a quick rap echoed inside the camper before the door swung open. "Vivian. Let's get dinner. I have big news." Maggie Orr's excited words bounced around the cramped space as Vivian's friend rushed inside.

Vivian straightened on the hard couch. The sun was already starting to set. Her cheeks were still damp. Tears weren't the solution. But Vivian couldn't seem to stop. Then again, giving up on a dream wasn't supposed to be easy. Otherwise, it wasn't the right one. At least, that had always been her grandmother's longstanding advice.

The door clicked softly behind Maggie. And

the champion roper stilled. Her smile dimmed instantly. Her gaze narrowed on Vivian. "How bad is it? One truffle or two?"

Vivian swiped at her eyes and met her friend's worried gaze. Her words sounded watery too. "Whole-truffle-box bad."

Maggie's eyes widened. "Nothing is that bad."

Tears swelled in Vivian's gaze again.

"Tell me and I'll prove it to you." Maggie grabbed the tissue box from the bathroom, then returned to sit on the sofa beside Vivian.

Vivian snatched several tissues, blew her nose and pulled herself together. Maggie and Vivian had been confiding in each other since they'd first met on the circuit several years ago. They'd both grown up in the shadows of their older sisters. Maggie understood Vivian like no one ever really had. Add in their shared passion for the rodeo and theirs was a friendship as strong as family.

She'd gotten no further than Dusty and his impending retirement when the tears started again. Maggie wrapped her arm around Vivian's shoulders and listened while Vivian listed Dusty's current health concerns. Finally, Vivian inhaled on a hiccup, then added, "And there's more than just Dusty."

"More." Maggie's eyebrows pulled together.

"It gets worse." Vivian met her friend's gaze. "It's the end of my three-year deal, Mags."

Three years ago, Vivian's future was neatly laid out for her. She'd attend graduate school to obtain a master's degree in marketing and work at her family's insurance business. That was the expectation. After all it was the same path her older sister had followed. The same path her father and her grandfather had followed. It was quite foolproof. A stable career at their solid family company would set her up for life. It was all upside. To everyone except Vivian. A free spirit who craved open spaces and adventure more than a cubicle and everyday comforts.

Vivian's grandmother had once told Vivian that she was like a frog in an aquarium of goldfish. *Nothing for a frog to do but leap, Vivian.* And so, to honor her late grandmother, Vivian had taken a leap for a future her family couldn't fathom. And a world of dust, dirt and everything they didn't like or even appreciate. While her parents accepted their daughter's need to go after her own goals, they never lost their practicality and negotiated a time limit on dream chasing. Three years to be exact.

Three years to earn back the entirety of her graduate school fund through barrel racing. Three years to prove her unconventional lifestyle was sustainable and profitable. Otherwise, Vivian would return home, take her place at Complete Milestone Insurance and, if she still must, ride her horse for pleasure, not work. But horses had never been work to Vivian. And none of it had been just a whim.

Maggie rubbed her palms over her jeans. Surprise worked over her face. "It's been three years already? Are you serious?"

"The Silk and Steel Cowgirl Stampede is my last chance." Vivian rubbed her forehead. "My parents have only ever seen my love for horses as nothing more than a hobby. The rodeo a fun pastime."

Her grandmother had understood Vivian's passion. Then Vivian had lost her grandma and her steadfast support. And the only place Vivian felt at home was with Dusty. When she competed, it was as if her grandmother was right there with her. Like she'd always been. Giving it all up opened that pit in her stomach wider.

"You're too good to walk away now. You've been winning more and more." Maggie's words and expression were heartfelt and encouraging. "Rodeo is what you're meant to do, Viv."

Vivian appreciated her friend's loyalty. Still, her practical side—the one inherited from the straight, sturdy branch on the Bryant family tree—stepped forward. "But now I don't even have a horse."

Maggie chewed on her bottom lip. The toe of her cowboy boot tapped against the scuffed floor.

"I was right, wasn't I?" Vivian nudged her shoulder into Maggie's and tried to work the defeat from her words. "This is seriously whole-truffle-box bad."

"I'm not conceding yet," Maggie said, her voice soft but insistent. Determination stiffened her shoulders. "And I'm not letting you give up either. Come on."

Vivian peered at her friend, plucked at the horsehair on the heavy blanket and remained seated. "Where are we going?"

"To Ryan's camper of course." Maggie leaned forward, grabbed Vivian's arm and tugged.

Ryan Sloan was a bronc rider and a stunt rider in the movies, currently number one in the standings on the circuit and too charming for his own good. He was also like the older, protective brother Vivian would've wanted growing up. The one that would've defended her love of all things Western in the face of her corporate-minded, city-dwelling-is-better family.

Maggie kept tugging until Vivian gave in and stood up. Tossing the blanket on the couch, she followed her friend outside.

"We are going to raid Ryan's truffle stash and make ourselves a plan," Maggie said. Resolve framed her tight smile. "A good, solid plan, mind you. That's what we need."

One other thing Maggie and Vivian shared was something Maggie always referred to as grit. Unfortunately, Vivian's grit was feeling a bit more like fine sand. Maggie didn't seem to care. And appeared more than ready to fight for Vivian until she bucked up herself. Vivian lifted her chin and matched her friend's quick pace. As for that buck, she would surely find it soon enough. After all, that's what real cowgirls did.

Maggie charged inside Ryan's camper. Vivian followed. The tall bronc rider was stretched out on his couch. His ankles stacked on one armrest, his head on the other. He never flinched at their intrusion. Simply adjusted his faded cowboy hat on his head and drawled out, "Didn't anyone ever teach you two how to knock? What if I had company?"

"Your dating dry spell has lasted for months now, Ryan." Maggie swiped her hand through the air. "And besides, you swore off relationships, remember?"

"Maybe you and Grant inspired me to get back into the dating game, Mags." Ryan chuckled, then lifted his eyebrows at Vivian. "Has my brother and his fiancée inspired you too, Viv?"

Grant Sloan was one of Ryan's younger brothers and now Maggie's fiancé. By all accounts, Grant was the ideal match for Maggie. Vivian was thrilled her friend had found the lasting kind of love. And might've been slightly envious if Vivian and love hadn't parted ways. After all, there was more to life than heartbreak. Vivian shook her head. "I'm afraid that while I'm happy for them, I'm just not inspired enough to want to date anytime soon."

"And that's why we get along, Viv." Ryan laughed, picked up the TV remote and turned the TV off.

"We aren't here to discuss your current single status or Vivian's either." Maggie opened and closed several kitchen cabinets. "Right now, we have much bigger problems. And we need all the truffles, Ryan."

Ryan had introduced Maggie and Vivian to the bourbon-chocolate-truffle decadence after his older brother, a distillery owner, had started dating a general store owner with a talent for crafting chocolate creations. Now that Maggie and Grant were engaged too, there always seemed to be a continuous truffle surplus at the rodeo. And Vivian thought they'd need every single one right now.

Ryan uncoiled from the couch, stood and stretched his arms over his head. His perceptive gaze skipped from Maggie and back to Vivian, where it held. He asked, "Who made you cry, Vivian? And where are they right now?"

If it was only that easy. Still Vivian appreciated Ryan looking out for her. She dropped onto the bench seat at the table and filled Ryan in on Dusty's injury and his questionable competition future. She skipped over the part about her own blurry future in the rodeo, preferring to keep her family issues between herself and Maggie.

"My younger brother Josh has horses, trained and ready to compete." Ryan tugged a purple ribbon off a white candy box, opened the lid and turned it toward Vivian. "You can ride one. If you like the horse, then you can make Josh an offer to buy it."

There were surplus truffles. The proof was on the table. In the unopened candy boxes. But cash. That, Vivian didn't have a surplus of. Vivian swallowed the last of her truffle, willing her words to sound more sugarcoated than sour. "I can't afford one of your brother's horses."

"Sure, you can." Ryan tipped back in his chair and speared his arms wide. "You just have to win at the stampede. Use the jackpot payout to purchase your new horse."

How simple Ryan made it all sound. Ride a horse she'd never competed on. Win. And get everything she wanted. Except a new horse wouldn't understand that Vivian fidgeted in the saddle before a race. Wouldn't sense that her nerves still got the best of her. But Dusty knew. Seemed to understand the stiller he stood, the more calm she became. Dusty knew her. She trusted him. What if she mounted a new horse and all her weaknesses were finally exposed? And the cowgirl she believed she was becoming turned out to be nothing more than a fraud. Vivian rubbed her throat.

"I have an even better suggestion." Maggie slid a bottled water across the table toward Vivian, then toasted Vivian with a white-chocolate-covered truffle. "When you win at the stampede, you will secure the open spot on the professional team sponsored by River Forge Saddlery—oh, and of course, the stampede jackpot."

Vivian stilled. "What?"

"That was my big news earlier." Maggie bit into her candy and grinned around the mouthful. "Aimee Perrson announced she's pregnant and stepping off the River Forge team. They decided to fill the spot to have a full competition team leading into the new year."

"Now, it looks like that spot is yours for the taking too, Viv." Ryan popped an entire truffle into his mouth and smiled.

A spot on a nationally sponsored barrel racing team would give Vivian exposure to coaches, training facilities and sponsorship opportunities. Not to mention the team was legitimate. Nothing her family could easily dismiss or even discount. Even better, Vivian would have the money to support two horses. She could keep Dusty with her after all.

Hope expanded inside Vivian. For the first time since Dr. Caslin drove away with Dusty in her trailer. Still Vivian sidestepped into caution. After all, hope alone was never a good strategy. "Are you sure your brother has a horse I can compete on?"

"Josh has the fastest horses around." Confidence surrounded Ryan's words. Then he shifted. The front legs of the chair he was sitting in dropped back to the floor and his earlier certainty dulled. "We just need to convince Josh to let you ride one."

There it was. The catch. Her hope tempered, Vivian returned her next truffle to the box, eyed Ryan and kept her words neutral. "What does that mean, exactly?"

Ryan lifted his cowboy hat, ran his fingers through his too-long hair. "Let's just say that Josh has a somewhat complicated history with barrel racing."

From the hesitation in Ryan's voice, Vivian guessed it might be more than somewhat complicated. "What does that mean?" she repeated.

"Well, it's in the past, so it might not mean anything," Ryan hedged.

Or it could mean everything. One more hurdle. Vivian wrung her hands together under the table.

"Don't worry, Viv. Ryan and I will handle Josh," Maggie stated, looking entirely too unconcerned. "You just need to get to Three Springs as soon as possible."

Yet Vivian was worried. For so many reasons. The least of which was convincing a stubborn horse trainer to let her ride one of his horses. Being given permission was one thing. Performing was another. Sure, she needed to win. But his business would be on the line too. She would need to showcase his horse's potential, otherwise, she could damage his horse-training reputation. Then whatever his history was with barrel racing would be far from forgotten. The truffles turned over in her stomach.

"Come straight to the farm, Vivian," Ryan

offered. "You can stay in one of our guestrooms at the farmhouse."

"I don't want to impose." Vivian frowned. It was all moving quickly. Falling right into place. From a horse to a place to stay. Too easy was too easy, wasn't it?

"You're not imposing," Maggie stressed, then chuckled. "Besides, Tess and I could use another cowgirl around the place to even the odds. There are too many Sloan cowboys as it is."

"You should have considered that before you went and fell in love with my brother, Mags," Ryan countered.

"Best decision I ever made." Maggie touched the diamond engagement ring on her finger and sighed. Then she glanced at Vivian. "Well, Viv, it seems you have a decision to make. Are you coming to Three Springs or not?"

You can live life or you can live with regrets, Vivian. The choice was always hers, according to her grandmother. Afraid or not, Vivian couldn't walk away. She'd given her word to her grandmother. There would be no regrets. She scuffed her boot heels on the floor as if checking for that grit, then said, "I'll be there."

"Who knows?" Maggie's eyes danced. "You might find a future you never imagined in Three Springs. The same as I did."

"All I need is a horse," Vivian assured her friend.

After all, the only future Vivian was interested in was the one where she became a champion barrel racer. Then those dreams her grandmother and her had always envisioned would finally come true. And Vivian would have everything she ever wanted.

CHAPTER TWO

IF WE WERE supposed to put all our eggs in one basket, it would be Easter all year-round.

Well, it wasn't Easter. It was December. The Christmas season was in full swing. And as of two hours ago, all Josh Sloan's *eggs* were now entirely in one basket.

Josh glanced at the empty passenger seat in his classic truck. Still, he heard his late grandmother's voice as if Gran Claire was riding shotgun after all. *Certainly not ideal, Josh. Best make sure you handle that basket with extra care.*

He was nothing if not diligent and deliberate. Every decision now had to be intentional and calculated. No missteps. No emotions. Unlike earlier that morning. When Josh had been more than a little disappointed with the staid loan officer at Amarillo Mutual Savings Bank. After being denied a loan, on account of no collateral and no cosigner.

The loan would have funded his future. And allowed him to fully fund the portion of his partnership stake in a brand-new equestrian training and therapy center. Bellmare Equestrian Center was slated to break ground at the start of the new year, just outside Houston. The investment group wanted Josh to help design and later run the center. It would give Josh a major platform to build his reputation on. Then, at last, Josh would prove he could stand on more than his family's last name. More than his brothers' successes.

Now it all came down to Josh's horses. It was fitting, he supposed. Some of the biggest moments in his life had started and ended with horses. He must sell his competition-ready horses for the highest price and earn the rest of his buy-in stake himself. To increase their value, he needed his horses to win in the arena. That meant he needed the best riders out there. Fortunately, he knew a few. That left one last piece. Bringing his potential buyers to the Silk and Steel Cowgirl Stampede to watch his horses perform.

All in less than two weeks. He'd bonded with a wild mustang in less time. And back then his future hadn't been at stake. There was no time to waste.

He eased his truck onto the side of the road, within feet of a crooked wrought iron gate and cut the engine. A stream of steam slipped from beneath the truck's glossy black hood. That wasn't the cause of his frown.

His grandfather and uncle were nowhere in sight, despite requesting help at that very location. Josh didn't have time to wait on the wily older duo. But he'd been tapped in to assist the cowboy pair by his busy brothers not an hour ago in their text group. Simply because Josh had been the closest to the pair's location. And his family came first. Always.

That didn't stop the frustration from rolling through him. He'd never been good at being idle. Too much tinkering in his blood, like his great-grandpa, Gran Claire had always claimed.

More steam puffed from underneath the hood. He climbed out, propped the hood open and waved at the white steam billowing from the radiator. Several quick checks proved it was nothing more than a busted hose. Simple fix. Everything he needed was in his toolbox. He rubbed his hands together, ready to get to work.

An unfamiliar silver truck pulled to a stop in front of his. He skipped his gaze from the Arizona license plate to the driver's-side door, ready to tell the helpful stranger he had everything handled.

Then a pair of brown cowboy boots appeared

and out stepped a cowgirl, who quite simply stole his breath. It wasn't her suede boots, which nearly reached her knees. Or her worn straw cowboy hat propped at an angle on her head. Or her braided dark hair that fell charmingly over one shoulder. It was her dimples that framed the widest, most genuine smile Josh had ever seen aimed at him.

Hers was a smile that could make a jaded cowboy like him amend all his vows never to fall head over boots in love again. Good thing Josh had been raised never to go back on his word. He collected himself and found his voice. "Can I help you?"

"I stopped to ask you the same." She tipped her head toward the overheating engine, then shifted her bright gaze back to him. "You look like you might need a hand."

And she looked like everything Josh hadn't known he was missing in his life. As if love at first sight really existed. But Josh had fallen hook, line and wedding rings for that instant-love bit before. Been there. Lived that. And those divorce papers in his desk drawer proved it was far from real. He crossed his arms over his chest. "It's nothing, really. Just a leak in the radiator hose."

"I've got duct tape and water in my truck." The wattage in her grin dialed up another notch.

"It's enough to get you down the road to town where you can get a new hose."

That hit of awareness expanded inside Josh. He struggled to remember she was a stranger simply offering her assistance. Which he didn't really need. Shame he didn't need a date or any of those messy entanglements. He should thank her and send her on her way. Instead, he blinked at her.

"I'm more than happy to tape the hose for you. I've done it on my own truck more than once." She eyed him, her eyebrows pulled together. She might've looked concerned if not for the doubt in her amber-colored gaze. She added, "It's not one of the messier engine jobs, but still."

As if Josh never got his hands dirty. He shifted, then remembered he wore tailored dress pants, a button-down shirt, silk tie and polished loafers. All of which belonged to his older brother, Grant, an orthopedic surgeon and best-dressed Sloan brother. Before Josh could defend his clean hands, she stepped around him and braced her arms on the truck frame.

"The chrome dress kit is a nice way to smarten up a solid farm truck like this one." Appreciation shifted through her words. Her gaze remained fixed on the engine.

Josh's gaze remained fixed on her. He didn't even try to hide his surprise that she recognized the chrome valve covers and such as a dress kit.

"Is this a '76 or '77?" she asked.

Josh had fully restored the truck from the engine to the steering wheel himself. There wasn't a bolt or part that Josh hadn't personally worked on. He understood every nuance of the classic truck. But the cowgirl running her palm over the two-toned black-and-red custom paint on the fender flustered him like nothing or anyone ever had. He cleared his throat. "It's a 1977 Ford 4X4."

"Nice." She nodded and leaned farther under the hood. "Is this a 351 Cleveland?"

Josh's eyebrows rose higher. Now she wanted specifics about the truck's engine. Josh wanted to know if his brothers were hiding in the bushes while they pranked him. But he was afraid if he looked away, this practically perfect cowgirl would disappear. He said, "It's a small block. V-8. Four-barrel carburetor."

She whistled softly. "Well, whoever did this should've upgraded the thermostat to accommodate for all that power. Then you wouldn't be overheating right now."

And right then, Josh might've considered the woman his dream come true if only he hadn't muted his heart and all its unreliable wishes. "You know your engines."

"My granddad and dad like to restore cars. They do mostly engine and bodywork on classic cars. I helped, growing up." Her smile and words softened into wistful. "But I've always been partial to old pickup trucks like this one. There's something about them."

Josh understood that. There was something about her too. He wanted to grab his cowboy hat and wave it around, claiming he was a tenderhearted cowboy and exactly who she needed. He squeezed his forehead and might've blamed the Texas heat for scrambling his common sense. He was more hardheaded these days than tender anything. And it was winter in the Panhandle. It was past time to bid his car-fluent cowgirl good day. Instead, he continued as if he wanted her to get to know him better. "This truck belonged to my Gran Claire."

"I bet she loves the restoration," she said.

Josh barely caught his flinch. He still missed his grandmother daily. But that was nothing he'd reveal to a stranger standing on the bypass. Even one as intriguing as her. "Gran Claire never saw it. She passed before it was finished."

"I'm sorry." Sympathy washed over her pretty features. "But you've honored your grandmother's memory with such a pristine restoration."

He'd certainly tried. His gaze skimmed over the truck. "I like to believe she would've loved this particular version."

She stuck her hands in the pockets of her long Aztec-print sweater coat and considered him. Her warm gaze shifted to his arms still crossed over his chest, then lifted back to his face. There was a wry edge to her words. "You don't need help with the duct tape or the radiator, do you?"

How was it possible he could find her any more appealing? One side of his mouth lifted. "My grandpa always says that turning down help is like asking Fate for even more trouble. If you're offering, I won't turn you down."

"How about this?" She laughed. "You tape and I'll pour."

Ten minutes later, Josh wiped his hands on a towel and watched his car-fluent cowgirl check out the truck's interior. She ran her fingers over the black vinyl-and-cloth bench seat, then across the dash before she gripped the original steering wheel. "Your grandmother would definitely be proud of what you did."

"Thanks for that and your help." Josh tossed the towel behind the driver's seat and considered his next words. He had things to do. Horses to sell. Money to earn. A future to secure. And lingering on the bypass with his cowgirl rescuer wasn't on his agenda. Not now. Not ever. "Would you…?"

The rest of Josh's words were cut off by the rumble of a tractor lumbering along the bypass. Josh turned and watched the tractor's approach. His grandfather waved from the driver's seat. His uncle leaned out the open doorway of the tractor cab and hollered a hearty hello.

"Looks like you've got company." His cowgirl waved to his family, then headed toward her truck. At the driver's side, she turned around and called out, "See you around."

That he doubted. Josh kept mostly to himself and his family these days. Still, he nodded, listened to the hum of her engine starting and watched until she drove away. His grandpa pulled the tractor up to the locked wrought iron gate, cut the engine and scrambled down beside Uncle Roy.

Time to get back to what mattered. His family. Josh set his hands on his hips and eyed the wily pair of brothers. "Does Carter know you stole his tractor?"

"Can't steal something I own," Grandpa Sam argued. Then he shoved the tractor keys into his shirt pocket as if afraid Josh might snatch them away from him.

Josh considered it. The older cowboys and tractors were not a trusty combination. It had all started when Uncle Roy had commandeered one of the tractors to dig up acres of land, looking for a lost moonshine recipe. The backyard had only just recovered that summer. Most recently, his uncle and grandpa had been taking the tractors to the distillery to sort whiskey barrels, or so they claimed. Josh suspected they wanted to borrow a barrel or two as they'd failed to convince Carter to let them distill their own whiskey. Perhaps Josh should've listened when his oldest brother suggested locking up the tractor keys. "So, you didn't ask Carter if you could borrow a tractor?"

"We aren't here to discuss your brother." Grandpa Sam waved to the wrought iron gate. "We need you to open the gate."

"You have the key to the lock," Josh countered. The land had been in Gran Claire's family for decades and passed from mother to daughter through the generations. Now the property belonged to Josh's mother. And as was his mother's long-standing custom, she neglected the land the same as she neglected her family.

"The lock is jammed. Can't get it to budge." Uncle Roy rubbed the back of his neck and frowned. "We tried everything."

"And we couldn't find any bolt cutters in your workshop," Grandpa Sam confessed.

Had Carter hidden the bolt cutters too? Josh asked, "What other locks have you two been cutting?"

There was more going on. Josh could see it in the wide-eyed glance Grandpa Sam slanted toward Uncle Roy. That silent connection that conveyed an entire conversation. Josh had shared that very same look with his own brothers over the years. Usually when Gran Claire had caught them up to no good again and she'd wanted a confession.

"Never mind about our business." Grandpa Sam plucked his cowboy hat off his head and swished it through the air. His bushy eyebrows lifted into his forehead. "After all, we aren't asking you who that cowgirl was just now."

"Well, that's simple." Josh watched the pair and kept his tone casual. "That was the woman I'd marry."

Grandpa Sam twisted around and stared at the empty roadway. Then he turned back to Josh. His eyes narrowed. Speculation curved over his face and into his words. "Is that so?"

Josh had been kidding just now. Sort of. There was definitely something about that particular cowgirl that had caught his attention. But she was gone now. And he had no plans to see her again. Still, he saw no harm in continuing what he'd started. "Yes, sir."

Uncle Roy's eyebrows bunched together. He tugged at his salt-and-pepper curls with one hand and motioned toward the road with the other. He sounded a little panicked when he said, "Then, why'd you let her go?"

"I said I'd marry her." Josh shrugged, then added, "I never said she'd marry me."

"Is that what you were doing then? All dressed up like you are." Grandpa Sam tapped his hat against his thigh. His gaze gleamed. "Asking your cowgirl to marry you?"

Not even close. Josh had no intention of standing at an altar ever again. Exchanging vows of love. Or promising forever. Those were promises people never kept. Besides, Josh had stopped wasting his time on love years ago.

Uncle Roy scratched his head. His gaze skipped around the roadside. "Not the most romantic spot for a proposal, is it?"

"But it is family land," Grandpa Sam mused.

Josh glanced around the overgrown, weed-infested property. Josh preferred it this way. The land practically swallowed the historic ranch house. *Finally*. The potential in the decades-old ranch house and property was almost completely lost now. *Almost*. Soon Josh would drive by and no longer see what it could have been. What it still could be. If his mother cared. If she wanted her family and this place more than her esteemed medical career.

"Still, it's probably why she turned you down just now." Uncle Roy scratched his cheek and wrinkled his nose. "There's absolutely no romance around here."

"Nobody turned me down." Except for the loan officer at the bank. But he hadn't told his grandfather or brothers about his potential business deal. It wasn't the Sloan way to keep secrets, but it was becoming Josh's way. He rubbed the back of his neck, but that pinch of guilt lingered. Then he added, "There was no proposal."

Not surprisingly, neither his uncle nor grandfather appeared to be listening to him. That was the way of the cowboy matchmakers, as the pair had dubbed themselves.

"Didn't you learn anything from your brother?" Grandpa Sam peered at Josh. "Grant turned the entire arena into a fairy garden when he proposed to Maggie."

"Now, that sure was romantic." Uncle Roy grinned. Satisfaction filled his weathered face.

Josh set his hands on his hips. He certainly wasn't learning anything now from the duo and their purpose. "How about we get back to you two and the tractor?"

Grandpa Sam stroked his fingers through his white beard and looked over the land. "Maybe if we cleaned up around here, then Josh could bring his cowgirl back and propose again."

Josh looked at the afternoon sky, inhaled, then returned his attention to the pair. And worked to keep his voice calm. "I'm going to try again. Why are we here?"

"You don't need to be here." Grandpa Sam propped his hat back on his head and motioned to the gravel driveway. "Open the gate and you can go find your cowgirl."

"But be sure to practice your proposal first," Uncle Roy warned, then arched a salt-and-pepper eyebrow at Josh. "After all, you only get one second chance."

Josh crossed his arms over his chest and considered the pair. "And what will you two be doing?"

"We've things to see to here." Grandpa Sam lifted his chin.

"Like digging up the property," Josh offered.

Grandpa Sam frowned. "There will be no digging."

Josh knew he was going to regret asking and yet he couldn't stop himself. "Then, what will you be doing?"

"Moving things, if you must know." His grandfather hooked his thumbs around his large belt buckle and narrowed his gaze on Josh. "Not that it's any of your concern."

But their safety was Josh's concern. His main one. It wasn't too long ago that the duo had found themselves in the hospital for several days after falling into the pond one night. That had happened after they'd taken things into their own hands. Hospital trips were not happening on Josh's watch. Neither was his own work. Looked like he'd be making those calls to his rodeo connections later that night.

Josh walked to his truck, grabbed his bolt cutters from his toolbox, then headed toward the gate. "Show me what you're moving then. It'll go faster if I help too."

"But what about your cowgirl?" Uncle Roy rushed after him.

"There is no cowgirl," Josh said, putting a note of finality into his words. At least, there wasn't a cowgirl he claimed as his.

Besides, he was good on his own. Because he was perfectly happy without love.

And that was a problem with someone like his cowgirl. A cowgirl like her deserved to be loved.

But Josh was a cowboy who'd turned his back on love years ago. And his family always claimed changing his mind was harder than making it snow on Christmas Day.

And not even his cowgirl had a direct line to Santa.

CHAPTER THREE

NIGHT HAD FULLY descended when Josh finally got to work on the tractor inside his workshop. Several warning lights had lit up on the tractor's dash that afternoon at the other property and Josh had stepped in to take control. He'd given his keys to his grandpa and uncle to drive his truck back home.

He had time only to park the tractor in his garage and complete a wardrobe change before he headed to the distillery. Where Carter had needed him for what was supposed to have been a simple still repair but proved to be nothing but quick or easy. At least Josh had entertained Carter with a recap of his animated debate with their grandpa and uncle.

Turned out his grandpa and uncle had wanted to move trees with the tractor. A half dozen to be exact. All to gain access to a two-story storage barn Josh hadn't even realized was on the property. Josh hadn't approved of their tree-clearing suggestions and that had launched a lengthy and loud debate. In the end, the trees remained, and Josh cleared a path to the back barn doors. Ones that Josh would need to repair before they could be opened safely. Josh had climbed through the broken window in the second-story loft and confirmed, to his grandpa and uncle's delight, that boxes filled the entire space from the plank floor to the rafters.

His grandfather and uncle refused to tell Josh what exactly they were hunting for. But the pair had given him their word that they wouldn't return to the property without Josh. That, however, wouldn't hold for long. Their impatience and curiosity would soon take over and the cowboy pair would be back at the storage barn, whether it was safe or not.

Josh checked the cabinets above his workbench for replacement tractor filters and quickly ran through his schedule for the next day. He needed to work in his grandpa and uncle between meetings with potential buyers for his three junior, friendly geldings, training sessions and now tractor repairs. Not to mention securing riders for his competition-ready horses. The ones that would get him the final portion of his $200,000 buy-in.

Some might say he needed a Christmas miracle. He disagreed. The only thing Josh required was no more outside interferences. Nothing else he'd need to repair or fix. No emergencies. No more: *Hey, Josh, can you...?*

"Josh, we need to talk to you," a woman called out.

Josh stilled. Whatever it was, he would say no. He worked the word around in his mouth and slowly shut the cabinet door. Then he turned to find his older brother Ryan and Maggie, his other brother's fiancée, heading toward him.

"You missed dinner again." Maggie held a tinfoil-covered plate out to him. "So we brought it to you."

Ryan frowned and his eyebrows lowered. "Seems to be something of a habit these days, little brother. Skipping out on the family."

He wasn't skipping out. Just getting his life in order. And soon enough, he'd be living in Houston, a nine-hour car ride away, and missing a lot more than family dinners. It was best they all got used to the distance now. He searched for a grin. "Thanks, Maggie. You can leave it on the workbench."

Maggie set the plate down, then touched the neatly folded clothes Josh had placed on the stool. The ones Josh meant to toss in the laundry room later before anyone, specifically Grant, noticed they were gone.

"These look like Grant's," Maggie said. "Do you want me to take them back to him?"

And have Grant figure out Josh had raided his closet without telling him? That would only lead to more questions he wasn't ready to answer. Not yet anyway. Josh was determined to do this on his own terms. No Sloan backup required. Proving himself wasn't supposed to be this complicated.

"What were you doing in Grant's closet?" Ryan stepped beside Maggie and touched the red tie with one finger, like he was testing the doneness of an uncooked cut of steak. Ryan added, "What exactly were you thinking? The Rudolph red silk tie is a bit much, don't you think?"

He'd been thinking a professional look might help his odds with the loan officer at Amarillo Mutual Savings Bank. But his morning meeting at the financial institution was another one of those best-kept secrets.

"I was trying out a new look." Josh grabbed the dinner plate, peeled back the tinfoil and picked up a chicken tender. As if Josh and dress clothes fit together as obviously as a hammer and nail. "You should consider it sometime, Ryan."

"You won't ever see me in a suit and tie." Ryan threw his head back and laughed. "Not in this lifetime anyway."

"I think Josh would look really good in a

suit. The red tie would accentuate his eyes." Maggie smiled at Josh, then poked her finger into Ryan's shoulder. "And what about my wedding? You're going to have to get dressed up for that."

"For generations the Sloans have been getting married on our land. It's bad luck if you change the location, Mags." Ryan stepped away from her and motioned toward Josh. "Ask Josh if you don't believe me."

Josh had married Isabel, his ex-wife, in New Mexico, after Isabel had won the national barrel racing title. Like his mother, Josh had skipped the tradition of reciting vows within Sloan borders. And like his mother, Josh's marriage hadn't lasted. Bad luck perhaps. Or more like inevitable. After all, those instant sparks never lasted longer than an instant. Josh finished the chicken tender and tried not to think of his car-fluent cowgirl. "Ryan is right."

"Of course we're getting married here," Maggie said, her exasperation clear. "Doesn't mean I can't have a formal evening wedding. With both of you wearing a tuxedo."

"Mags." Ryan grabbed her shoulders and turned her around toward the open steel rolling doors. "Look around out there. There's a distillery. Wheat fields. Pastures. And horses."

"What's your point?" Maggie crossed her arms over her chest.

"Nothing about our land is formal," Ryan explained. "That goes for us too. And that includes Grant, even though his closet looks like it belongs in a penthouse in the city."

Maggie shook her head and countered, "We are talking about one night."

"But that's all it takes to start things changing," Ryan argued. "We're good as we are. Boots and jeans and no fuss. Tell her Josh."

You're good as you are, aren't you? Getting by in life on your family's name and your brothers' successes. Well, that's not good enough for me. Josh's then-wife had ended her accusations that night by handing Josh divorce papers. He was better now. Without Isabel. He'd been building a solid horse training reputation and business. But it wasn't enough. Definitely not good enough yet. But he would be. "It's Maggie's wedding day. She gets to make the final decision on the dress code."

"There's a good tailor in Belleridge. I'll make you an appointment for a fitting." Maggie nudged her elbow into Ryan's side, then beamed at Josh. "We need a favor, Josh."

"We're not done discussing your formal wedding, Mags," Ryan stated. "I'm asking

Grant what he wants when we get back to the farmhouse."

"He's going to tell you whatever I want is what he wants." Maggie held out her hand and raised an eyebrow. "Want to bet on it?"

Ryan never hesitated. The wager placed, he glanced at Josh. "We have a friend, Josh."

This was the part where he told them no. Josh aimed another chicken strip at them. "I'll wear a tuxedo to your wedding, Mags. But I'm not taking a date, even if she's your best friend."

"Got it. And this isn't a setup." Maggie chuckled then paused. "Well, I suppose it is a setup." At Josh's frown, she rushed on, "But we need you to set her up with one of your fastest horses."

Josh put the plate down and wiped his hands on his jeans. To say he was protective of every single one of his horses would be a slight understatement. "Have I met your friend?"

"No." Maggie pursed her lips first, then brightened. "But she's a natural in the saddle. Hardworking. And a really great person."

That didn't tell him anything useful. Like whether she could handle one of his horses. Or if she recognized that a horse was not simply a tool to get what she wanted. Or if she understood what good horsemanship even meant.

"Her competition horse needs to retire. Arthritis and too many injuries," Ryan explained.

"And she needs to compete in the Silk and Steel Cowgirl Stampede."

"Come on, Josh," Maggie urged. "You've got a stable of performance horses ready for a chance. She's one of the best up-and-coming barrel racers on the circuit."

Josh stilled, slid his gaze to his brother and shook his head.

"It's been five years." Ryan yanked off his cowboy hat and ran his hands through his hair. "Can't you bend on your old vow this once?"

"What vow?" Maggie glanced from Ryan to Josh, then tilted her head to study Josh closer.

"I vowed never to get involved with a barrel racer ever again." Minutes after signing his divorce papers. When his heartbreak had been entirely too fresh. Josh supposed it hadn't been the most appropriate time to make such a sweeping declaration. But it hadn't changed the fact that he'd stuck to his word for the past five years and meant to keep to it now. There was too much riding on his future right now. He couldn't afford to let anything, or anyone, upset his plans.

"We aren't asking you to get involved with Vivian." Maggie wrinkled her nose and frowned at him. "We just need you to give her a horse. One she can ride in the rodeo next weekend."

There was no *just* about that. Horse and

rider were a team. A partnership that when built properly over time led to things like national championships, belt buckles and jackpots. When those wins happened on one of his horses, well, that increased Josh's value as a horse trainer and the worth of his horses. That mattered right now. He needed every dollar he could get to fund his investment stake.

"She's good, Josh," Maggie stressed.

Josh didn't need good. He needed a rider who was at the top of their game. Who knew how to quickly learn the nature of a horse and communicate with it to win. He couldn't bend on that. Not even a little. And not even for a family friend. He asked, "How long has she been competing?"

"Three years." Maggie shifted from side to side but held Josh's stare.

"That's not long in the competition saddle. Or the circuit," Josh countered. Barely more than a rookie. The last thing he needed was a hobby rider. One who hadn't mastered her own fears in the arena. Or who couldn't quiet herself enough to focus an anxious horse.

"She's full-time on the circuit," Ryan added. "Dedicated. Smart. A quick learner."

But with limited competition time.

"She can win on one of your horses," Maggie jumped back in. "With your help, she can do it."

Help her out. There it was. Train the rider too. But Josh would rather take in an entire herd of wild mustangs than coach another barrel racer. Five years. He would've thought he had gotten *past* his past by now. Apparently, time healed on its own timeline. Go figure.

"Vivian is here now. She's staying in one of the guestrooms. She's going to be in the arena tomorrow morning." Maggie walked over and gripped Josh's arm. Her words insistent. "Just come over and meet her. Watch her ride. See what you think, then decide. Please."

Josh took in Maggie's strikingly pale gaze and understood why Grant couldn't resist his fiancée. Fortunately, Maggie was his older brother's problem. Josh had stopped surrendering to captivating eyes and pretty cowgirls years ago. Five to be exact.

A flash of beguiling amber eyes and a dimple-framed smile flashed in his mind. But he hadn't given in to his car-fluent cowgirl either. He'd let her drive away. Because he had things to do. His own future to secure. Josh sighed. "Fine. I'll meet her in the morning."

"Thank you. Thank you." Maggie hugged him, quick and tight. "You and Vivian can work together all week."

He added an extra hit of caution to his words to temper Maggie's enthusiasm. It would do no good to get Maggie's hopes up. "It's not about Vivian and me, Maggie. It's about the horse and the rider. They need to match, or it won't work."

"Stop looking for reasons that this won't work." Ryan tapped his fist against Josh's shoulder. "Vivian can ride. She can win. I'd wager she can win on any horse."

"Then, let her ride your horse," Josh countered and quickly returned his brother's light punch. Josh had trained Ryan's grullo mustang. He knew exactly what Mischief could do. "Or don't you trust your barrel racing friend that much?"

"That's you, my brother, who doesn't trust barrel racers." Ryan chuckled. "And as I keep reminding you, it isn't fair to paint all barrel racers with the same broad brush."

Fair or not, that seemed to be Josh's default. Call it bad wiring. Or simply the aftereffects of a marriage gone wrong.

"Well, I know this is going to work out." Maggie hugged Josh again. Her words confident and sure. "Josh, you'll just love Vivian."

Love her. He didn't even like her. She had him breaking his vow to himself. Nothing to like about that. Then again, loving her or even liking her wasn't necessary.

All Josh needed was for Vivian to prove she could win. Then maybe he'd consider changing his mind about her.

CHAPTER FOUR

VIVIAN RODE WINSTON, a ten-year-old gelding from the Sloans' personal stables, around their indoor practice arena. Working slowly through the cloverleaf pattern smoothed out her jitters. She'd already lost too much time. She'd lingered in Oklahoma the past week, holding out in case Dr. Caslin changed her mind and released Dusty. All Dr. Caslin had done was extend Dusty's therapy another week. And left Vivian to head to Three Springs alone.

Now the stampede was one week out. Her own false hope had cost her precious practice time. She looped around a barrel and refined her pitch. The one that would convince Josh Sloan to help her.

At least she had an ally in the arena. Maggie stood at the railing next to Sam Sloan. His beard rivaling Santa's for its pure white color, Sam had greeted Vivian with a warm hug and insisted Vivian call him Grandpa Sam. Vivian had liked the older cowboy instantly and very much wanted to consider him an ally too. But

Josh was his grandson. And loyalty was more than a word to families like Sam's, with roots that ran deep.

Vivian adjusted the reins and readied Winston for another turn around the barrels.

"Hold up, Viv," Maggie called out. "Josh just walked in. Come on over and meet him."

Time to make her case. Vivian dismounted, ran her hand over Winston's strong neck, then turned toward the railing. Her gaze collided with a very familiar pair of striking blue eyes. Her mouth dropped open. Her well-crafted pitch slammed together in her mind.

Her handsome roadside businessman.

It was him. Only turned full cowboy, from the black hat, plaid shirt, faded jeans to his cowboy boots. Her businessman-turned-cowboy looked anything but happy to see her. He didn't acknowledge that they'd met only yesterday on the bypass. Neither did she. Vivian lifted her chin and said, "I was told you don't like barrel racers."

His eyebrows lifted beneath the rim of his cowboy hat. He remained silent, not confirming or denying her claim. Yet his focus remained steady on her.

Vivian searched his face for that warmth she'd seen on the bypass. When she'd stepped out of her truck. And her roadside businessman had looked as if he'd been waiting for her all along. All she found now was a cool reserve. Vivian reined in her runaway imagination.

"Well, that can't be true." Sam chuckled. Then his words gained speed and that glimmer in his shrewd gaze flashed bright. "Why, Vivian is the woman Josh told Roy and me he was gonna marry."

Now it was her turn. Vivian's eyebrows spiked high on her forehead. How was she supposed to respond to that outrageous claim? Why wasn't Josh correcting Sam? The older cowboy was his grandfather. Vivian was a guest. It wasn't her place to tell the kind older cowboy he'd obviously misheard his grandson.

Maggie gaped at Vivian. "What did I miss?"

Vivian shook her head at her friend. Maggie gave her a this-conversation-is-far-from-over stare.

"Don't you remember what you said yesterday, Josh?" Sam paused, then added, "You certainly couldn't have forgotten Vivian already."

"I remember everything I said yesterday, Grandpa." Josh tapped the rim of his cowboy hat higher on his head as if he wanted to see Vivian better. "And I remember her."

There was that warmth. Just a flash in his faded denim–tinted gaze that fixed on Vivian like a promise.

Vivian's throat dried. She felt her cheeks heating. *Get it together, Viv. You never let a man turn your head before.* And starting with her businessman-turned-cowboy would be worse than missing the pattern in a race. She'd get disqualified for an error like that in the arena. But an error with a cowboy like Josh Sloan, well, those kinds of mistakes broke hearts. And she'd already made that mistake once before. And she always prided herself on being a quick learner.

"Now that we've cleared all that up, let's decide on a horse for Vivian. She's got good balance, alignment and no bounce in the saddle." Satisfaction widened Sam's grin. "I'm thinking Vivian and Fox would work well together."

"Fox's thoroughbred blood still runs hot." There was a tension along Josh's jawline. His words were firm. "Fox needs an experienced rider."

And he didn't believe that was Vivian. That much was clear. Vivian shifted, firming her boot heels into the sandy ground and her resolve. He knew nothing about her. If he did, he would already know nothing he said now would discourage her. She'd found her grit and wasn't letting it go this time.

"What about one of your Appendix Quarter Horse geldings?" Maggie suggested. "They both have the speed and agility."

"But not the discipline." Josh widened his stance and crossed his arms over his chest as if preparing to block every suggestion and Vivian's resolve. "They certainly won't find it in a week."

And Vivian doubted she'd find any soft spots in her rigid cowboy anytime soon either. How was she going to convince him she could handle one of his horses?

"There's Artie." Sam drummed his fingers on the top rung of the railing. "That Arabian was made for competing."

Josh looked less than pleased by that comment.

And Vivian was beginning to think it wasn't the horses with the issues. But rather their owner. She hadn't really believed Josh didn't like barrel racers. Now she was beginning to believe it might be true. But she was here. And she wasn't about to let one stubborn cowboy keep her from competing. Winning meant more than a jackpot. It meant she could support Dusty and keep her team intact. "What about Winston here?"

"He's reliable and has speed," Sam mused. "Quiet too."

"Too quiet." Josh frowned. "That'll be a problem for Vivian."

Vivian narrowed her gaze. Oh yes, Vivian

had a problem alright. He was tall, blue-eyed and spoke with a slow Southern drawl that made her imagine slow drives on backcountry roads to nowhere and long moonlit strolls. Worse, he made her want to both shout at him and kiss him. Anything to scatter his reserve and make him see her. Really see her. Anything to get him to bend enough to give her a chance.

"Josh is right." Sam chuckled and nodded. "Winston can run the pattern clean, but he won't be the fastest. He lacks that hurry switch."

Well, Vivian was starting to lack patience. But airing her frustration would be like tossing vinegar on a beehive. Vivian smoothed her expression into polite. "I don't think it's barrel racers you don't like, but rather it's me." Vivian stepped up to the railing and braced her arms on the cool metal. "Because if it was barrel racers, you wouldn't have sold your buckskin quarter horse, Scout, to Erin Singsen and Huey, your bay roan quarter horse, to Ruthie Urtz this past spring." *Oh yes, Josh Sloan. I know who you are.*

One corner of his mouth tipped up. "I'm not saying you're right, but does that bother you?"

"It should bother you," Vivian countered. She held his gaze, then pushed even more confidence into her words. "I have more wins in the arena than both Erin and Ruthie combined."

Appreciation widened his eyes. "As I told Maggie earlier, success is about finding the right fit between the rider and horse."

We could be the right fit. Vivian sidestepped that foolish thought. "Well, prove you're as good as they say you are, Josh Sloan. Find me a horse to win on."

Josh rubbed his chin, moved closer.

Just then, the side door behind him swung open. A tall, attractive woman in high-heeled boots and a holly berry–colored, knee-length coat, stepped inside.

"Hey Josh." The woman, her strawberry blond hair falling in rich waves down her back, walked straight into Josh's arms. Bold and forward as if she belonged there. Now and always. The woman held on to him and said, "Josh. It's been a while."

Vivian glanced at Maggie. Her friend looked equally as surprised as Josh. Maggie moved beside Sam at the railing as if wanting to make sure she had an unobstructed view.

Josh's gaze connected with Vivian's over the woman's head.

And that was when Vivian lost him. Not to the stunning woman, who he held as if she were a dusty sack. But rather to himself. It was as if he'd retreated inside himself. His gaze cooled and dimmed even more.

He set the attractive woman away from him. His voice was guarded. "Isabel. What are you doing here?"

The woman never answered. She brushed her silky hair over her shoulder and studied Josh. "Didn't know you were coaching barrel racers again, Josh."

"I'm not." Josh crossed his arms over his chest.

"Hello, Isabel." Sam braced his arm on the top railing. His words were reserved. "We were just discussing which horse Josh's girlfriend was gonna ride in the Cowgirl Stampede next weekend."

Girlfriend. Before that inaccuracy fully sank in, Vivian took in the woman and realized exactly who she was. Isabel Sampson-Spero was rodeo royalty, a champion barrel racer, and one of Vivian's idols.

Isabel's smile was pageant worthy as she stepped to the railing. She reached over to shake Vivian's hand. Her grip warm and friendly around Vivian's cold fingers. Isabel tipped her head, her gaze assessing. "I recognize you from the circuit. It seems you're my competition."

In the arena. Yes. Out of it... Vivian slanted her gaze toward Josh.

"So, what do you say, Vivian?" Isabel said into the sudden stiff silence. The rodeo queen's smile never faltered. "Are you up for a run against me?"

Vivian's fingers tightened around the railing. "Right now?"

Isabel untied the belt at her waist. "Fastest gets first pick of Josh's horses to compete on at the stampede."

"You're retired, Isabel." Josh's words were clipped and almost impatient.

"Seems I have some unfinished business." Isabel's shoulder lifted in a small shrug. "And things change."

The way Isabel watched Josh, Vivian wondered if he was part of her unfinished business.

"You can't just…" Josh trailed off.

"I tried calling." Isabel's words were relaxed. "For the last few days. Same as I tried calling after our divorce. You never answer. Not then. Not now. I had no choice but to come here. To see you in person."

Divorce. Josh and Isabel had been married. Vivian should leave. She admired Isabel's rodeo success. Wanted to ask the woman for advice. And less than five minutes ago, she'd been challenging Isabel's ex-husband and considering kissing the stubbornness right out of the cowboy. This wasn't good.

"There's nothing to talk about, Isabel." His expression was resigned.

"There's a lot to say. But not here and not right now." Isabel motioned toward Vivian, seemingly unflustered. "First, Vivian and I need horses."

That settled things for Vivian. Josh was most likely Isabel's unfinished business. The only question that remained was whether Isabel was his too. All Vivian knew for certain was that it wasn't any of her business. Her handsome businessman-turned-cowboy was off-limits.

Besides, Isabel was exactly who a cowboy like Josh should be with. As for Vivian, she was still earning her right to be called a cowgirl. And an actual relationship with Josh Sloan was as far-fetched as glass slippers, pumpkin carriages and love at first sight. Not that it mattered in the least to Vivian.

Vivian wasn't in town to go on a date. Or find a boyfriend. Or even remember that she once wanted all those things. But that was before she'd declared independence from her heart. She was at the Sloans' ranch now to sharpen her focus and practice for the stampede. All to ensure when she entered the arena next weekend, she had the race of her career. Nothing less would do.

"Well, are you going to stand around and

talk? Or practice and pick your horses?" Grandpa Sam pushed away from the railing. "Dinnertime will be here soon, so you best get to deciding."

"This is not how this works." Josh yanked his cowboy hat off his head and tugged at his dark brown hair.

"Vivian, you should know that Josh likes to have the final say on things, especially when it comes to his horses," Isabel explained. "But I'm still game to ride a round or two if you are."

"Sure." Vivian glanced from Isabel to Josh. He smashed his cowboy hat low on his head, the rim shadowed his face. And Vivian wanted to comfort him. Take his hand. Hold on. As if he needed her. As if that was her right. Vivian pushed away from the railing. "Sure, Isabel. Let's ride. I could use the practice." And more than a moment to clear her head.

Maggie pulled out her phone, stared at the screen, then frowned. "Hold up. Looks like you might not need Josh's horses or practice runs after all."

Silence descended around the small group.

Vivian tightened her grip on Winston's reins and took in her friend's worried expression. "What are you talking about, Mags?"

"The Silk and Steel Cowgirl Stampede is

being canceled." Maggie tapped on her phone, then swiped her finger across the screen as if scrolling through an article. "There was an electrical fire at the arena on the Belleridge Rodeo Grounds."

No. Vivian shook her head. She had to compete. The stampede was her last chance. To keep her rodeo family together. To keep her promise to her grandmother. Panic pressed around her words. "They can't just cancel, can they?"

"If they don't have a venue, they have to cancel." Sympathy washed over Maggie's face. "And from reading this press release, it would take a miracle to get the Belleridge arena repaired and cleared by the inspectors in time."

And Vivian thought the hardest part was going to be convincing Josh to let her ride one of his horses. Now she needed a miracle too. All to keep her rodeo career alive. She could hear her parents even now. Practical and sensible as always. *Vivian, how many more roadblocks do you need to hit before you admit you're going in the wrong direction?*

"Three Springs has rodeo grounds," Isabel offered. There was an anxiousness to her words that replaced her earlier calm.

"But it's one week away." Maggie chewed

on her bottom lip. "That's a heavy lift to move it here last minute."

"But could it be moved to Three Springs?" Vivian pressed and swung around the roadblock. And that hope she could never quite rein in wove through her.

"Abby Tanner is the town assistant manager." Sam stroked his beard. "Abby will know if it's possible and exactly what to do."

"Except Abby is expecting her second child any day now," Josh explained. "Not to mention it's December. Most of the locals are busy preparing for Christmas and other holiday town events."

Vivian curled that barely there thread of hope around her finger like a blue first-place ribbon. And worked the desperation out of her words. "What if Abby didn't have to organize the rodeo by herself?"

"What are you suggesting?" Josh tipped his head and watched her. "That you can put on a rodeo in seven days?"

His tone was far from encouraging. She couldn't care. She had to try. Vivian nodded.

"It's not a bad idea." Maggie's grin started small, then expanded. "After all, this isn't our first rodeo. Not for any of us. Yes, that pun was absolutely intended."

"I like your spirit, Vivian and Maggie." Sam

nodded his approval and smiled. "The rodeo would be good for the town and local businesses."

"I helped Abby with the Three Springs Reunion Rodeo Days this past Labor Day weekend," Maggie explained. "I got a good look at what goes into putting it all together behind the scenes."

"I will definitely help too." Isabel smiled.

Vivian inhaled. That hope expanded inside her. "We can be Abby's boots on the ground, so to speak."

"It could work," Sam mused. "If we all come together."

"Ryan will help," Maggie declared. "And my sister, Kelsey, of course. I'm sure we can find others if we need too."

"What about you, Josh?" Vivian lifted her gaze to Josh and locked on. "Are you in?"

Josh considered her for a beat, then another and finally nodded.

"Okay, then let's get Abby on the phone." Grandpa Sam's gaze twinkled like so many Christmas lights. As if he truly was a cowboy Santa in training. "And see if we can't make our own Christmas miracle."

CHAPTER FIVE

TEN MINUTES LATER, Abby Tanner, Three Springs's assistant manager, had agreed to make some calls to the stampede organizers in Belleridge. Josh had taken Winston to the stables. And Vivian was swept inside the farmhouse with the others.

Only to find herself boots to blue eyes with an identical copy of Josh. Same vivid, perceptive gaze. Same strong features. Same good looks. Only this cowboy wore a charming half grin that paired nicely with his long auburn hair brushing against the collar of his volunteer firefighter sweatshirt.

Vivian blinked and blurted, "No one told me…"

"You don't need to say it," her cowboy's look-alike interrupted. Amusement curved around his words. "Everyone knows I'm the better-looking twin, even Josh."

Vivian blinked, then laughed. Another charmer. And hard not to like. Same as his grandfather. And same as his twin. But when it came to Josh, Vivian needed to remember she had no "couple" goals. Her goals only required a fast horse and an arena, not a life partner.

"You must be Vivian." His grin grew wider. "The barrel racer who's here for my brother. Sorry I missed meeting you last night." He touched his sweatshirt and introduced himself. "Duty called. Now, back to my brother."

"I'm not here for…" Vivian paused. "I fear I'm more of a bother to your brother than anything."

"Trust me." He waggled his eyebrows at Vivian. "Josh could use a lot more bother in his life."

"Caleb, leave Vivian be. We've got no time for questions," Sam announced. His words clipped out in time to his boots tapping against the hardwood floor as he walked through the kitchen. "We've got important rodeo business to see to."

Caleb gave Isabel the barest of nods in greeting as the woman passed him. But his gaze turned even more alert, and his grin slipped.

"We've got a rodeo to rescue, Caleb." Maggie opened a drawer in the kitchen and pulled out a notebook. Then she aimed a pencil at Caleb. "It's all-hands-on-deck for this one, and that includes yours too."

Vivian followed the others to the massive oak kitchen table and took a seat next to Maggie and across from Isabel. The former rodeo queen was beautiful at first glance. But Vivian noticed a fragility around her smile. A dull cast to her blue eyes, like fog streaming across a blue sky. And Vivian found herself wanting to comfort Isabel. Champion her cause too.

Caleb reached for the chair next to Vivian. Sam's words stopped Caleb before he sat. "Caleb, let your brother sit next to his girlfriend."

Caleb's eyebrows rose. Speculation shifted across his face before he moved and took a seat beside Isabel. The former rodeo queen never reacted to Sam's words. Never flinched. Never cast Vivian a jealous side-glance.

But that girlfriend tag bounced around inside Vivian. Not entirely as unwelcome as it should be. But Josh and Vivian weren't a thing. They were... Vivian wasn't entirely sure. Business associates she supposed. Time to set the record straight. Vivian opened her mouth.

"It's Abby," Maggie cut in. She set the phone to her ear and greeted the assistant town manager. After a series of yeses and I-got-its, Maggie covered the speaker on her phone with her hand, then smiled wide. "It's a go. The stampede is coming to Three Springs."

"We're going to need more than a notebook for this project." Sam pushed his chair back and stood. "Caleb, get that large whiteboard from Carter's office. I'll find the pens."

Vivian was about to offer her help when Josh walked inside and called her name. Vivian joined him in the laundry room and said, "The rodeo is happening."

"That's good." Josh opened the back door and motioned outside. Both his expression and words bordered on bewildered. "There's someone here to see you."

"Me?" Vivian shook her head. "I can't imagine who would be here to see me." She'd only told her mother where she was going. And she'd left out the bigger details, only telling her mom that Maggie had invited her to stay at the Sloan farm until the stampede.

Not two steps out the door, Vivian came to a full stop. The kind that was statue still. Mouth open. Eyes too wide. Breath stalling. The kind that came with those internal warning bells blaring.

No. It can't be.

Josh stood behind her. His words were soft. "Do you know them?"

Vivian took in the massive, brand-new, shiny silver-and-black motor home idling in the driveway. And the excited driver and passenger waving with more enthusiasm than children waiting in line to see Santa. Vivian tried to swallow.

Tried to nod. What were her parents doing here? Her voice sounded thick, and dust coated. "That's my family."

Josh's hand landed on her lower back. His touch steady and stable. "I take it you weren't expecting them."

"Let's put it this way." Vivian tried to mute those insistent warning bells. "I would've been less surprised to see Santa's sleigh with Rudolph and his other reindeers gliding down your driveway right now."

Before Josh could reply, the side door on the RV swung wide.

Vivian's older sister stepped down the stairs. Her sister's natural blond hair gleamed as if the strands trapped the sunshine. Happiness sparkled in her wide eyes and even fuller smile. Heather spread her arms wide and shouted, "Surprise, Vivian. We are here."

Surprise. It was an ambush. Then Wade, her sister's husband, stepped from the RV and tucked Heather into his side. That was when Vivian noticed the small swell of her sister's stomach. And the surprises just continued coming. Vivian swayed, pressed back into Josh's hand and whispered, "She's pregnant."

Suddenly Josh was at Vivian's side, his arm curving around her waist. His embrace more anchoring than affectionate. His gaze skimmed over her face, a mixture of worry and concern crossed his features. "Are you okay?"

I will be. If you could hold me. For real. For a minute. Or forever. Not that Vivian wasn't more than capable of standing in her own boots. Leaning on her own strong shoulders. Vivian inhaled and straightened. "Sorry. Just surprised."

His gaze searched hers for another beat before he took her hand in his. "We should probably greet them."

Vivian nodded, then glanced at her hand joined with his. When Maggie and Ryan had told Vivian to make herself at home on the ranch, her friends certainly hadn't meant like this. Still, Vivian tightened her grip. Later, she'd blame the stress of her family's ambush, the fear of losing Dusty and the holidays. Later, she'd remember she was meant to hold reins, not hands. Especially not Josh's.

But not right now. Right now, she was going to kick up even more dust than her parents' new motor home and make the air even cloudier. Her whisper was urgent. Desperate even. "I'm going to apologize in advance for what happens next." A brief pause. One last inhale of clean air, then Vivian added, "And I'm going to owe you a really big favor and an explanation later."

Josh never flinched. Never dropped her hand.

Vivian exhaled and forced herself to smile. Squeezed Josh's hand one last time. Then spun around and crossed the porch to hug her parents. "Mom. Dad. What are you guys doing here?"

"We decided to lease a motor home for the month and test out our retirement options." Her dad beamed and presented the motor home with a flourish of both hands. "And we decided the maiden voyage should be to see you in the rodeo."

Her family had never come to watch Vivian compete in a rodeo. Not once in three years. Now they were here. To see what could very well be Vivian's last rodeo. Her gaze skipped to her father. If he wanted her to win or fail, he gave nothing away.

"We decided if we came early, we could spend some quality time together as a family too." Warmth and excitement rushed over her mom's words.

Her father continued, "This family has been apart entirely too long."

What he didn't say was that Vivian had been in the saddle entirely too long, when she needed to be seated at her desk at Complete Milestone Insurance. Right where her father wanted her. Right where Vivian never felt she belonged. Vivian locked her grin in place.

"Besides, traveling is going to be hard in a few months for some of us." Her older sister laughed and touched her stomach. Pure joy filled Heather's smile. "We wanted to tell you in person, Viv. And now is as good a time as any. We're having twins."

Vivian worked to smooth her smile into genuine. Her words into heartfelt. "Congratulations. That's incredible."

"Well, it looks like the surprise might be on us." Heather wrapped Vivian in a tight embrace then extended her hand out to Josh. "Vivian, aren't you going to introduce us?"

Keep on leaping, Vivian. And one day, you'll land on your perfect lily pad. Vivian was about to leap alright, like her dear grandma always told her to. And if it was a jump too far, well, she'd simply have to adjust her landing later.

Vivian aimed an apologetic look at Josh and smiled at her family. "This is my boyfriend, Josh Sloan."

Josh never missed a beat. He simply stepped forward and shook hands with Vivian's sister, her mother, Catherine, and father, Ted, then finally Wade, Vivian's brother-in-law.

"Vivi, I warned them." Wade set his arm around Heather's shoulders and added, "I kept telling them we should've called you first.

Filled you in on our plans. I know how much you dislike surprises, Vivi."

Vivian stiffened. She never liked that particular nickname. Not at all. She shifted and found herself moving even closer to Josh. She also disliked that Wade presumed to know her better than her own family.

Vivian had introduced Wade and Heather when Vivian had been in college and besties with Wade's younger brother, Jared. Vivian and Jared had met during freshman orientation and had become fast friends. But Vivian had let her heart overstep those friendship boundaries with Jared. All while Jared had been quietly falling for Vivian's roommate instead. But that was all in the past. *Water under the bridge*, as her dad often said. Everyone had moved on. Vivian had moved so far on that she'd skipped graduate school and headed out into the professional world of rodeo.

And while Vivian chased her barrel racing dreams for the past three years, her sister created the life Vivian had once imagined sharing with her best friend, Jared. If the dreams-achieved score was being tallied, her sister was certainly winning. Still, Vivian wanted her sister to be happy. And her parents too. She truly did. Yet Vivian also wanted the same for herself. Surely that wasn't so wrong.

What was she supposed to do now? Vivian glanced at Josh as if her fake boyfriend was truly her knight. Her champion.

"Vivian and I continually surprise each other." Josh's arm curved around Vivian's waist, and he tucked her more firmly into his side. His words sounded genuine. Easy. "I find there's something refreshing about that."

There was something all too welcoming about her handsome cowboy and standing in his embrace. Vivian wanted to blame it on her gratitude to Josh for going along with her scheme. But that butterfly feeling in her stomach hinted she just might be feeling more than grateful. *Nice going, Viv.* Already blurring those fake-relationship boundaries. But she had no time to collect herself.

"Oh, Vivian. Is that beauty over there your horse?" Heather pointed toward the closest pasture. "She must be your horse. You would look so good together. Picture perfect."

Vivian shifted and saw the proud, quite regal, dappled gray Arabian prancing close to the fence railing. Head held high. Its white tail lifted. He was quite stunning. And most definitely not hers.

"Come on, Viv." Heather turned and headed toward the pasture. "Introduce us to your horse."

But she didn't have a horse. One more thing

Vivian couldn't confess. No doubt her family would be thrilled by that bit of news. If her horse was retiring, surely then, Vivian would be as well. And if Vivian was hanging up the reins, then she could finally return home. To the family business and stable life her parents always envisioned for their youngest daughter.

"She is actually a gelding." Vivian joined her family at the pasture fence and eyed the Arabian. Wishing she could slide onto his muscular back, open the gate and ride. Far and fast.

Delight smoothed across her mom's face. She tipped her head toward Vivian. "What's your horse's name again, Vivian?"

Panic pushed into Vivian's throat. Those warning bells blared. *Confess. Confess. Confess.*

"Artie," Josh said. Once again, he was at Vivian's side as if he never intended to leave. He smiled at her mom and added, "It's short for Aristocrat."

And the very same horse Josh hadn't wanted Vivian to ride earlier. The same one he'd hinted she was too inexperienced for. He hadn't seemed to like her in the arena. Now he kept coming to her aid. She hadn't much cared for him in the arena either. Now she couldn't get through this without him. What had she been thinking? What was Josh thinking? *Time to come clean.* Vivian blurted, "Dad, you should see Josh's '77 Ford truck that he fully restored. It's incredible."

"I would like to see that sometime." Her dad grinned. "I'll admit I know more about engines and horsepower than I do horses and rodeos."

"That's fine, sir, we can teach you a little about both here," Josh offered.

Her father nodded. But before he could respond, Sam shouted a hearty greeting and strolled over to join the group. Introductions complete, Sam smiled. "Well, now let's all head to the house. We've got snacks and drinks ready to serve."

"I know it's only lunchtime, but I wouldn't mind something on the stronger side." Her father touched his stomach. "The salesman insisted we'd appreciate the extra two feet on the motor home. But I'm not ashamed to admit, there were a few moments on the drive I wondered what I'd gotten us into."

"You'll get the hang of it soon enough." Sam chuckled, then started walking toward the farmhouse. "In the meantime, my grandson Carter owns Misty Grove Distillery. He's got one of the smoothest bourbons on the market, if you're of the mind for a taste."

"Sam Sloan, I definitely like the way you think." Her father strolled beside Sam and the pair fell into easy conversation.

Vivian turned toward Josh. But her mom and sister got to her cowboy first. And the trio headed for the house. Their conversation lively. That left Vivian and Wade to walk together.

Wade brushed his fingers over his polo shirt. "You never mentioned Josh before."

His observation sounded more like a reprimand. Vivian stiffened. "We've kept things quiet. It's relatively new."

"Yet here you are." Wade's words were mild. "Staying at his family's ranch."

"Maggie and his older brother Ryan are my good friends from the circuit." *They supported me when my family couldn't. Or wouldn't.* She added, "They live here too."

"Right. The circuit." Wade nodded, his words were drawn out. "Still trying to make this lifestyle fit you, I see."

There was no trying. Vivian forced herself to sound cheerful. "This is my life."

"But for how much longer?" he asked. "Or is that what this is? Josh is your instant access. Your fast pass, so to speak."

As if Vivian couldn't succeed on her own. As if she couldn't make her own dreams come true. In a world her family seemed uninclined to understand. "What does that mean?"

Wade shrugged. "Just that you have a fine life waiting for you in Phoenix. A corner office with your name on the door. A family who needs you."

"From what I've heard, the business is doing well," Vivian countered. *Without her.*

"There's always room for improvement." Wade shrugged. "Look, Vivian, we've got opportunities coming. Big ones. We could use your help convincing your dad that these opportunities are the right strategy to move the business forward."

"Surely Dad trusts Heather and you," Vivian argued. "Trusts your business decisions."

"Yes, but don't forget there have always been two Bryants at the helm of Complete Milestone Insurance Company." Wade smoothed the wrinkles from his polo shirt. "Since your greats founded the company. That's the legacy."

And her parent's vision. Their two daughters taking over the family insurance business and running it together. Just as her father and his older brother had done. Just as her grandmother and great-uncle had done before that. Vivian crossed her arms over her chest.

"Your dad still believes in the checks and balances with two family members at the helm," Wade said. "That's how it has always worked. How it can only work for the future in his mind."

But what about Vivian and what she wanted?

What made her happy? None of it made her feel good. That was for certain. The thought of moving back to the city made her queasy. Yet disappointing her parents made her ache. Keep running or return? She wasn't ready to decide. She said, "But you are part of the family now, Wade."

"Yes, but I'm not a true Bryant," Wade countered.

She stopped and faced Wade. "What are you saying?"

"It's simple." Wade's expression was reserved. His words straightforward. Direct. "Your dad won't retire until you're back at the table full-time, Vivian."

Wade didn't mean the kitchen table either, sitting down for family meals. Wade meant sitting at the conference table in the boardroom of Complete Milestone Insurance Company. Taking an active role in the family business and its operations. Vivian searched Wade's face, looking for a catch. An out. Was it possible her dad didn't agree with Wade's new strategy for growth? That her dad was only standing behind Vivian as his excuse for not retiring. Or perhaps Vivian was just reaching. She asked, "What do my sister and Mom think about all this?"

"You should talk to them." Sympathy splashed

over Wade's reserved face as if he understood her struggle. "Isn't it past time you remembered who you are, Vivian? Who you are meant to be?"

Vivian's temper frayed around the edges. She shouldn't care what Wade thought. Still, she felt like she was failing everyone all over again. Just once she wanted to measure up. She rubbed the back of her neck and tried to keep calm.

"Believe it or not, I do have your family's best interests at heart. And that includes you." Wade stopped and lowered his voice. "I'm not the enemy here."

But Wade wasn't telling her anything she wanted to hear. He wasn't supporting her rodeo career. He was reminding her of family loyalty. Reminding her that she'd given her word to them three years ago. Now her time was almost up. And it was more than clear she needed that win at the stampede. Then her family would need to keep their word to her.

"Everyone is inside. You can go right in, Wade." Josh stepped beside Vivian. His words were neutral. Then his gaze landed on Vivian, gentle and searching. He held his hand out to her. "Vivian, Grandpa Sam needs our help in the kitchen."

"Think about what I said, Vivian." Wade

never waited for her response. He turned and disappeared inside the house.

Vivian linked her fingers around Josh's and pressed her palm against his. His touch was warm. His grip sure. And everything inside Vivian quieted. Settled. Steadied.

Just like that, Vivian knew.

She could give her heart to a cowboy like Josh Sloan. If she let her heart jump first. If she let her heart take the lead. But the risk wasn't worth the inevitable heartache. Because when it came to love, there was no ribbon for a second-place finish. Nothing to celebrate. And Vivian needed wins now more than ever.

And something about her cowboy told her she didn't have enough grit to recover from his kind of heartbreak.

It was all a pretense anyway.

That perfect fit of their hands. *Pretend.*

That hit of awareness. *Pretend.*

Even that hint of a connection. *Pretend too.*

Vivian loosened her hold and let her fingers slip free from her cowboy's. After all, Vivian certainly had enough grit to keep from falling for a fantasy, didn't she?

CHAPTER SIX

VIVIAN BRUSHED PAST Josh in the doorway and stopped as Maggie and Caleb walked into the laundry room.

"Maggie and I are heading to the Owl to pick up food for everyone." Caleb grabbed his keys from a hook on the wall and set his cowboy hat on his head. "Now, Josh, you can get to know Vivian's family better." When Josh's frown appeared, Caleb's laughter spilled free. "Quality time with your future in-laws is always a good thing, my brother."

"Caleb, keep it down. They'll hear you." Vivian grabbed Josh's twin and nudged him toward the back door. Caleb dragged his boots and laughed louder. Vivian kept prodding him in the back. "You're not helping at all."

"I am." Amusement flashed in Caleb's gaze when he glanced down at Vivian. "I told you, Vivian. Josh needs this in his life."

Vivian finally got Josh's twin outside. No sooner had she turned around than Maggie wrapped her in a tight hug. Her friend whispered, "Don't worry, Viv. I'll fill Ryan and Josh's other brothers in on the particulars. Your fake relationship with Josh will feel real in no time at all."

That was exactly what Vivian feared. If her friends started to act like it was real, Vivian might start to believe it too. Vivian clung to her friend and steadied herself. *No.* She would trust herself not to get tripped up again. Her gaze slipped to Josh and held. "Don't say anything, Mags. I need to come clean. I shouldn't have done this to Josh."

"Just go with it, Viv. Josh doesn't seem to mind." Maggie released her and squeezed Vivian's shoulders. "You found the perfect cowboy for you. This was totally meant to be."

Her perfect cowboy. No, she hadn't done that. Vivian wasn't interested in finding *her one*. That implied things like relationship labels, declarations and opening herself up. *Not happening.* Vivian chose to take her risks in the arena rather than with her heart these days. Vivian shook her head. "Nothing about this is perfect."

"Besides being a really good guy, Josh *is* a cowboy. It's all he knows. Who he is." Maggie tugged her closer to the washing machine and whispered, "Josh can help convince your family this is the only life for you. Josh is perfect for Operation Rodeo Life or Bust."

Vivian squeezed her forehead. "Operation what?"

"You heard me." Maggie raised her eyebrows. "It's catchy, isn't it? I just came up with it."

"I panicked out there, Mags." There was an urgency to Vivian's words. "I had no master plan. There is no Operation Rodeo Life or Bust."

"There is now." Maggie hooked her thumb over her shoulder. "Your sister is pregnant with twins. And your family could very well be expecting to pack you up into that RV out there and take you home with them permanently."

Right. Hadn't Wade alluded to that much? Vivian needed wins. In the arena. In her personal life. To prove to her family that she hadn't made a mistake skipping graduate school. That her life was definitely on the right track. But how far was she willing to go?

"Viv, we'll talk later." Maggie squeezed her arm. "Just promise me you won't reveal anything yet."

"Vivian," Sam called out. "You coming? Josh and I need help in here."

Gotta keep on leaping, Vivian, or you'll never get where you intend to go. Vivian whispered, "Fine. I won't say anything. But the same goes for you too, Mags."

Maggie was already out the door when Vivian realized she'd never gotten her friend's word to keep quiet. Vivian searched for her smile and walked out of the laundry room. How much worse could it get, really?

Her family was gathered around the large kitchen island. Sam ladled hot chocolate into an oversize mug and handed it to Isabel. Wade dropped marshmallows into Heather's cup, then into his own. Josh stood at the end and prepared a cheese tray. Vivian headed toward her cowboy.

Her mother sipped her hot chocolate. Her words and smile were warm and soft. "So, Isabel, how do you fit into the Sloan family?"

That was when Vivian realized *worse* was something of a sliding scale. And it was slipping in the wrong direction.

"I'm Josh's ex-wife." Isabel dropped that truth and sipped her hot chocolate as if she'd just confessed her secret addiction to mini marshmallows. "I'm just here for a horse to ride in the rodeo. I'm a barrel racer like Vivian."

Not quite like Vivian at all. Isabel was also a former rodeo queen with unfinished business. Who'd once claimed Josh as her husband and was now suddenly back. Vivian couldn't forget those facts. No, Vivian and Isabel were nothing alike. Yet, there was a bravado in Isabel that Vivian recognized. That hinted of a loneliness Vivian understood.

The silence became more awkward.

Wade frowned into his mug as if the chocolate had suddenly seized. "Then, you're competing against Vivian next weekend."

"I hope to." Isabel casually dropped more marshmallows into her mug as if Wade's assessment didn't faze her. She added, "It all depends on Josh and his fastest horse."

"Josh is a horse trainer," Vivian explained. She met Josh's gaze and smiled. "One of the best in the South."

Vivian's father accepted a tumbler glass filled with two fingers of bourbon from Sam. Then offered the older cowboy a grateful smile. Sam lifted his bourbon glass in a toast to his grandson. Pride in his gaze.

"Sounds like a conflict of interest," Heather offered with a small chuckle. "Giving your ex-wife your fastest horse to use to compete against your new girlfriend."

"There's more to barrel racing than a fast horse," Josh offered. He leaned against the counter, his arms loose at his side. His stance relaxed as if he was content to give her family an in-depth lesson on horses and horse training.

She didn't want him to waste his time. Her family wasn't interested in the details. Vivian poured hot chocolate into a mug and chose her words carefully. "Well, I want Isabel on the fastest horse. I imagine she wants the same for me. Then we know we've earned our victories against the best."

Isabel tipped her chin at Vivian. Her smile there and gone.

Heather wrinkled her nose. "Still doesn't feel right to me."

What didn't feel right was Josh and Vivian being together. Her family only needed to look at Isabel standing next to Josh to realize they were the obvious match. Cowgirl and cowboy from their appearances to their backgrounds. Vivian used a spoon to dunk her marshmallows to the bottom of her mug, willing her interest in her cowboy to dissolve too.

Isabel pulled her phone from her pocket and glanced at the screen. "Sam, is there a place I can take this? It's Kelsey. She's all in to help with the stampede."

"I'll show you to Carter's office." Sam motioned toward the hall and waited for Isabel to join him.

The pair walked away and left Josh and Vivian alone to face off with her family. On one side of the island stood her cowboy and the Western lifestyle she wanted. On the other, her family. With their casual attire that tipped into the more formal side of business wear. Still, they'd never pretended to be anything other than who they were. Smart. Accomplished. And tight-knit. Vivian brushed at the horsehair on her sweater. If only Vivian could've figured out where she fit.

"We've certainly got expert assistance for our rodeo rescue." Sam returned and smiled wide. He headed toward the large whiteboard lodged like a misplaced Halloween sign among all the unopened holiday bins in the family room. "I'll wager it comes together in less than a week."

"Rodeo rescue." Her mother glanced toward the family room. Interest skimmed over her words and face. "What exactly is that?"

"We're moving the Silk and Steel Cowgirl Stampede to Three Springs. The original location in Belleridge suffered an electrical fire and had to be shut down," Sam explained. "We'd only just created our task force when you arrived. Individual duties are yet to be assigned."

"Task force." Her dad turned and walked into the family room to join Sam. "Catherine and I have been on our fair share of task forces over the years back in Phoenix."

"We could always use more help." Sam stroked his fingers through his beard.

"No," Vivian blurted. All eyes were once again on her. Vivian held out both hands and softened her words. "I mean, you're supposed to be on vacation. Relaxing and all that in your new motor home."

"We're not really the relaxing type though." Her dad laughed off Vivian's words. "We keep trying and it never seems to hold for long."

Sam lifted his eyebrows in understanding.

"A rodeo rescue sounds much more exciting than figuring out water hook-ups for the plumbing in the motor home anyway." Her mom stood in front of the dry-erase board and picked up a marker. "Sam, where do we put our names? Count us in."

"Wait." Vivian stood behind the couch. "You don't have plumbing?" Why would they? Her parents' travels always included five-star hotel accommodations, room service and spa appointments. Working plumbing was always a given. Yet they'd leased a motor home and driven to Texas. What were they thinking?

"Plumbing that works. No, we don't have that." Her mom waved her hand and pointed the marker at Vivian. "Just don't use the bathrooms in the motor home and everything will be fine."

"Or the sinks either." Heather walked over to the love seat couch and sat down.

"Those too." Her mom chuckled then eyed Vivian. "It's not that bad, Vivian. We figured it out. We just took advantage of rest stops on the drive here."

But if they'd broken down, what would they have done then? She asked, "Didn't the salesperson at the dealership walk you through instructions on operating a motor home?"

"He gave us a link to the tutorial videos on the internet." Her dad sat on the other couch and grinned up at Vivian. "We planned to watch them this week and get ourselves fully immersed in the motor home know-how."

"Where did you plan to stay tonight?" Vivian worked to keep her words even. These were successful, professional people. Surely, they had made arrangements. Surely, they didn't just jump into the motor home and hit the road.

"I'm sure there's a hotel in town." Her mom swirled the marker around in the air.

Sam shook his head. "Afraid not."

"A quaint bed-and-breakfast, then," Heather suggested. Hope filled her face.

Josh moved beside Vivian and rubbed the back of his neck. "Unfortunately, it closed over ten years ago."

"We have ourselves quite a nice campground," Sam offered. "Starfall campground is only twenty minutes from our front doorstep."

"Campground, it is." Worry and something close to doubt crossed her father's features. "It is why we leased a motor home after all. We've always talked about getting one when we retire."

Heather and Wade looked slightly less than thrilled and more than a little ill-at-ease. Not Vivian's concern. Served them right for ambushing her like they had. Still, they'd never camped in their entire lives. Not even a tent pitched in the living room. Not one of them. She'd have to go with them. Stay in the motor home too. Show them how things worked. Now Vivian was the one feeling ill.

"Or you could stay right here," Josh offered.

Sam smiled. "We have more than enough space to park your motor home and more than enough extra rooms."

No. No. Abort. That would put them in Vivian's backyard, literally. She had to practice, not watch over her family, who didn't know the difference between a suburban backyard and a ranch. "That's really generous but I'm sure my parents would rather spend the time getting acquainted with RV living."

"It's just one option for our retirement." Her father leaned his elbows on his knees and swirled the ice in his bourbon glass. "Since we are all practically family, I believe it's okay for me to be honest." He glanced around the room. At everyone's nods, he added, "That motor home out there scares me."

Her mother tucked her blond hair behind her ear and looked almost sheepish. "That motor home terrifies me too."

Sam reached over and squeezed her mother's shoulder as if offering her reassurance.

But this was absolutely not the time for renter's remorse. Her parents could have all the remorse when they returned to Phoenix. Not now. Not here.

"I, for one, would love a decent bed." Heather touched her stomach. "And a working bathroom."

Wade dropped his arm around Heather's shoulders. "Morning sickness still catches her."

Sam gave her sister a sympathetic smile.

Vivian glanced at Josh and widened her eyes, silently willing him to understand. Her family could not stay at the farm. There had to be another solution. Josh set his hand over hers. "You can all stay in my apartment. It's a two-bedroom, two-bathroom over the workshop."

No. He just gave up his apartment for her family. Now Vivian felt even more guilty. He was a good guy. A really decent one, in fact. Important characteristics for a boyfriend—fake or otherwise. Now she had one more reason to like him. And one more reason to owe him.

"But where will you stay, Josh?" her mom asked.

"Josh still has a room here." Sam picked up his own marker and nodded at Josh. "And I think it's a fine solution."

Vivian thought nothing was going to be fine.

"Well, now that the sleeping arrangements are settled, we must get back to our task force," Sam declared.

"Wonderful." Her mother beamed. "Put us to work, Sam, so we can earn our room and board."

Vivian braced her hands on the back of the couch. This was so not good.

"Maggie is handling the rodeo and moving it to its new location." Sam picked up a clipboard. "My grandson Ryan knows the Belleridge rodeo coordinator and already introduced Maggie. The two women hit it off. So the process should be fairly seamless, with them working together."

Isabel returned from the office and raised her hand. "Kelsey and I will handle the donations for the kids' midway games and the silent auction at the gala." No sooner were those words out than Isabel was answering another phone call and heading back to the office.

Sam read over the list on the dry-erase board, then checked it against his clipboard. "That leaves the games and the gala itself."

Her mother's hand shot into the air. "We can handle the games."

Vivian worked to keep the surprise and doubt out of her words. "Mom, what do you know about carnival games?"

"Don't you remember when you were in grade school?" Her mom picked up her hot chocolate from the coffee table and took a sip. "Your dad and I worked the fall festival each year."

Heather and Vivian had attended a private school in the city. The fall festival was set up and organized by professional event planners. The booths and games were brought in and assembled by the organizers. The food catered by local restaurants.

"You sold raffle tickets," Heather said, siding with Vivian for once.

"And I cued the music for the musical chairs game." Her dad lifted his bourbon glass and took a sip. "I used to set aside those caramel apples and pumpkin–cream cheese cupcakes from the bakery down the block."

"Dad," Heather scolded. "Those were for the kids."

"I figured my time was worth a cupcake or two." Her father laughed and shrugged.

"We should have musical chairs, Sam." Her mother started a carnival game list on the whiteboard. "It was always a favorite for the kids."

"It's a rodeo," Vivian cautioned. "Not a school gymnasium." There was dirt and dust. Not to mention, Three Springs wasn't the city. Vivian wasn't certain where the donations would come from.

"Right." Her mom snapped her fingers. "Let's make it western themed. The kids can jump from horseshoe to horseshoe."

"Call it Holiday Horseshoes Musical Chairs," Heather amended. "The prizes can be all about Christmas. And the horseshoes wrapped in red and green ribbons."

"Now, I like your thinking." Sam quickly wrote notes on his clipboard. "We can call the whole thing The Cowgirl and Cowboy Christmas Carnival."

"The stampede goes Christmas." Josh moved to stand beside Vivian and crossed his arms over his chest.

He looked and sounded about as thrilled as Vivian. Which was not at all.

"Hmm, we certainly can't stop at musical chairs." Her father tapped his fingers against his knees. "The kids need to have more things to do."

"How about Rope a Christmas Tree?" Wade suggested.

Not Wade too. Her whole family was jumping into the Christmas carnival with both feet.

Yet they were all insurance brokers. Skilled in premiums, contract lingo and underwriting. Not ring toss, milk can tumble or hole in one. Not to mention, Vivian had always handled the company parties and employee fun days when she'd worked there in college. The past few years, they'd used an outside event planner. Yet someone suggested Snowball Bushel Toss. Race a Reindeer. And Christmas Wreath Cornhole.

Vivian wanted to put her hands into the letter *T* position and call time-out. Then remind her family that ideas were wonderful and welcome. But execution was where it counted. Yet she feared they just might look to her for the execution. Vivian had to find a horse and start practicing, not build carnival games. If her family was going to dive into the carnival deep end, they were going to have to swim too.

Her mother finished listing the rest of the game ideas on the whiteboard at the same time Sam finished writing on his clipboard. He lifted his head. Satisfaction lifted his smile into his white beard. Then he aimed his shrewd gaze at Vivian and Josh. "You two are awfully quiet over there. And I think I know why."

Vivian glanced at Josh. He never flinched under his grandfather's steady regard. Vivian straightened her shoulders and looked back at Sam.

Sam pressed his pencil against his clipboard. His words held a tinge of alarm, but his gaze was alert. "You two are worried we forgot about the gala, aren't you?"

Vivian was worried it all had gone too far. Way too far. And it didn't appear to be stopping anytime soon either. "Gala. What gala?"

"The one happening after the rodeo." Sam's smile sparked in his eyes "It was supposed to be a barn dance when the stampede was happening in Belleridge."

"That's quaint." Heather leaned into Wade's side. "We've never been to a real barn dance."

"You won't have your chance here either. A barn dance wasn't fancy enough for our Abby and Maggie," Sam explained. "They changed it to a gala with a silent auction."

"Holiday galas are lovely this time of year." Her mother sighed and touched her button-down blouse as if it was a ballroom gown. "Everyone gets dressed up. There's dancing. Good food."

"They become annual affairs when done right. The hottest invitation of the season," her dad added. "The silent auctions make for solid fundraisers too."

Vivian yanked off her cowboy hat, suddenly

feeling too hot. Or maybe that was simply the bad feeling tumbling through her. Time for that time-out.

"That sounds like a lot of work." Josh drummed his fingers on the back of the sofa. "Can't we just cancel it?"

"Tickets were already sold for the barn dance." Sam shook his head. "Maggie and Abby promised to honor those tickets for the gala. Give folks something special to look forward to."

Josh's fingers stilled. "Isn't the rodeo supposed to be that something to look forward to?"

Vivian smashed her straw cowboy hat. Nothing squashed her unease.

Sam looked as if he had something up his sleeve. "The gala and silent auction will raise money for repairs at the Belleridge rodeo arena."

"Sounds like the show, or rather gala, must go on," her dad announced, sounding all too delighted.

"That takes us full circle." Sam leveled his gaze on Vivian and Josh. "Right back around to Vivian and Josh."

Josh's shoulder brushed against Vivian's. Her grip tightened on her cowboy hat.

"I should mention that Vivian helped plan our company holiday parties with me for years," her mother offered.

"That experience will be good to have. And

Josh knows the area well," Sam added. "He can help find a venue."

"What are you saying?" Vivian kept her focus on the older cowboy. Felt Josh go entirely too still beside her.

"Welcome to the task force," Sam announced. "You two are our new gala cochairs."

"We need to write their names down." Her mom was back at the dry-erase board, happily filling up the entire white space.

And Vivian was back to that sliding scale and wondering exactly how much worse *worse* could get.

CHAPTER SEVEN

COCHAIR. A GALA. With Vivian.

No way. Josh shook his head. As if that would dislodge his surprise and free his refusal.

His grandpa beamed at him brighter than a star topper on a Christmas tree. Josh found himself trapped in the glare. And unable to voice all the reasons he was the complete wrong choice to put on a gala.

He worked with his hands. Had an affinity for power tools. And smelled like horses most days. His dress boots were more scuffed than most people's work boots. *Fancy* wasn't in his vocabulary. And his Gran Claire always accused him of misplacing his manners.

Vivian's shoulder bumped against his. She leaned closer and whispered, "If we run now, could we claim we never heard any of this?"

He shifted toward her. "Like, deny we were ever here."

"Exactly." Her pretty amber eyes were too wide. Her face too serious. Her cowboy hat almost unrecognizable in her tense grip.

She no more wanted to plan a gala than he did. And somehow that made everything better. He tilted his head toward the cunning pair at the whiteboard and kept his voice low. "Your mom and my grandpa look quite determined."

Her gaze slanted toward the pair. Her mouth dipped down. "My mom works out every day. She would definitely chase us down."

"Grandpa Sam would too," Josh whispered. He eased her cowboy hat from her grip and set it to rights. "Only he'd drive a tractor to catch us."

Vivian caught her laughter in her hands. Her eyes sparkled. And Josh settled in beside her.

Grandpa Sam glanced over his shoulder and narrowed his gaze on Josh. "Have something you'd like to share with us, Josh?"

"No, sir." Josh rubbed his cheek to keep his smile in check. "Vivian and I were just discussing themes for the gala."

Everyone shifted to look at him. No one bothered to hide their surprise. Well, if that didn't chafe, just a little bit. He might lack manners. And prefer to spend his time outside with his horses. But that hardly meant he didn't know the basics of things like galas and dances. True, he practically lived in a barn, but he hadn't been born in one. He worked the wrinkles out of Vivian's cowboy hat. "We need a theme. And it should be something more romantic than the Cowgirl Stampede."

Sam tapped his marker against his chin. "You're not wrong. What are you suggesting?"

Vivian picked up a snow globe from the end table and shook it, sending the fake snow swirling inside. "Winter wonderland."

Josh watched Vivian's fingers trail over the glass dome as if she wanted to escape inside the globe. Then he grinned at his grandpa. "Or how about this? A Cowgirl's Christmas Wonderland."

"That's good." Heather shifted on the couch and flicked her fingers as if she was tossing snowflake confetti into the room. "I can see it now. Rustic, upscale decor. Luminaries to light the outdoor paths and ballroom. Dozens of snowflake lights twinkling from the ceiling. Flocked Christmas trees with blue-and-silver ornaments and sleigh bells. So many sleigh bells."

"Sounds like maybe you should be chairing the gala instead, Heather," Josh remarked.

Heather laughed and shook her head. "That's where I stop. Vivian is the one you want."

Vivian. The one he wanted. Not at all. What he wanted was to continue going it alone. Like he had been. Because there was nothing wrong in Josh's world as it was right now. He balanced

Vivian's cowboy hat on the back of the couch. Still his gaze tracked back to Vivian and held.

"Vivian has always known how to turn my ideas into something fantastic," Heather continued. "She'll create a winter wonderland unlike any we've ever seen."

Vivian glanced away as if uncomfortable with her sister's praise.

Suddenly Josh was looking forward to seeing Vivian's wonderland gala too.

Vivian's mother wrote the theme on the dry-erase board. Grandpa Sam checked his clipboard. "We've still not settled on carnival food."

"I'm going to head out." Isabel returned from another phone call and interrupted the next carnival debate. She pulled her car keys from her coat pocket. "I'm meeting Kelsey for dinner and we're going to put together our donation to-do list."

"Let us know if you'd like help," Vivian's mother offered.

"That's our out," Vivian whispered to Josh, then she said louder, "Josh and I will walk you out, Isabel." And then she hurried after Isabel to the back door.

That left Josh no choice but to follow. The back door had barely shut when Vivian stopped on the porch and faced him. "I was serious earlier."

About running away together? Creating a winter wonderland for two. For just us. Josh waited.

Vivian continued, "I want Isabel to have your fastest horse."

That was not what he'd been expecting. Josh opened and closed his mouth. He hadn't even decided if his ex-wife was riding one of his horses. Let alone his fastest.

Isabel touched Vivian's arm and offered her a soft smile. "I don't even know if I'm allowed to saddle up one of Josh's horses yet."

Apparently, his ex-wife still knew a few things about him. Josh wasn't sure if that bothered him or not. What did bother him was that he wanted to know more about Vivian. Like everything. But a fake boyfriend shouldn't really be interested. And a gala cochair should be focused on the event, not his partner. But Josh was first and foremost a cowboy. One who clearly liked a cowgirl. Now he just needed to decide what he was going to do about it.

"Why wouldn't you let Isabel ride, Josh?" Vivian set her hands on her hips and stared him down.

And now Josh was back to learning a few things about himself this day too. Like how much he preferred a wisp of a cowgirl who refused to back down. Who seemed more than intent on continuing to challenge him.

Vivian jammed her finger against her chest and never released his gaze. "I get me, but not Isabel. I don't get that, Josh."

What Josh couldn't get was the exact color of Vivian's hair. The strands were far from a simple, plain brown. That, he'd realized when she'd removed her cowboy hat inside the house earlier. And he'd been fascinated trying to name all the different colors from the lightest wheat to the deepest chestnut. Now, with the late afternoon sky, he was once again captivated.

Isabel moved to stand beside Vivian. "What do you mean, Vivian?"

"I'm still a relative novice in Josh's eyes." Vivian swiped at a long strand of her hair floating against her cheek. Her frustration clear in her movements.

Her hair fell back against her skin, distracting Josh again. No doubt about it. His cowgirl had caught his attention something good. And that was definitely *not* so good. Especially for a cowboy like him who knew firsthand that love and happiness were in fact mutually exclusive. And that he could be perfectly happy without love. Staying single and on his own.

"That hardly means you can't handle Josh's

horses, Vivian." Isabel set her hands on her hips, mimicking Vivian's stance. Irritation ran through her words. "I've seen Vivian compete, Josh. She has all the skills you look for."

Josh finally pulled his gaze away from Vivian. It was surreal, really. Having his ex-wife and his fake girlfriend defend each other to him. As if they'd become fast friends in the past few hours. And just how was he supposed to respond to their accusations?

"I appreciate that, Isabel," Vivian cut in. "But this isn't about me."

It was becoming more and more about her. More than Vivian could even imagine. More than he cared for, really. Josh linked his hands to stop himself before he reached over, tucked Vivian's hair behind her ear and grazed his knuckles across her cheek. Just the briefest, lightest of touches. That was all he'd need to discover how soft her skin was. "Vivian, you should know that Isabel and her second husband have stables on their ranch that rival ours."

"Our geldings are too green for this competition," Isabel countered. "You have the best-trained horses in the Panhandle, Josh. I'm sure you have a horse you want to see compete. Really compete."

Full disclosure, he had three. His words came

out on a long sigh. "The horse will decide if he wants to compete or not, Isabel. You know it's not my decision."

"Agreed." Isabel's grin was small as if she wasn't quite certain of their victory yet. She added, "Think of it this way, Josh. You've got a veteran barrel racer and an up-and-comer. What could be better to showcase the versatility of your horses?"

"Isabel is right. We are good for your business." Vivian stepped right back into the fray. "With both of us riding your horses, you've hedged your bets. We're both aiming to win."

"And I would bet on us." Isabel bumped her shoulder against Vivian's. Both women notched their chins higher.

A united front. His past and what could possibly be his future. Josh was certain his grandfather would have something to say about this. But all he knew was that he was most comfortable standing still. Right there in the present.

"If you coach us this week on your horses, Josh, we'll be even better prepared." The challenge was there in Vivian's words. In her direct gaze.

Josh never flinched.

"I'm staying with Kelsey at her apartment in downtown Three Springs," Isabel said. Hope worked through her words. "I can definitely come here to practice."

"We can practice together," Vivian added. "That way we won't take up too much of your time, Josh."

Careful what you wish for. Josh scrubbed his hands over his face. He'd wanted to be in demand as a horse trainer. He'd wanted the same for his horses. But not quite like this. Nothing like this. Coaching both his ex-wife and his fake girlfriend. Surely even they understood that might just be a line too far. He worked his refusal around in his throat and said, "I cannot believe I'm agreeing to this."

Isabel's eyes widened. Her mouth dropped open.

He was as stunned as his ex-wife. Even more so when Vivian launched herself into his arms with an enthusiastic thank-you. And Josh finally had his cowgirl in his embrace. And he wanted to hold on. Instead, he released her and added a warning to his words. "There's no guarantee you guys will find a match with my horses."

Vivian nodded and gave him one of her dimple-framed smiles. The one that made him consider sunshine, rainbows and second chances at love.

Vivian asked, "When do we get to meet your horses?"

Nothing for it now. One day he'd learn to put his boot down and stand his ground and simply tell people: *I'm sorry. That's not possible.* That day was clearly not today.

Josh focused and ran through his schedule, which horses were to be worked and which were to be turned out. But that only happened if his horses were 100 percent in the morning, and no one was off their feed. If their evening hay remained in the morning, then all bets were off. He said, "Let's meet at the stables sometime before noon tomorrow."

"We need to add gala planning to tomorrow's agenda too." Vivian tugged on her ponytail, freeing more strands. "My mom excels at putting together to-do lists. She's probably building one right now for us."

Right. The gala. The event he and Vivian were going to now put together. He'd convince Vivian there should be a time limit for gala planning. Whatever they got accomplished in that time frame was what they would do. Nothing more. Nothing less. Satisfied with his decision, he said, "We can work on the gala after our practice session."

Isabel touched Vivian's arm. "I'll text you my schedule in the morning after Kelsey and I figure out exactly what we need to get done for the rodeo." Then she offered Josh a quick smile and a thank-you before heading to her SUV.

Josh waited for Isabel's car to start then turned toward Vivian.

Vivian grabbed his hand. "You aren't going to regret this. I promise."

Josh glanced at their joined hands. There were going to be regrets. Of that he was quite certain. What he didn't know yet was whether they were the kind he could live with or not.

"Oh man. Real nice, Vivian," she muttered then looked at him. Her eyes wide. Her shoulders lowered. "You already have regrets, don't you? I mean how could you not?"

He could've stopped her, but there was something appealing about her voice. About all of her, really.

"I mean I introduced you to my family as my boyfriend without even asking you first," she continued on. "Now I talked you into coaching me too. What is wrong with me? I like a good adventure, but…"

Josh reached up, tucked her hair behind her ear. Skimmed one knuckle across her cheek. Finally appeased his curiosity, and in the process, captured her full attention.

He watched her breath catch—the smallest hitch. She trailed her fingers over her cheek as if capturing his touch. Then she blinked and seemed to draw herself up before her words started spilling out again, both vibrant and sweet. "I'll fix this, Josh. No one else knows. Maggie promised not to tell anyone. It'll be fine." She wrapped her free hand around their joined ones. Her grip and words earnest. "We just won't bring our relationship status up anymore. And we'll keep our distance from each other. It won't look like we're even together. That'll work, right?"

He quietly closed the distance between them.

She never retreated, edged even closer, then said, "Never mind. That's not a good plan. I don't like it either."

As for him, he very much liked that Vivian seemed less inclined to release his hand than he did hers.

"I'll just go inside and tell everyone I misspoke earlier. I meant friend, not boyfriend." Vivian blew out a breath. Her cheeks turned a delightful pink color. "Or I'll convince them that they misheard me. I mean your grandpa misheard you when you told him that you'd marry me. It happens all the time."

Josh squeezed her hand. "About that…"

Too late. One by one, his brothers' trucks rolled into the wide, circular driveway, followed by several more vehicles. Headlights flashing and horns honking.

Uncle Roy was the first one to hop out from Ryan's truck. His cheerful voice boomed across the driveway. "There's no avoiding Christmas this year. Tess and Maggie got trees for every room in the house, including your place, Josh."

His place. More engines were cut off. The rest of his family emerged and headed for him and Vivian. Josh said, "I don't need a Christmas tree."

"What? You want your girlfriend's family to feel welcome, don't you?" Uncle Roy was the first to reach them. His eyebrows boomeranged up into his forehead. His gaze sparkled. "Or is it fiancée?"

Vivian's hand clenched down on Josh's before she quickly recovered and extended her arm toward Uncle Roy. "It's just Vivian."

"Well, Just Vivian, it's a true pleasure." Uncle Roy patted Vivian's hand that he held and grinned. "I think I'll head inside to meet the others. And don't linger out here too long, you two. We've got decorating to do."

Ryan jogged across the porch and held the door open for their uncle then called back, "I can't wait to hear all about Josh and Vivian. I feel like I hardly know anything, and I've known Vivian for years and Josh his whole life. You'd think I would've known something about their romance."

Josh frowned at his older brother. Ryan only grinned wider. Beside Josh, Vivian fidgeted with the buttons on her sweater as Josh's other brother approached.

"Maybe Vivian and Josh were worried you'd gossip too much on the circuit, Ryan." Grant tucked his truck keys into his scrub pockets, then pulled Maggie into his embrace for more than a brief kiss. Grant kept his arm around Maggie's waist as if he wasn't ready to let her go while Maggie introduced her fiancé to Vivian.

"So, you can be honest with us, Vivian." Amusement curved from Grant's eyes to his smile. "Ryan really is the biggest gossip on the circuit, isn't he?"

"I can hear you!" Ryan called back.

Grant accepted a food bag from Maggie, then looked at Vivian. "We'll chat later, Vivian. And just know, your secrets are safe with me. It's that doctor-confidentiality oath that we take in medical school."

"Don't listen to anything Grant tells you, Vivian," Ryan said. "We've been friends too long, Viv. You've always told me everything."

"Stop teasing Vivian," Maggie chided. "She has Josh now. He'll keep her secrets."

Josh wasn't certain he'd ever seen cheeks as pink as Vivian's. But there was no stopping any of it now.

Carter, the oldest Sloan brother and his wife, Tess, beelined for Vivian. They skipped handshakes and went straight to welcoming embraces. Tess apologized for smelling like chocolate and for her husband smelling like his distillery. Tess laughed as she called it an occupational hazard and gave Vivian another quick hug. They each grabbed more dinner bags from Maggie's truck and headed inside.

"The food is getting cold, brother." Caleb took a to-go bag from the back seat of Maggie's truck and shoved it into Josh's arms. Then he grabbed the last one.

"We better hurry up." Maggie shut the truck door and smiled brightly. "We've got a busy, fun night ahead of us. I, for one, cannot wait."

Maggie and Ryan disappeared inside.

Josh adjusted the food bag and set his hand on Vivian's lower back. He leaned in and whispered, "Vivian, I think they know the truth about us."

CHAPTER EIGHT

LAUGHTER RUSHED FROM deep inside Vivian and spilled into the crisp air. Josh's family had just green-lighted Vivian and Josh's fake relationship. It was nothing to laugh about. None of it was. Yet her laughter rolled on. And she gave in to it, not caring what Josh thought about her. She let it fill her up until all her panic was finally pushed aside.

She was fooling her family. With a pretend boyfriend. And all of Josh's relations were seemingly in on it now too. It was such a bad idea. A very bad one. Vivian needed to back away, not keep leaning into it. As if she liked the pretense. As if she liked Josh.

Liked Josh. There was the one truth at the core of the entire mess of her own making. She liked Josh. But Vivian didn't have any goals to be a couple. All Vivian chased these days was another rodeo. A belt buckle. And a jackpot.

Not to mention there was that unfinished business of his. With a former rodeo queen who happened to be his ex-wife. Now she'd wedged herself between them. And bad just got worse. She had to give Josh an out. Let him off the hook. Vivian buried her face in her palms. "This is so wrong."

Josh tugged on her hands. "What was that?"

Vivian took in his appealing eyes and his gentle smile. Lost herself in her cowboy and the what-ifs. "We have maybe five minutes before they come looking for us. But we can't go in there without knowing something about each other."

"We have time for favorite food. Favorite color." He tapped his chin. "And our first fake date."

"Grilled cheese." Vivian smiled and pointed at him. "But bread and cheese only. None of those grown-up add-ins allowed."

"Old school. Got it." He chuckled. "Gran Claire's bacon-potato soup. Real bacon only."

"Is there any other kind of bacon?" Vivian returned, then added, "Red and silver are my colors. Christmas is my favorite season."

"No favorite color. But I'm starting to see the appeal of auburn," he mused. "I'm partial to New Year's."

"Always looking to the year ahead." She tipped her head and studied him. "Rather than celebrating the moments that already passed."

"Something like that." His gaze skimmed

over her face. "That leaves us with our first date."

"An outdoor concert in the park. Picnic basket and blanket and sunshine." Good music. Easy conversation. And no pretense. One perfect afternoon with one perfect cowboy. Vivian pulled her wayward thoughts back in line and asked, "What's your idea?"

"First date would be a trip to the farmers market and cooking dinner together at home." He paused, then dipped his chin in a small nod. "Yeah, I'm going with that."

"I'm a bad cook," Vivian confessed. As if that was important information for him to have. As if they were discussing an actual date.

"I'm not." One of his eyebrows twitched. "And we'd be cooking together."

Vivian swallowed her sigh. Told herself to stop. Told herself it was all just made up. Still, she couldn't help asking, "Candle-lit dinner?"

"Definitely. And a fire in the fireplace." A slow grin shifted across his face. "And mistletoe. There'd be that too."

"I like that." *I like you.* That whisper came from her heart. Vivian stepped back. Let her mind grab the reins. *Stick with the plan, Viv.*

The one that would use a fake relationship to keep her out of an office chair and in her saddle. The one that would get her what she really wanted—that spot on the national barrel racing team. Then she'd keep Dusty with her. And her small rodeo family would remain intact along with her current career.

Josh lifted his gaze over her shoulder then glanced back at her. "Vivian."

Yes. I want to have that date. With you. Instead, she managed a breathless *hmm* sound.

"Our five minutes are up," Josh said.

His words were barely out when the porch door swung open. Vivian turned around only to find the Sloan brothers crowded behind her. Each one was a presence all on their own. But together, standing shoulder to shoulder, they were a wall of impressive cowboys. She asked, "What's going on?"

"Josh, give the food to Vivian," Carter ordered. "We need to bring in the Christmas trees."

"All the Christmas trees," Ryan added. "It's time to get our Christmas spirit on."

"How many trees did you get?" Vivian asked.

"Too many." Caleb shook his head and narrowed his gaze on Ryan. "Because Ryan and Tess argued over which tree was the best one. Then Carter bought both. But Maggie wanted to pick a tree too and chose the most unfortunate one on the lot."

"So, we had to find a companion for the unfortunate tree." Ryan laughed. "Uncle Roy and

I figured we could tie the two together to make a better tree. But Mags refused and picked out another one."

"Then Uncle Roy spotted a tree he had to have. Something about the branches being sound enough for his purposes." Caleb set his hands on his hips. "Whatever that means."

Vivian skipped her gaze around the group. None of the brothers looked the least bit put out or even that bothered by the Christmas-tree mayhem. Vivian's family had stopped putting up their artificial Christmas tree years ago when they'd started spending Christmas holidays in private cabanas at oceanfront resorts instead.

Now the Sloans had several live Christmas trees to put up. She'd always wanted a live tree growing up, but her parents refused. White carpet and pine needles were not a good look according to her mother. To her father, there was a better-value proposition in artificial tree ownership. Now Vivian was being invited to join in. Excitement flickered inside her.

"Maggie and Tess just declared it was going to be a dining-and-decorating evening since the whole family is together." Carter started across the porch toward the trucks.

Vivian wanted to get straight to the decorating. The Sloans probably had long-standing

Christmas traditions, like the same angel tree topper and homemade popcorn garland. Her excitement flared brighter. Something else Vivian had craved as a kid. But her mother didn't like clutter in the house or the attic. *Keep memories, Vivian, not things. After all, you're less apt to lose or break memories.*

"The only rule tonight is that you can't eat if you don't decorate." Ryan took the food bag from Josh, handed it to Vivian, then aimed his frown at Josh. "Don't even think about it, little brother."

Josh lifted his hands as if surrendering. "What am I thinking?"

"That you're not hungry," Caleb said, his words flat. "And if you're not eating, then you don't have to decorate."

Irritation worked across Josh's face. And if Vivian wasn't mistaken, a hint of guilt.

"It'll be okay, little brother. We are all here for you." Grant wrapped his arm around Josh's shoulders. "Tonight you can get over your decorating phobia."

"It's not a phobia." Josh shoved Grant away. "It's a preference."

Vivian adjusted her grip on the handle of the food bag and eyed Josh. "What kind of preference is it, exactly?"

"The kind that prefers not to get swept up

in all this holiday stuff." Josh folded his arms across his chest and held her stare.

Holiday stuff. He made it all sound like some tedious nuisance. He never cracked a smile. Never shouted: *Just kidding.* Vivian's mouth dropped open. And the truth burst inside her like a blown Christmas bulb. Her cowboy was a scrooge. Of all the Sloan brothers, she chose the anti-Christmas cowboy. "But I love the holidays. The Christmas season most of all."

"You can have it. You can all have it." Josh flicked his hand out. "I'll take a tree inside. Then you can count me out."

He jammed his cowboy hat lower on his head, spun around and walked away. Vivian shoved the food bag at a startled Caleb and took off after Josh. She supposed she should've let Josh's twin and his other brothers handle things. It wasn't really her place. Fixing his aversion to the holidays wasn't her responsibility. But that didn't stop her from chasing her cowboy scrooge down.

She waited for him to lift a tree out of the truck bed, then moved to stand directly in his path. "You have to at least eat with your family, Josh."

Around them, his brothers quietly removed the rest of the Christmas trees and headed back inside the farmhouse.

Josh lowered his tree until the stump touched the gravel near his boot. Then he wrapped one arm around the center, propping the tree against his side. His words were firm. "You aren't going to convince me to decorate."

"I'm not trying to." She was trying to make sure he wasn't alone. Because she'd seen a flash of loneliness before he'd walked off. Just the smallest hint in his gaze that echoed inside her. That drew her to him. Made her want to comfort him. But he wasn't really hers to comfort. Or even look after. Still, that didn't stop her. "I'm trying to get you to eat with your whole family and mine."

"And then what?" he asked, clearly not convinced she wasn't up to something.

"Then we can leave together," Vivian offered.

He eyed her. "But you just told me Christmas is your favorite holiday."

"My favorite season," she clarified. His eyebrows dipped together as if he didn't understand the distinction. She wasn't about to explain. It was hard to put into words. She just knew this time of year gave her hope and more warm feelings than any other. And those feelings weren't exclusive to one day only. She continued, "And it's no big deal. I don't mind leaving. My family hasn't decorated a Christmas tree since I was a little kid."

He wiped the back of his free hand across his mouth. "Why not?"

"We spent Christmas in hotel suites growing up." Vivian shrugged, trying not to sound ungrateful. The locations had been beautiful, even if there hadn't been a chimney for Santa. "There was no point in putting up a tree or decorating when we weren't going to be home."

"What about now?" he asked. There was an intensity in the way he watched her. "You don't live at home anymore."

"I live in a camper." She brushed her hand through the air. Christmas in her own home was buried deep on her priority list these days. "There's hardly any space for me and my gear in my camper. Let alone a Christmas tree." She paused and lifted one shoulder. This wasn't her home. Or her tradition anyway. No sense borrowing what she couldn't have. "It's fine if we leave."

He studied her another minute, then lifted the tree back onto his shoulder. Once it was secure, he extended his free arm toward her. "Let's go."

"Do you need help?" she asked.

"No." He adjusted his hold and chuckled. "I left the biggest trees for my brothers and grabbed the smallest one."

"I'm guessing you might have Maggie's unfortunate tree," Vivian said, unable to keep her laughter in check and her hand out of his. Tomorrow she'd remember to stop holding his hand when no one was around to see.

"Most likely." He held her hand until they reached the back door. She propped it open for him, and he paused in the doorway and looked at her. "I almost forgot. You better have those facts about us straight."

"Why is that?" she asked.

"Because we're not leaving after dinner." One side of his mouth tipped up. "And I'm afraid both families are going to have a lot more questions."

around the table, he made Jana's e-glass full
returning to his chair.

Josh pulled out the stool, flashing Jim that
smile. "All your bz most precious ornament...

Josh had been avoiding the table because...
Vivian certainly didn't feel the discomfort the...

CHAPTER NINE

THE WHOLE FAKE relationship thing was becoming more trouble than untangling strand after strand of Christmas tree lights. And it was all because of his pretend girlfriend. Who Josh wanted to see happy. Not simply fine. Not just okay. But genuinely happy. Like she was right now. Surrounded by his family in the living room, learning every story behind every ornament before she hung it on a tree.

And that was why Josh returned to the kitchen table—the last place he needed to be—after taking Heather and Wade to his apartment. He had potential buyers to call. Horses to check on. Client appointments to confirm. Instead, he plugged in another strand of lights and set about replacing blown blubs. Because there was no end to his family's stories. No end to the decorating. And no way was he going to be the one to dim Vivian's delight.

"I have your most precious ornament and a red-velvet brownie to share." Vivian held a napkin with the brownie in one hand, a glass bell ornament in the other.

Josh pulled out the chair beside him and asked, "Did you say my most precious ornament?"

"Your brothers used the word *guarded*." Vivian carefully set the bell ornament on the place mat. "And explained that you are the only one allowed to hang it on the tree."

"This was one of Gran Claire's favorite ornaments. Gran Claire always claimed when the bell rang, another child made Santa's 'good' list." Josh traced the faint crack in the clear glass ornament that ran from the base of the bell to the top. Tiny crystals covered the top of the bell like snow and still shimmered. He touched the three-dimensional, star-shaped chime and heard the wistfulness in his own words. "I used to listen for the bell to ring and ask Gran Claire if I had finally made Santa's 'good' list."

"That's sweet." Vivian broke the brownie in half and handed it to him.

"It was, until I broke it." Josh set the bell down and took the dessert.

"You didn't." Vivian tugged the place mat closer to her as if to protect the bell ornament from him again.

"We were playing football in the house.

With a foam football," Josh added when Vivian arched an eyebrow at him. "Anyway, Caleb went long. I went high. Had to make the catch and score. We were finally going to beat Grant and Ryan."

A smile played around Vivian's mouth. "And…"

"And I had a little too much awkward zeal in my jump. And Caleb put too much height in the throw." Josh touched his forehead. "The ball and I crashed into the Christmas tree. Me head-first into the lower half. The ball at the top."

Vivian's eyes widened as she chewed a bite of brownie. "Did you knock the whole tree over?"

"Amazingly no. It wobbled something good. I grabbed several branches to stop the fall." Josh tapped the bell ornament. "That's when the bell crashed on the wood floor along with the football." He pointed to the corner of the family room where Maggie and Grant were adjusting lights on the tallest tree. "Right there, in fact. And that's when I knew the bell was not ringing for me that Christmas."

Vivian covered her mouth with her hand.

"My brothers fled the scene, of course." Josh chuckled and shook his head. He still marveled at what could only be described as his grandparents' endless store of patience. That was far from the last messy incident the brothers had caused. "I'm sure my brothers figured there was still a chance they could get on Santa's 'good' list."

Vivian laughed. "There's always hope, I suppose."

"I was left holding the foam football and the broken bell." Josh grinned at her. "All while trying to explain to Gran Claire that I had absolutely no idea what happened."

Vivian finished her brownie. "Did she believe you?"

"Gran Claire knew what we were up to before we did. In this instance, I was covered in flocked pine needles and tinsel. I'm sure she had a fairly good idea all on her own." Yet Gran Claire had taken it in stride. Expressed her disappointment in Josh's poor decision-making skills. And hugged him while doling out Josh's punishment. He added, "We were grounded from all electronics and TV for two weeks. But I convinced my grandma it was all my idea, so she let my brothers off after a week."

"What did you do in the evening with no cell phone or TV?" Vivian asked.

"Fixed the bell." He'd spent hours testing different glues to find one that wouldn't show the cracks. And even more time searching the stores for matching crystals to cover the worst crack. "The next year, I told everyone only I could handle the bell. Because if it broke again, I would know how to fix it."

Vivian touched his arm. "And make your Gran Claire feel better."

That too. Gran Claire had cried when he'd given her the repaired ornament. "I bought Gran Claire a new glass bell ornament every year for Christmas after that. Just in case." He'd forgotten how much fun he'd had finding a unique holiday bell to add to her collection. He picked up the bell again. Set it ringing. The soft chime settled around his memories like one of his grandmother's warm hugs.

"Well, did you ever hear the bell ring for you?" Vivian bumped her shoulder against his. The tease in her words drew him back to her.

"Sadly, no. But it was my own doing," Josh admitted, not even slightly regretful. He was grateful for every bump and bruise and the childhood his grandparents had allowed him to experience. "I really tried to be good each December. But things just never worked out as planned."

"And still Santa came," Vivian said.

"Every year. On time. Despite our antics all month." Josh replaced one last bulb and plugged in the lights. The entire strand sparkled. "That, I suppose, is the magic of the season."

"More working lights." Maggie grabbed the strand from the table, dropped another in his lap, and rushed back to the living room. "Thanks, Josh. Can you fix those, please?"

"What about you?" Josh untangled the colored lights to find the end and settled even more into the evening. Something about Vivian made him content to linger. "Did you get everything on your Santa wish list as a kid?"

"Vivian only ever wanted a horse." Vivian's mother dropped into an empty chair across from them. "She was around four and she'd watched an animated horse movie at her best friend's house. And that was it. She put a horse on her wish list every year after that."

Josh worked on the lights and imagined a younger Vivian writing *horse* on her letter to Santa. He slanted his gaze toward her. "When did Santa bring you your first horse?"

Vivian rolled her lips together. Her eyebrows pulled in slightly. Her fingers bent the napkin, declaring joy to the season, in half. "Santa never did bring me a horse."

Josh wanted to take Vivian's hand in his. Somehow bring back the cheer that was slowly dimming from her gaze. But Josh wasn't the holly, jolly sort of cowboy. At least, he hadn't been since his divorce. Since his wife left him two weeks before Christmas. Yet sitting there with Vivian, he wanted to… He leaned over and plugged in the lights instead.

"A horse was not practical," Catherine explained. Her words were clear-cut and brushed lightly with indifference. "We lived in the suburbs. There was no suitable place for a horse."

Josh didn't think Vivian's mother was intentionally being unkind. Vivian's parents came across as pragmatic and straightforward. And unafraid to explain the truth, even if it meant crushing their young daughter's biggest wish.

Catherine continued, "Vivian understood."

"I got horse-riding lessons when I turned eight." Vivian shifted beside Josh and added, "Mom made sure I never missed a lesson." She paused, her smile and words surprised. "Not once in all those years."

Her mom had found a way to make her daughter's wish come true. There was something to admire about that.

"I took a lot of client calls during the hour drive out to the ranch and the hour back." Catherine tipped her head and considered her wineglass. "I suppose I was remote working before it was a buzzword. And Vivian was my assistant. She took the most meticulous notes for me. I couldn't have done those calls without her."

"I took down every word my mom said on those calls," Vivian stated. "I was worried if I messed up, Mom might not take me to my lessons anymore."

"It's funny," her mom mused. "I started wishing Vivian was with me for every single call and meeting, taking notes. I knew if she'd been taking notes, I wouldn't forget anything."

"Is that why you continued to drive me?" Vivian asked. "So I could be your assistant?"

"That, and it made you happy. But I'm afraid those lessons only encouraged her horse obsession." Catherine swirled her wine in her glass. Her mouth pursed. "We put Vivian in dance. Swimming. Soccer. Band. Theater. All the typical things normal kids like. All the things her older sister loved doing. Yet Vivian only wanted more time with the horses."

Catherine looked baffled. Her words sounded perplexed as if she still couldn't understand where they'd gone wrong with their youngest daughter. Vivian tucked her hands in her lap, her shoulders dipped in and she seemed more than a little uncomfortable now.

Josh reached over, covered Vivian's hands with his own. "Vivian found her passion early. There's nothing wrong with that."

Vivian glanced at him. Surprise in her gaze. Gratitude in her quick grin.

"But passion projects only go so far, don't you think, Josh?" Catherine asked.

Vivian shifted until her palm touched his and her fingers curved around his hand as if she was anchoring herself to him. Then she sat back, looking resigned.

"Everyone knows you can't pay bills with passion alone." Vivian's father handed Catherine a brownie and took a seat next to her. Then Ted added, "And if your passion is a financial burden, are you really a success?"

"There are other measures of success than money." Josh kept his hand in Vivian's and sorted the strand, looking for blown blubs with his other.

"True," her father allowed. Yet his words leaned into professional and unemotional. "But you cannot discount financial stability either."

"Without it, you're trapped in, say, something like an old, cramped camper." Her mother broke off a small piece of brownie.

Vivian's fingers flexed around Josh's hand. "I happen to like my camper."

"That's no way to live, dear." Catherine blinked at Vivian. Her expression puzzled as if her daughter still mystified her. Her words were measured. "But this—" with an elegant flare,

Catherine waved her arm around her "—all this—is a way to live."

"I don't need all this," Vivian argued and glanced at Josh. "Not that I don't appreciate what your family has built here. Especially the hard work it has taken."

Josh squeezed her hand to let her know her explanation wasn't necessary. That he wasn't judging her.

"But if your passion was making money, you would already have something like this," Ted countered. His fingers tapped against his bourbon glass. His words were objective and sensible, as if that was his approach to every part of his life, business and personal. He continued, "You're approaching thirty, Vivian. Isn't it time to have more than a horse and a trailer? Time to be realistic about passion and be responsible about your life."

Vivian pulled her hand from Josh's and set her palms flat on the table. "I can get the lifestyle I want when I win at the rodeo next weekend." Her determination was clear.

"But we just heard at dinner that Isabel is a former barrel racing champion." Her mother leaned forward and lowered her voice. "How do you plan to beat her?"

Vivian inhaled. Her shoulders straightened. She looked as if she was bracing for impact.

The impact of not being good enough in her parents' eyes.

Josh knew that look well. Knew exactly how Vivian felt. He'd felt much the same when his ex-wife had accused him of not being good enough. Right before she'd handed him divorce papers. And no matter how hard Josh had shoved his shoulders back. Or how high he'd lifted his chin. The impact had still shaken him.

He shifted until his shoulder touched Vivian's. To her parents, he said, "Vivian will be riding Artie in the rodeo. He's the fastest horse on the property. And that's how she plans to win."

He didn't allow anyone to respond. Simply pushed his chair back, stood and gathered the lights. Then he held his hand out to Vivian. "Why don't we go hang these lights and get back to the decorating before everyone else does it all."

When her hand landed in his, he wasted no time pulling her to her feet and into his side. And if he had to decorate the entire farmhouse inside and out until Vivian's joy returned, that was what he would do.

Tomorrow he would get back to his priorities. To remembering he had more important things to do than stringing lights and trimming trees.

Tomorrow he would reestablish those fake-relationship boundaries. The ones that would keep his heart out of trouble.

As for tonight, well, Gran Claire always told him: *It's all trouble of your own making, Josh. That's exactly what you've gotten into.* Then she'd hug him and add, *You best enjoy it now. Because getting out of it is a trouble all its own.*

CHAPTER TEN

"Josh. Good morning." Vivian paused in the upstairs hallway outside her bedroom and smoothed a hand over her braids. The ones she'd put into her hair when she'd woken before sunrise, restless and needing something to do. Now the sun was up, and she was even more out of sorts. Usually, she started her day with Dusty.

Though it wasn't a typical morning. She'd spent most of her night, staring at the stars through her bedroom window, sighing and ordering herself to stop. Mostly because of her cowboy. Josh had defended her. Stayed with her until the last ornament had been hung. Looked after her as if she was all that mattered. It'd been sweet and entirely too appealing. And she had to remind herself over and over again what she felt was only pretend. Like the racing of her heart now. Just her imagination. She started, "Josh, I was going to—"

Josh closed the door to his bedroom, held up his hand and stopped her, "Coffee first, then conversation."

Her cowboy wasn't a talkative morning person. But was he a good-morning-kisses-are-okay kind of cowboy? Vivian pressed her lips together and smothered that thought. Certain there was a warning label somewhere stating not to mix fake boyfriends and real kissing. She managed a nod, then turned and hurried down the hall. Willing her cheeks to stop heating on her way downstairs.

In the kitchen, Josh started the coffee machine, then set flavored creamers and a sugar bowl on the kitchen island. Within minutes, he had a large mug of coffee pressed into her hands and one in his own.

He poured hazelnut creamer into his mug. Took a test sip, then added another dash of creamer. It wasn't until he was well into his first cup of coffee that he leaned against the counter and grinned at her. "Sorry. I'm usually the first one awake and I don't see anyone until I've had two cups of coffee."

"I'm sorry for intruding on your coffee metime." Vivian watched him over the rim of her mug. "And I'm not much for talking in the morning either." Kissing, well, that was another matter. Vivian blew her sigh into her coffee, then rushed on, "I've been up for a while and had time to wake up."

"Missing your camper." There was a teasing gleam in his gaze.

"More like my horse, Dusty," she admitted.

His eyebrows flexed. "Where is your horse?"

"With Dr. Caslin in Oklahoma City." Vivian ran through Dusty's injuries and condition, then tugged on her braid. "I know it's only one more week. And he is better off in Dr. Caslin's care. It's just…"

"You'd rather have him with you," Josh finished for her.

Vivian nodded. "And I'm sort of lost without him. I was hoping you might need help in the stables this morning before we practiced."

"I could always use help." He finished his coffee and poured another cup full. "But you should consider bringing Dusty here. Then he'll be with you."

"I don't know," Vivian hesitated.

"We have space," Josh said. "Dr. Paige Bishop is our local veterinarian and a close friend. We can take care of Dusty's rehab together, and if there's anything we can't handle, Paige is only a phone call away."

"I don't want to impose," she said. She was already staying at the farmhouse. Borrowing his horse. And claiming him as her boyfriend. Not to mention her family had taken over his apartment. The imposition line had long since been crossed.

"I don't want you to worry," he countered. "You'll worry less if Dusty is here. You'll be able to sleep. And a well-rested rider is a focused rider."

She was going to need every ounce of her focus if she wanted to win next weekend. Even more if she wanted to win on Josh's Arabian. To say she was nervous about riding Artie was an understatement. He was the fastest horse on the property. And Josh was entrusting him to Vivian. She wanted to earn Josh's trust and Artie's. But she'd only ever competed on Dusty. Vivian tightened her fingers around the coffee mug and worked to calm her unease. She had to get over herself quickly. The stampede was fast approaching.

Josh set his mug in the sink and touched Vivian's arm. "Trust me on this. You need to bring Dusty home with you, Vivian."

Home. Vivian liked hearing that word too much. But this wasn't her home, or Dusty's. And getting too comfortable here would not be good for either of them.

Vivian stepped around Josh and set her coffee mug next to his in the sink. "I'll call Dr. Caslin later. But I don't think I can spare the time to drive to Oklahoma City and back."

Roundtrip was seven hours. That would cut an entire day out of her practice schedule. She had to make every minute with Artie count.

"What's in Oklahoma City?" Uncle Roy walked into the kitchen and snapped the buttons together on his blue-and-red, fleece-lined flannel jacket. Ryan was right behind him, finger-combing his hair into place and yawning.

Josh handed the older cowboy a cup of coffee before Roy reached the stools at the kitchen island. Ryan pulled a professional-looking waffle maker from the cabinet. Then he grabbed a mixing bowl, a box of waffle mix and got to work on the batter.

"Dusty, my horse, is in Oklahoma City," Vivian explained. She tugged the place mat with the creamers and sugar closer to Roy and added, "Josh thinks I should bring him here."

"You certainly should." Uncle Roy nodded and scooped several teaspoons of sugar into his black coffee. "Horses need their family when they're on the mend. Same as people do."

"But you can't leave, Viv." Ryan cracked several eggs into the bowl and whisked the ingredients together. "Grandpa Sam was still talking about the rodeo and gala on his way to bed last night. He's got a gala clipboard with your name and Josh's on it and all the action items listed in red pen."

Right. The gala she was now cochairing. The one that needed to be organized and put together. She'd hoped to discuss that with Josh while getting to know Artie.

"We can get your horse, Vivian," Uncle Roy offered, then glanced at Ryan. "After we finish filming our movie."

Ryan poured batter into the double-sided waffle iron and closed the lid. Steam hissed from the sides of the iron. Ryan frowned. "You're not in the movie, Uncle Roy. I am."

"But the last time I went with you to a movie set, I got a walk-on part. Don't you remember, Ryan?" Uncle Roy smoothed his hand over his lined jacket and waggled his eyebrows at Vivian. "The director and producer liked my look. They called me dashingly Western."

"Well, they were right," Vivian said. She liked the older cowboy and his brother. Roy and Sam had entertained Vivian last night with stories from Christmas pasts. They'd also taught her how to make a spiked white hot chocolate with bourbon. And above all else, they clearly cherished their family.

"I always thought you had a certain star quality, Uncle Roy." Josh set forks and plates on the island. Ryan flipped the finished waffles onto a plate and refilled the iron.

"Hear that, Ryan." Uncle Roy accepted the

plate of waffles from Ryan. "Someone thinks I've got what it takes to be an actor."

"My director buddy called in a favor. One of his stunt riders came down with a bad case of the flu yesterday." Ryan explained. "Production is scheduled to wrap in a few days. They asked me to be a rider for the last set of scenes."

"They're filming outside Tulsa." Roy spread butter over his waffles then dusted them with powdered sugar. "Close enough to your horse, Vivian."

"My trailer is there too," Vivian said. At this rate, she was going to owe the entire Sloan family a favor. She only hoped she could properly pay them all back for their generosity.

"We can handle it," Ryan said, not looking the least bit put out. "Just give me the keys."

Still, Vivian hesitated. She'd been doing things on her own for so long. Accepting help didn't come easily. Even when she knew she needed it. She asked, "Are you sure about this?"

"He's sure." Josh's words were certain and confident and amused. "Because if Ryan stays, he's worried we might put him to work on the gala."

Vivian shook her head but couldn't stop her smile. "Ryan, what if I said my horse was in Kansas City?"

"He would've driven there too," Josh stated.

"It's really unfortunate I'm going to miss putting on a dance. But what can I do?" Ryan spread his arms wide and failed to look the slightest bit remorseful. "Hollywood is calling. I'm an actor in demand."

"You're a stunt rider, big brother." Josh crossed his arms over his chest, but his words lacked any heat. "And I'll remember this."

"Hey, I'm helping your girlfriend out," Ryan countered. He plopped a waffle on another plate and thrust it at Vivian. "There has to be bonus points for that."

"We're reuniting a cowgirl and her horse," Uncle Roy stated. "That's the important part."

"Your bonus, big brother, is that Vivian and I won't put you to work decorating for the gala." Josh laughed, then his cell phone rang. He answered, surprising Vivian by using a formal greeting she would've expected from an executive in a high-rise office suite. His words crisp, professional and to the point. Even his Southern drawl sounded less easygoing. Phone to his ear, Josh walked into the family room and out of listening range.

"Now, Vivian, how does my hair look?" Roy fluffed his salt-and-pepper curls and pulled Vivian's attention back to him. Roy continued, "And tell the truth. I told Ryan we need to stop at Bec's Salon on our way out of town this morning and get our hair tidied up."

Vivian thought Uncle Roy looked like a windblown, cowboy Jack Frost. Charming and all too endearing.

Before she could compliment the older cowboy, Ryan cut in, "We are not stopping at Bec's for haircuts." Ryan aimed his frown at Vivian and added, "Viv, do not encourage him."

"I need to look neat and proper for the camera," Uncle Roy argued, then eyed Ryan as if he was a casting director for a major movie. "You should really consider it."

"I like my look." Ryan ran his hand through his hair, then patted his head as if surprised his cowboy hat was missing. He tugged on his hair, where the wavy strands touched the collar of his long-sleeved shirt. "Just as I am."

Ryan was a cowboy and unapologetic about it. He lived for an eight-second ride on a bucking bronc. Never claimed to want more than the rodeo and his family. And inspired Vivian to embrace the rodeo lifestyle with the same bold conviction.

"What if you meet someone who doesn't like so much cowboy?" Uncle Roy waved his fork at Ryan.

"Then, she isn't the one for me." Ryan squeezed syrup onto his waffle and grinned at Vivian.

"Ask Viv. She agrees with me. We're cowboys and cowgirls from our hats to our boots. We don't change for anyone."

Vivian agreed, of course. And when she was out chasing rodeos, she almost believed it. Yet doubt inevitably crept in. An inner voice whispered she just might not be strong enough. Fast enough. Skilled enough to be the cowgirl her heart always wanted her to be. And she wondered if her dad was right. Had she taken her passion to its limits? Exhausted her dream and still come up short?

Her gaze landed on Josh. He stood in front of the tallest Christmas trees and looked to be arranging the lights while he talked on the phone. He'd told her parents she was riding his best horse. He wouldn't have just said that. He could've picked any other horse in his stables. He must believe in her. Vivian sliced into her waffle and took a bite. Not that she needed Josh's endorsement. It was simply nice to have. Especially since she wasn't throwing in the towel or her reins yet.

"It's a haircut, Ryan." Uncle Roy shook his head and finished his waffle. "It's not like I'm telling you to hang up your boots, move to the city and put on a business suit to go to work in some stuffy office."

No, that life wasn't for Ryan. That was what Vivian's family wanted her to do.

"I can't listen to this." Ryan took Roy's empty plate over to the sink and turned on the water. "We leave in an hour Uncle Roy. And there will be no more talk of cities and offices and things that hurt my soul."

The thought of leaving the rodeo behind hurt Vivian too. Disappointing her family didn't feel good either. Now there was the Sloan family. Her gaze tracked back to Josh and stuck. And something told her saying goodbye to them was going to hurt more than she cared to admit.

"Oh good, Vivian. You're up and already finished eating." That came from her mother. She hurried into the kitchen wearing a blueberry-colored, fitted, insulated jacket, matching leggings and running shoes. "We need you over at the apartment."

"Is there a problem?" Vivian set her plate in the sink and washed her hands.

"Just a family thing." Her mom flicked her hand out in front of her and grinned at Ryan and Roy. But she ruined her air of nonchalance by tugging off her knit hat and squeezing it in her grip.

"What's going on?" Vivian dried her hands, tried to still her sudden unease and studied her mom. "I was going to help Josh in the stables and then practice."

"It'll be better if we just talk at the apartment and let everyone here enjoy their breakfast." Her mother tapped the kitchen island and smiled at Ryan. "Those look good enough to be served in any restaurant."

"Gran Claire told us we had to learn to cook five things before we graduated from high school." Ryan whisked his waffle batter like a seasoned sous chef. "She claimed it helped prove we could be self-sufficient. And that our partners would appreciate that."

"She wasn't wrong." Vivian's mother laughed.

"I honed my waffle-making skills." Ryan motioned to the stack of thick waffles. "You're welcome to help yourself."

"Thank you, but Vivian and I need to get going." Her mother gripped Vivian's arm, then nodded toward the hallway. "It sounds like everyone is awake and you're going to need more waffles than what you have."

With that, her mother tugged Vivian outside before she could even signal to Josh that she'd be right back. On the gravel driveway, Vivian matched her mother's quick steps. "Mom. You said nothing was wrong, but we're practically running to the apartment. Is Heather okay?"

"Your sister is fine. She and Wade are waiting

for us in the apartment." Her mother frowned at the motor home and quickened her steps as they passed by the massive RV. "Her morning sickness woke her up, but her stomach has already settled."

"Then, Dad?" Vivian asked.

"He's inside the motor home, rummaging around," her mother said. "Sam is going to walk him through the basics there this morning."

That was the last her mother said until Vivian stepped inside Josh's apartment and shut the door. Then her mother announced, "Vivian is here. She will save us."

CHAPTER ELEVEN

BY THE TIME Josh hung up the phone with Miles
Nesci, his potential buyer for Artie, he'd rear-
ranged the lights on two Christmas trees, fixed
a half dozen ornaments with precarious holds
on their respective branches, and watched the
rest of his family eat and run.

Now he was back in the kitchen where he'd
started the day. But without the cowgirl he'd
started his morning with. He frowned at the
piled strawberries he guessed Ryan had sliced
onto his waffle. "Where's Vivian?"

"Her mom came over." Ryan washed dishes
in the sink and loaded the dishwasher. "Needed
her for some family thing. Didn't sound serious. Shouldn't take that long."

Josh nodded and debated adding whipped
cream to his waffles.

"Hey, I know it's all fake between you and
Vivian." Ryan cut off the water and turned to
look at Josh. "But Viv is a really good person.
You'll like her if you give her a chance."

He already liked her. Too much. He skipped

the whipped cream and poured himself another cup of coffee that he didn't need. Same as he didn't need his attraction to Vivian. Surely that would go away also if he didn't encourage it. He said, "I know Vivian is a good person. She talked me into coaching her and Isabel."

Ryan didn't brother to hide his surprise.

"Which is why I need you to stay." Josh left his plate of untouched waffles on the island. "I need your help with the coaching."

"Caleb can do it." Ryan pointed at Caleb as soon as Josh's twin appeared in the hallway. Then Ryan announced, "Caleb, your twin needs you."

"I've got fifteen minutes. Twenty, max." Caleb pulled a volunteer firefighter sweatshirt over his head and continued, "Grant and I need to get over to see Sheriff Hopson about safety staffing for the stampede."

Caleb was a volunteer fire-and-rescue responder for Three Springs. Grant worked as an on-site doctor for the rodeos. Grant's orthopedic patient list already included a large portion of the rodeo circuit competitors. And Grant liked that he could work while also being able to watch Maggie compete in breakaway roping and team roping. Grant claimed he was living his best life.

Josh was certain one day soon he would

be making the very same claim as his older brother, once he was established in Houston at Bellmare Equestrian Center. Then he would be living his best life too. Without his cowgirl. Who he might think of as the best thing to happen to him recently, if he was in the mind to listen to his heart. He frowned into his coffee cup.

"Well, Josh needs you to help coach Isabel and Vivian with him." Ryan grabbed an apple from the basket on the counter and polished it on his shirt.

"Can't do it." Caleb grabbed Josh's untouched plate of waffles. "I have neither forgotten nor forgiven Isabel for what she did to you, Josh."

Ryan took a large bite out of the apple and spoke around the mouthful. "When it comes to Isabel, I feel exactly the same."

Clearly his brothers weren't in the mind to forgive or forget what Isabel had done. Caleb had been Josh's first call the night Isabel had left him. His twin had gathered their other brothers and they'd all rallied around Josh. That had always been their way—having each other's backs.

Still, there were things Josh's brothers didn't know about the weeks after Isabel had left. Or about Josh's dogged determination to prove he could stand on his own. Some truths were personal and hard to share, even with his brothers. Josh ground his teeth together, then asked, "What was I supposed to do when Isabel just showed up?"

"Ask Isabel to leave." Caleb swirled whipped cream over the top of the waffles and picked up a fork. His words anything but sweet and syrupy. "And then kindly tell her never to return."

"But instead, you're coaching your ex-wife on one of your own horses." Ryan crunched into his apple and studied the apple core as if it held the answers. "Seriously, what were you thinking, Josh?"

I wanted Vivian to smile. That, he wasn't admitting to his brothers. He also hadn't told his brothers about Houston. His possible buy-in. Or his potential relocation. He'd planned to do all that when the deal was finalized. But to get to the contract-signing stage, Josh needed his horses to sell. For the highest prices and quickly. He kept it close to the truth. "I have to build my horses' competition résumés. Isabel is an excellent rider and competitor."

"Then, it's not personal." Caleb watched him.

It was getting more and more personal when it came to Vivian. Still not going there. Josh said, "It's personal because horses are my business."

"Not what I meant, and you know it." Caleb's eyebrows lowered. "I want to know if it's personal, like, you-want-a-second-chance-with-Isabel personal."

Josh gaped at his twin.

"Well, your ex-wife came back yesterday..." Caleb lifted his hands in his typical hear-me-out gesture, then he continued, "Seemingly out of the blue. You invited her into our house. And she wasn't wearing her wedding ring."

Caleb let that fact drop like a prosecutor with the last piece of evidence that would seal a guilty verdict. Josh's mouth dropped open farther. He searched for an appropriate response and came up blank.

"Didn't you notice Isabel wasn't wearing her wedding ring?" Suspicion crossed Caleb's face.

Josh shook his head.

"Really?" Caleb moved closer and eyed Josh like he used to do when he was convinced Josh was hiding the last chocolate chip cookie—his twin's favorite—from him. "You really never noticed."

"I never noticed," Josh stated. He'd been too busy watching Vivian. That was something he was going to get in check today. Or his brothers would read way more into things between him and Vivian than there was.

Caleb suddenly smiled and his shoulders relaxed, as if he knew precisely where Josh's attention had been yesterday. He picked up the plate and devoured the waffles.

Ryan wasn't as easily swayed. He worked on his apple and studied Josh as he would one of his uncooperative horse rescues. "Just to clarify. Josh, you are not wanting a second chance with Isabel, right? And this thing with Vivian isn't some ploy to make Isabel jealous."

Josh turned on his older brother, then reached up and squeezed his own forehead, as if that would bring the absurd conversation into focus. He shifted his gaze from his twin to his older brother. "Is that what you both think?"

"Look at it from our perspective," Caleb argued. Ryan nodded in support.

Josh wanted to laugh. He could've ended the discussion right there. But then he wouldn't be a good Sloan brother if he didn't push a few buttons of his own. "What if I said yes, I want a second chance with my ex-wife."

"We'd unmake your mind up for you," Caleb said, his tone matter-of-fact.

"What if my mind is already made up?" Which it was. Josh had never considered a reconciliation with Isabel. Not once in the past five years. And he wasn't about to consider it now. No, what he wanted from Isabel was strictly business related. But when it came to chances, he was beginning to think he'd like a first one with a different cowgirl.

"Isabel is not the one for you." Ryan walked over and squeezed Josh's shoulder. "Don't get us wrong, little brother. We want you to have a second chance at love, just with the right person."

But his big brother wouldn't know the right woman if he found her seated atop his favorite horse. As it was, Ryan always joked the gossips on the rodeo circuit knew who he was dating before he ever did. Josh set his hands on his hips and worked to sound uninterested. "And who would the right person be?"

"Vivian, of course," Caleb announced. "Grandpa Sam and Uncle Roy called you and Vivian a good pairing last night."

"Just to be clear," Josh stated. "Vivian and I are not a good pairing." Yet his words stuck in his throat and sounded stiff and somehow wrong. Still, he added, "And I'm good as I am."

"Staying single is an option," Caleb mused, grinning at Josh. "But not for you, brother."

"Why not?" Josh frowned at his twin.

"Because you believe in soulmates and all that stuff." Caleb tapped his knuckles over his own heart. "You believe in romance and hearts and true love."

Ryan nodded. Sympathy slipped through his words. "He's not wrong, little brother."

"I used to believe. *Used to* being the operative phrase here." Josh didn't believe anymore. Now he believed only fools trusted in love. And instant attraction was no more sustainable than holding fog. And building a foundation on that was like building a house on quicksand. Eventually it would all sink and completely disappear.

"You just need the right woman in your life." Caleb's tone was confident. "Then you'll believe once again, and all will be right in the world."

"I don't know about all that." Josh poured his coffee down the sink and rinsed the mug. "But I do know that seeing Isabel was good for one thing. It reminded me I'm better off alone."

Better off not getting entangled again in love's deception. And seeing Isabel also had reminded him why. Love hurt. And it wasn't a pain he ever wanted to feel again.

"All I know is that it's fortunate you have this thing with Vivian going on," Ryan said. "Just in case Isabel wants you back, Josh."

Caleb tapped his fork against his plate as if considering Ryan's words. "Isabel's real motive might be Josh, not a horse for the rodeo."

Ryan added, "If Isabel believes Josh has finally found someone else and moved on, then she'll reconsider her win-back-Josh plot."

"We don't know for sure that she's here to win me back," Josh countered. The words sounded ridiculous when uttered out loud.

"Until you do know, I'd keep your girlfriend close," Caleb advised. "Girlfriends make a good shield against scheming ex-wives."

Like his twin knew anything about ex-wives, or exes, for that matter. Caleb quit relationships before any labels were ever discussed let alone established. Josh shook his head. "I don't need protection from my ex-wife."

"Yes, you do." Caleb stressed his words, insistent and serious. "Because no matter what you claim, brother, you never stopped believing in love."

That was the old Josh. The one who had blindly fallen in love minutes after meeting the newly crowned rodeo queen. He'd grown up since then. Josh wiped his hands on his jeans. "I'm not debating this with you anymore. I need to get to the stables."

"And I need to get to the sheriff." Caleb dropped his plate in the sink and headed outside.

"Before you go, there's something else." Ryan brushed his hand over his mouth and frowned at Josh. "Mom is in town next weekend. She's been invited to speak at Wright Well University."

'Tis the season for his past to pop up. Josh said, "You never thought to lead with that or fill me in last night?"

"And disrupt the evening?" Ryan shook his head. "No way. You were hanging ornaments and having fun. I wasn't about to ruin that."

Now Josh knew the real reason Ryan was heading out of town. Like Josh, Ryan wasn't interested in seeing their mother either. It was that whole forgiving-and-forgetting piece all over again. Before Josh could get more details about their mother's visit, Uncle Roy carried his suitcase into the kitchen and said, "Now that I'll be gone for a few days, Josh, you need to help your grandfather at the other property."

"What's happening over there?" Ryan's expression shifted into wary.

"Nothing, I hope." Josh rubbed the back of his neck. First his ex-wife. Now his mother.

"So, Mom isn't moving back in over there, is she?" The wariness worked into Ryan's voice, thick and heavy.

"Don't look at me. I'm not spreading that rumor." Uncle Roy set his suitcase near his boots. "Your grandpa and I are just looking for something over there. That's all."

"What?" Ryan asked. "A reason to make our mother stay?"

Direct hit. Right on point. Josh raised his eyebrows and watched his uncle.

"Sticking around here is entirely up to Lilian," Uncle Roy said. "Your mom will decide that all on her own. In her own time."

"Well, if history repeats itself like they say it does, we already know what will happen," Josh said. Frustration tightened around his chest. Their mother wasn't sticking around. Not for good. And the sooner everyone accepted that, the better they all would be.

"If you've got it figured out, then there's nothing to fret about," Uncle Roy stated and eyed Josh. "Help your grandpa at the property and let that be that."

Josh forced himself to relax. His uncle wasn't to blame for their mother's unexpected return to Three Springs and her even more surprising desire to connect with her sons. The very ones she'd left behind all those years ago while she pursued her medical career. As if her sons weren't important enough to include in her life. He said, "Uncle Roy, you still haven't told me what you two are looking for at the property."

"We will know it when we see it." Uncle Roy shrugged one shoulder.

"That's not helpful," Josh returned.

"It's all I've got." Uncle Roy slipped his boots on, picked up his suitcase and headed for the door. "Let's go, Ryan. We've got hair appointments and we don't want to be late."

Ryan chased after his uncle, following him outside and shouting about not stopping.

Sam walked into the kitchen and laughed. "Now I wish I was going on that drive. Care to make a wager on who wins the haircut war?"

"I don't want to lose money." Josh chuckled and shook his head. "We both know Uncle Roy is wiser and sneakier than Ryan. Uncle will get his way."

"He sure will." Sam stepped over to the kitchen window and laughed again. Then he glanced at Josh. "Vivian is tied up with an important project. She won't be practicing this morning."

What could be more important than practicing? Josh frowned at his grandpa. "What is she doing?"

"Her family needs her," Sam said simply.

Josh needed her too. Now he'd be alone with Isabel. For the first time in five years. And it was all Vivian's fault. The least she could do was be there with him. He said, "Well, it's her rodeo to lose then."

"Cut Vivian some slack," Sam scolded. "I'm

sure she'd rather be in the saddle than punch-
ing keys on a keyboard for her family."

And you don't turn your back on family. One
of the cardinal rules in the Sloan household.
Josh couldn't fault Vivian. He sighed. "Right.
We will figure it out later."

"While you're of a mind to figuring things
out—" Sam pointed to the window "—you
might want to see this."

Josh stepped beside his grandfather and
watched Isabel's SUV pull into the driveway.
Vivian stepped from the RV, holding a laptop,
and stopped when Isabel climbed out of her
car. The women shared a brief hug.

"Your past is staring your future in the eye,
Josh," Grandpa Sam declared before nudging
his elbow into Josh's ribs. "And you know the
problem with that, don't you?"

Josh remained quiet, sensing his grandfather
was just warming up.

Grandpa Sam charged on, "You can't look
both ways at the same time. It's impossible."
His elbow tapped Josh's ribs again. "So that
means you gotta make a choice, Josh."

"What's that, exactly?" Josh asked.

"It's about looking forward or backward.
Certainly can't have it both ways," his grandpa
said. "Got to make a choice which direction
you're going."

"What if I like exactly where I'm standing right now?" Josh asked.

"Where you are now is on the sidelines, Josh." Grandpa Sam paused then added, a warning in his words. "You certainly can't sit on the sidelines indefinitely. Best to know where your heart is leaning before you get called back into the game."

Josh knew where his heart stood. Where he wanted it to remain. In the background. He glanced out the window and watched Vivian head toward his apartment. His home. And his heart might've wanted to welcome his cowgirl. But he stepped in and blocked it.

"Best get to it, Josh." Grandpa Sam rocked back on his heels and eyed Josh. "After all, futures aren't made standing still. Standing still only works for statues."

CHAPTER TWELVE

VIVIAN PACED AROUND Josh's apartment from the family room into the modern kitchen and back. The furniture was tasteful, though sparse. The vibe was more like an upscale hotel room. Not exactly cold, but it lacked the inviting, homey feel of the farmhouse. And it was neat. Not an empty glass in the kitchen sink. Or stray magazine with a water ring on the coffee table.

She wasn't finding comfort in her fake boyfriend's apartment. That was to be expected. That her family was putting her even more on edge, well, that was unavoidable. Her mother had claimed Vivian would save the family. And Vivian was still trying to come to terms with that bold proclamation.

Heather and Wade sat together on the leather sofa. Her mother held her computer, which Vivian had retrieved from the RV earlier, and perched on the edge of the leather recliner.

Vivian stopped on the other side of the coffee table and said, "Let me make sure I'm following. Wade received a request for proposal from…"

"South Trek Enterprises," Heather supplied for her. "We need to provide South Trek with a comprehensive business insurance proposal that covers all their commercial insurance requirements while being affordable, but also exceeding their expectations."

No small feat. "And you have forty-eight hours to submit your response?" Vivian eyed her family. They nodded in sync as if they'd rehearsed this particular part earlier. Vivian continued, "And you want me to work my magic on the presentation?" Those had been her mother's exact words.

"And save the family." Her mother slipped in that piece again as if it required repeating. As if she fully expected Vivian wouldn't hesitate to take up the charge.

"That about sums it up." Heather leaned her head back against the couch. Her morning sickness had passed, yet she still looked too pale to Vivian.

The situation might've been summed up, but nothing was clear. Vivian pinched the bridge of her nose.

"Look, Vivian. This contract with South Trek Enterprises gives a solid first step in the corporate business sector," Wade explained. He reached over and touched Heather's leg like a silent checking in. Her sister set her hand on top of his. Wade added, "This contract is part of that growth strategy I mentioned to you last night."

Oh yeah. When they'd been walking back to the farmhouse, just before Wade had told Vivian it was time to remember who she really was. Certainly, this wasn't her family's misguided attempt to remind her who they wanted her to be. Vivian disliked her cynicism and worked to shove her suspicions aside. Her mother looked genuinely worried.

"We're sustaining with our residential clients and sole proprietors," Heather added. "But it's barely enough to cover salaries and day-to-day operations of the business. We have to expand into the commercial sector."

Barely sustaining. No one had mentioned anything to Vivian. Then again, Vivian had skimmed around the topic of the company when she'd called home. For her own selfish reasons. Still, shouldn't they have told her? *You can't be in and out when the mood suits, Vivian. If you're chasing your dream, then go all in.* Those had been her father's words, then he'd set down the three-year time limit—the same time it would've taken her to earn her master's degree in marketing. Vivian looked at her mother. "What does Dad think?"

"Your father still believes in handshakes over lunch to close deals." A weariness settled around her mother's eyes. "But the landscape has changed out there with more options for customers to buy insurance. Heather and Wade are right. We need to change and adapt our business if we want to stay relevant."

That they were sitting there now without Vivian's father spoke volumes.

"Without this contract, we risk not growing." Heather unscrewed the cap on a bottle of ginger ale and took a small sip. "And when a business stops growing, it can't exist for long."

Vivian wanted to blame Heather's morning sickness for her dire words. But there was too much truth there. Vivian had never considered the potential closing of the family company. The potential end of the Bryant family legacy. Although Heather's sober expression told Vivian her sister was more than serious. Her parents would be crushed. Her dad most of all. Vivian spun around and moved to stare out the window that overlooked the pasture and back of the stable barn. She took care not to look at her mom or Wade. Knew she would see the truth—the one she didn't want to even consider—on their faces too.

"If you work on this Vivian, then dad will know you buy in." Her mom's words were earnest and tinged with a splash of hope. "Your dad will know this is the right direction if we show a united front."

That selfish side within Vivian waved its arms and wanted the business to close. That would free her, wouldn't it? Such disloyalty left a bitter taste in her mouth. Vivian needed to take a breath and leaned against the windowsill. "You guys have been managing the business. Why do you need me?"

"You've been doing this exact thing for us over the past few years," Heather argued. "Vivian, this is nothing you haven't done before when we've sent you presentations and proposals to review."

"You've always enhanced them for us," her mom added. "Fixed our mistakes and improved what we had put together. You have an eye for the details."

But those were one-offs. Quick read throughs for Vivian at night in her camper. They weren't make-or-break proposals. Not like this one. Vivian touched her stomach, wishing she hadn't added so much syrup to her waffles earlier. Breakfast seemed like a lifetime ago, when all she'd been worried about was her treasured horse.

"Even more, you know the software, Vivian." Wade stood up, walked into the kitchen, and opened the soda cracker box. He handed several crackers to Heather, without her having to ask.

Vivian wanted to ignore him. But he looked after Heather like her sister deserved. And that was how love, when it was the right kind, was supposed to work. Vivian crossed her arms over her chest.

"Your dad doesn't want to hear about portals, secure websites and automation." Her mom watched Vivian over the top of her computer. "And he's not interested in learning either."

Heather arranged her crackers on a napkin on her lap. "Viv, you know how to best represent our business."

"We're just asking for your help, Vivian," her mother stressed. "Just a few hours of your time. That's all. It's not too much to ask."

Her mother had given more than that during all those years of driving Vivian to her horse-riding lessons out in the country. No, this wasn't too much to ask now. Because while Vivian was selfish, she loved her family.

Vivian pushed away from the window and sat on the couch next to her sister. She held out her hand toward her mom and took the laptop, then said, "Let me see the request-for-proposal documents."

Her mom stood and leaned over to wrap her arm around Vivian's shoulders. She squeezed Vivian tight. "I'm going outside to learn about the motor home with your dad and Sam."

Vivian read through the request documents from South Trek Enterprises. Beside her, Heather chewed on her crackers and Wade tapped on his phone screen. It was two more passes through the documentation before Vivian finally set the computer on the coffee table and looked at Heather and Wade. She said, "This is way more than a growth strategy. It's a ten-year contract."

Heather reached over and took Wade's hand. He nodded.

Vivian ran her palms over her jeans. "If you get this book of business, you could fund mom and dad's retirement. Buy that motor home outright and pay them a substantial pension."

Wade exhaled as if he'd been holding his breath. "Now you understand exactly how important this is."

"Mom and Dad let us pursue our dreams, Vivian." Heather leaned over and touched Vivian's arm. Her words earnest. Her gaze understanding. "It's time Mom and Dad had the freedom to do the same. And without having to carry the business on their shoulders too."

Vivian wanted to deny her sister's words but couldn't. Her sister was right.

"You should also know what Mom didn't say." Heather glanced at Wade. At his small nod, her sister continued, "Dad can't handle the stress any longer. His heart isn't what it used to be."

Vivian opened her mouth.

"Nothing serious has happened yet. We would've told you—" Heather squeezed Vivian's arm "—but his doctors, and we, as well, want to help prevent something from happening."

"We want your dad to be around for our kids," Wade added.

"And your children someday." Heather offered Vivian a gentle smile. "I know this sounds like a guilt trip. It's not intended to be. We really just want you to have the full picture of what's going on."

Their father's brother and business partner had passed away from an undiagnosed heart condition five years earlier. Her father was now the same age his brother had been when his heart gave out. Vivian worked to calm the unease and worry working through her. Nothing bad had happened yet. That mattered. Except that *yet* made her all the more concerned. She would do this. Do her small part to give back to her parents, especially her dad. As for her practice and those things she needed to do, well, she'd make it up later somehow. Her family needed her.

"We have work to do," Vivian said. "Those proposals we've done in the past are like introductions to what we need to put together now."

Wade disappeared into one of the bedrooms and returned with two laptops. One he handed to Vivian. "You're going to need this. Heather and I can use hers."

The trio settled in at the kitchen table and got to work. More than an hour later, Vivian stood up to stretch her legs. She walked to the window, saw Isabel and Josh together with the horses. Told herself that was for the best anyway. After all, she didn't want to stand in their way of a reconciliation. Still, it took her a few minutes to squash down her disappointment beneath workers' compensation premiums and liability umbrellas and saving her family.

Lunchtime was closing in when Wade called a timeout and declared they all needed fresh air and food. Vivian tossed her truck keys to Wade, and the couple went on a food run. Vivian finished the last of her notes, then closed the laptop and picked up her jacket.

"Where are you going?" Her mother came through the front door, holding what appeared to be one of Sam's clipboards. "We need to discuss the gala. Sam and I did some preliminary organizing since you were tied up here. And Josh was busy too."

"Heather and Wade are picking up lunch." Vivian zipped her coat up. "I'm heading to the stables to find Josh." And finally work in a short practice.

"He's not there." Her mother tapped her watch on her wrist. "Isabel and Josh left not twenty minutes ago."

Vivian looked out the window. Isabel's car was gone. This was what Vivian wanted. Not to be in between Josh and his ex-wife and their unfinished business. That was true, she hadn't wanted to be in their way, but she also hadn't wanted to be so far out of the way, she'd been forgotten. Even that was for the best, wasn't it?

"You okay?" Her mom tipped her head and studied Vivian.

"Just hungry." And tripping herself up in the make-believe exactly like she'd sworn not to do. Vivian moved back to the square kitchen table. "Let's talk about the gala while we wait for Heather and Wade."

Her mother pulled out a chair and sat down heavily. Then she frowned at Vivian. "Between you and me, Vivian, the gala needs to return to a barn dance. Because that's the only available space in this town. A barn."

Her mother's expression matched the thick, forlorn note in her words. Vivian pressed her lips together and caught her laughter. "There's a town hall. I saw it when I drove through downtown." The building was historic-looking but not small by any means. "The town hall should have conference rooms. Maybe the rooms even connect."

"According to both Abby and Sam, it would be standing room only for the two-hundred-plus guests expected to attend." Her mother wrinkled her nose. "And by that, I mean the guests could eat off each other's appetizer plates, they'd be so close to one another."

That wouldn't do. Vivian tapped her fingers on the table. Perhaps a barn dance wasn't all that bad.

"Abby's husband, Wes, owns the Feisty Owl Bar and Grille." Her mother's mouth pursed. "But they should be preparing for their new baby's arrival, not a gala."

Vivian nodded. "There has to be a suitable place in town that isn't a barn."

"You need to get with Josh," her mother urged. "And scour the town until you find a venue. It can't wait."

How was she supposed to do that? Josh was

with his ex-wife. Unfinishing whatever their business was. Vivian stilled in the chair and stared at her hands. Then her sweater jacket. She felt green, then she chided herself. Jealousy was never a good look. On anyone. And if Vivian wasn't mistaken, she also sounded jealous.

How bad was that? She'd just face-planted in a mess of her own making. Nothing to do now but get herself out of it. Step back. Way back. Far enough that she wasn't interested in her cowboy any longer. Vivian reached for the clipboard. "I don't need Josh. I can take my truck and scout out places around town myself."

"It might be faster if Josh went along with you," her mother said.

"He's got clients he needs to work with." An ex-wife to reconcile with. Vivian stood up. "I'll just get on my way and call you when I find something."

"What about lunch?" her mother asked. "Heather and Wade just got back."

"I'm not that hungry after all." With that, Vivian grabbed her spare set of keys and hurried outside before her mom could stop her. She was in her truck and headed downtown within minutes. Determined to put distance between her heart and her cowboy.

CHAPTER THIRTEEN

THE LUNCH HOUR was quickly closing in the following day when Vivian eased her truck over to the side of the bypass and cut the engine. Four miles out from downtown Three Springs. Steam poured from under the hood of her truck. No doubt from the radiator. The one Vivian had patched last month rather than replace. The same one she'd been bandaging for the past few months. There always seemed to be another priority that required her money and dipped into her radiator fund.

Yesterday's extended jaunt around town had certainly not helped the cause. All Vivian had found on her own was barns. Just as her mother had claimed. Then she'd returned to the Sloan property, only to spend the rest of the day and a large chunk of the evening working on the business proposal for her family. She'd missed dinner last night. Slept in that morning and missed breakfast. And missed Josh at every turn.

He'd placed Artie on "no exercise" after the

Arabian had skipped his evening feed too. Then left for an emergency at the distillery. Vivian had practiced on Winston with Isabel riding Fox. Even with Winston's unrushed attitude, Vivian had spent more time righting barrels than on anything else. Isabel ended her session early after getting a text, mentioned something about stopping at the distillery too and left. Vivian assumed Isabel was meeting up with Josh.

Frustrated and wanting to do something productive, she'd set out on another venue search. But in her haste to be alone, Vivian had never considered topping off the radiator.

She reached under the bench seat and came up empty. The bottled water she usually stashed under there for situations like this one was gone. She'd used the water on Josh's truck days ago and hadn't replaced it. Vivian popped the hood and climbed out to figure out her next steps.

A black SUV with tinted windows and reindeer antlers honked and pulled over. The door on the driver's side swung open. A spry retiree, wearing a Santa hat, hopped out and called out a hearty hello in the off-key notes of a Christmas carol. Her bright smile filled her petite face. "I'm Breezy Baker and my sister, Gayle, is in the shotgun seat." Breezy's laughter swirled on the wind. "And my oh my, we've been waiting to meet you, Vivian Bryant."

Vivian wiped her hands on her jeans, caught by surprise. "How did you know my name?" Because she certainly would've remembered meeting Breezy.

Breezy wedged herself next to Vivian, peered at the engine and let out a clucking sound. "Your Arizona license plate gave you away, dear."

Before Vivian could respond, Breezy's shotgun rider climbed out of the passenger side of the SUV and shouted, "Got him."

Vivian twisted around. Gayle Baker wore snowmen-patched denim overalls, cuffed around her boots, and moved with the speed of Santa's elves on Christmas Eve.

Gayle pointed at the cell phone pressed against her ear and grinned at Vivian. "He wants to know what the diagnosis is, Breeze?"

"Radiator." Breezy clucked again beside Vivian. "Poor thing has more leaks than an old dog on a walk."

Vivian watched more water weep from even more holes in her radiator and wished Breezy wasn't right. She doubted her inexpensive leak sealant was going to cut it this time.

Gayle relayed that information to her caller, nodded, then extended her arm with the phone toward Vivian. Her eyes were saucer round behind her even rounder glasses. "He wants to talk to you, dear."

Vivian accepted the phone and glanced between the lively sisters. Their expressions encouraging, Vivian lifted the phone to her ear and offered a hesitant hello.

"Vivian." Josh's slow drawl streamed across the speaker like a welcome embrace. He added, "You okay?"

I am now. Vivian shut down her silly reaction to the concern she heard in Josh's words. She said, "Yeah. Nothing I can't handle." Same as her misplaced attraction to her fake boyfriend.

"How bad is it?" Josh asked.

Bad. My heart is racing. Those butterflies are flapping. Nothing too serious. Just the beginning stages of once upon a time, a girl liked a boy. Nothing world-tipping like a cowgirl loves a cowboy. She could still come back from this. Vivian rubbed her throat. "I forgot to top off the radiator when I left earlier."

There was a scraping sound, then Josh said, "I'm with Tess at the Silver Penny."

"Tess," Vivian blurted. But he was supposed to be with Isabel, his ex-wife, not Tess, his sister-in-law. At least that was who she'd assumed he was with. Vivian shouldn't be happy. She should be irritated about her truck. Frustrated at her misstep. Still, she felt lighter. Relieved. Cheerful even.

"Yeah, Tess has a problem with one of her refrigerated chocolate displays in the general store," he explained. "I shouldn't be more than an hour. Then I can get you."

"An hour," Vivian repeated, feeling that cheer inside her expand. "I can wait." For as long as it takes.

Gayle frowned and shook her head at Vivian. "Not out here on the side of the bypass."

"Let me talk to him, dear." Breezy waved a hand at Vivian and held out her thin arm. Her gaze, steady and resolved, latched onto Vivian's like a challenge.

Vivian surrendered the phone to the rather determined retiree.

Breezy wasted no time getting to the point. "Your Gran Claire taught you better manners than this, Josh Sloan. I did too. You won't be leaving your girlfriend stranded on the side of any road."

His girlfriend. Vivian really had to stop liking the sound of that so much. She had to stop letting it get to her. Otherwise, before she knew it, her cowboy would be getting to her too.

Breezy drew a deep breath that seemed to fill her entire petite frame from her bold white hair to her boots. Purpose filled her words. "We will be taking Vivian to the diner for lunch. You may meet us there." Breezy paused, her smile expanded across her papery cheeks before she tapped on the phone screen. "Come on, ladies. Josh is covering our lunch. He's such a thoughtful cowboy."

In less than a minute, her truck hood was shut, her doors were locked and Vivian was bundled into the back seat of the Bakers' SUV. And feeling like she'd climbed inside a balsam fir instead. One flocked in cinnamon and cloves and every seasonal warm spice available.

"Pardon our Christmas potpourri." Breezy settled into the driver's seat and slipped on a pair of fire-engine-red sunglasses. "It's our wreaths scenting us up something good."

Vivian shifted and gaped at the dozens of fresh wreaths stacked inside the back of the SUV.

"We've been delivering all morning to businesses and homes around town," Gayle explained. "It's a long-standing Three Springs tradition. Handmade wreaths for front doors to welcome the joy of the season and friends, old and new, inside."

The Baker sisters certainly made Vivian feel welcome. No wreath required. "Can I ask how you knew me? Other than my Arizona plates."

"We heard all about you the other night at the tree lot." Breezy pulled out onto the road and drove into town. "We were there selling hot chocolate for Whitney Carson. Whitney owns the farmers' market and sells the best Christmas trees each year. Well, her son got sick. Poor thing. Right there in the parking lot for everyone to see."

Vivian quickly sorted through Breezy's story. Fortunately, Vivian's grandmother and her friends had the same habit of backfilling their own retellings with more details than necessary. Vivian had quickly learned to filter the essential bits from the fluff. But, oh, how Vivian always enjoyed the fluff.

"Too much peppermint bark, if you ask me," Gayle offered. "Peppermint soothes a tummy, but not one that's too full of chocolate and marshmallows."

Breezy nodded, met Vivian's gaze in the rearview mirror, her expression downcast. Then Breezy quickly picked up where her sister had left off. "We filled in for Whitney all evening at her tree lot. Then, when the hot chocolate ran out, like it always does, even though we encourage Whitney to make an extra pot, well, we helped customers choose their Christmas trees."

"Maggie and Tess wanted more than one

tree," Gayle volunteered. "And that sure took us some time to find the proper ones, but we finally did. Have to make sure your customer is happy when they leave. Otherwise, they might not come back."

Vivian connected the dots. Clearly Maggie and Caleb had been talking to neighbors and friends about her and Josh. Vivian watched Breezy inhale and waited, in case Breezy's tale wasn't over.

Gayle tapped a sparkly blue nail on the center console, drawing Vivian's attention to her. The lively retiree announced, "I was a barrel racer in my day too, Vivian."

"Gayle, the only thing you chased around a barrel was Harold," Breezy accused.

"Caught my cowboy too." Gayle gave Vivian a one-sided grin and eyebrow waggle. "Harold and I were married for more than fifty years."

Both women released deep laughs that spun around Vivian like cotton candy. Vivian was delighted to be waiting with the spirited duo and not alone on the bypass. The rest of the drive into town was filled with more stories about the town's holiday traditions.

At the Lemon Moon Diner, Vivian ordered a pumpkin bacon quiche on Gayle's and the waitress's recommendations and settled into the vinyl booth across from the Baker sisters.

Their lunch orders arrived between introductions to the local patrons and even more stories. By the time dessert arrived, Vivian's cheeks hurt from laughing.

"Now, Vivian, what's this we hear about a gala?" Breezy asked and sighed into her napkin. "I sure do like putting on a fancy dress and my dancing shoes."

"Although our dancing shoes now look nothing like they did when we won the square-dancing title that year in Amarillo." Breezy chuckled and tapped her coffee cup against her sister's. "Isn't that right, Gayle?"

"I can still do-si-do and promenade better than most anyone in this county. I do hope the gala's dance floor is big enough for square dancing." Gayle plucked a candied orange from her winter citrus tart. Her pencil-thin eyebrows had slingshot into her forehead. "But what we really must know, Vivian, is about our plus-ones. Plus-ones aren't all that easy to come by around here."

Breezy waved her fork at Vivian and lowered her voice into an urgent tone. "We have to know if we need to secure our dates for the gala now."

Vivian pressed her napkin against the corner of her mouth to capture her laughter. "First, we need to secure a venue for the gala."

"You haven't got yourself a venue?" Gayle's lips pursed. "We can't get gussied up and have no place to go."

"That wouldn't be right," Breezy added.

"We haven't found a venue yet," Vivian admitted, trying to sound optimistic. Her phone vibrated on the bench beside her. She opened the new text from Josh and frowned.

Breezy stirred more creamer into her coffee. Her spoon clanking against the ceramic. "Something wrong, dear?"

"Josh got called over to Paige Bishop's clinic." Vivian read the text again. "There's a problem with the ventilation system in the kennels. He's going to be a little longer."

"Nothing for it now, ladies." Breezy slapped her palms on the table. "We're going to have to multitask this afternoon."

Gayle grinned and nodded. "We sure are."

Vivian blinked at the pair. Certainly, they weren't suggesting they intended to help Vivian change out her radiator on the bypass. "What are we doing?"

"You're coming with us, Vivian. To deliver the rest of our wreaths." Breezy polished off her last bite of cranberry-chiffon pie. "And while we're delivering, we'll scout out a gala location."

"Josh can meet us when he's done at the

clinic," Gayle added. "We can show him the venue we find, and he can give us his opinion."

The spirited pair looked confident and sounded assured that they could locate a venue. Josh had told her that Sam always claimed turning down help was asking for more trouble. And Vivian knew enough to know she needed help. She picked up her phone. "Let me just text Josh and tell him our plan."

"Splendid." Gayle concentrated on finishing her tart.

They were down to their last wreath drop-off several hours later and Vivian wasn't feeling quite so splendid. The Christmas potpourri inside the SUV had faded along with Vivian's confidence. She was ready to throw in the towel and declare the barn dance back on the table. She'd seen more than half a dozen barns around town that looked more than solid enough to hold up for a one-night barn dance. Her mother certainly hadn't been exaggerating earlier. What Vivian hadn't come across was a venue for a gala.

And she certainly couldn't afford another afternoon of an aimless search. Even if she'd thoroughly enjoyed the sisters' company. She needed time in the saddle, not the Bakers' back seat. And there was still the proposal for the family business to finalize. Although her mother had been more than pleased when Vivian had texted her about the ongoing venue search when she'd left Lemon Moon.

Breezy drove through a tall wrought iron, arched gate with a sign for Doyle Farm. Gayle peeked around her seat. "Marlena Doyle is a dear friend. She's been having a bit of a rough patch since her husband passed two years ago. The farm became too much to handle alone, and she's had to close down. Sure do miss her prized heirloom tomatoes and Christmas poinsettias."

"Marlena has been talking about selling in the new year, but it's hard to let go of so much family history." The rings on Breezy's fingers flashed in the late-afternoon sunlight streaming through the windshield. "We were hoping to bring her some of our own Christmas cheer."

The pair certainly knew how to do that better than anyone Vivian had met. House after house, the Baker sisters had greeted everyone with inviting hugs and genuine affection, as if they were all family. It was difficult not to feel the spirit of the season with the pair. And even more difficult not to want to feel a part of it. But this wasn't her hometown. Or her home. Just the place she was passing through. She was always passing through, it seemed. She'd never minded so much until now.

Vivian took in the two-story house with a wraparound porch, an intricate stone exterior and etched glass framing the double front doors. A half dozen, commercial-sized greenhouses stood in a neat line on the far side of the house. And open land spread for miles on the other. A woman stepped through the front doors. Her red hair fell around her shoulders and her smile stretched wide.

Introductions complete, the women wasted no time centering a wreath on each of the front doors then hung the last one over the original stone fireplace inside the family room. Marlena poured hot spiced apple cider into cups and toured Vivian through the old manor-style house. Then she led Vivian out onto the back porch where Gayle and Breezy sat in a wide porch swing.

Gayle pushed out of the swing and grinned. "Now it's time for my favorite part of the tour. The greenhouse."

"I've kept one going." Marlena headed down the porch stairs and chuckled. "I couldn't quite let go of everything. There's something inspiring about watching my plants thrive and bloom. Even after all these years, I still feel the thrill."

Marlena went on to explain her having the greenhouses built and the fire that had collapsed the roof on the last one the year prior. She walked them through an empty greenhouse that connected to the one she'd kept running. Gayle and Marlena got into a conversation about a Christmas cactus with yellow blooms.

Vivian walked the long length and back again. Then stopped beside Breezy and another Christmas cactus with deep ink blooms. She whispered, "Breezy, do you think this space is big enough for square dancing?"

"I've never considered it." Breezy straightened, tapped her chin, then tipped her head toward Vivian. "Do you mean square dancing for something like a gala?"

"Maybe." Vivian clenched and unclenched her hands. "Do you think it's possible?"

Breezy scuffed her boot heel on the plank floor. "It certainly has the floor for it."

"The floor for what?" Gayle asked over the crowded plant table.

"A promenade." Breezy sashayed a few steps and swirled her hips. "Or a two-step perhaps. Or even an old-fashioned waltz."

"You want to waltz in here?" Gayle set her hand on her hip and pushed her glasses up her nose. "It's a greenhouse."

"But what if for one night it was transformed?" Vivian walked through the connecting door into the empty greenhouse. The trio followed her, their boots echoing on the concrete floor. Vivian lifted her gaze to the windowed ceiling and turned in a slow circle. "What if for one night this space was transformed into a glass ballroom?"

"I'm listening." Interest shifted across Breezy's face.

"We could hang lots of soft lights around the walls. Keep the ceiling clear. Set up the DJ in the far corner. Rent a proper dance floor." Vivian bit her bottom lip and let the image form in her mind. "Snowflakes falling from the rafters and swaths of silver garland. Of course, Christmas trees too."

"What if you want to sit down for a spell?" Gayle stuck her hands in the deep pockets of her overalls. "Rest your feet between sets."

Vivian grinned. "Marlena, does this greenhouse connect to its two neighbors?"

"Through those doors." Marlena pointed to two doors on both sides of the greenhouse. "They look much like this one. In fact, the greenhouse floorplans are identical."

"Then we could set up a seating area in there with the silent auction. Heat lamps as well." Vivian warmed more and more to the idea. "In the next one, a dining space and bar. All decorated in the winter wonderland theme. Soft lights. Silver and blues."

"Are you saying you want to put the gala here?" Wonder worked across Gayle's face and into her words. "In Marlena's greenhouses?"

"A gala? Here?" Marlena ran a finger across her eyebrow and considered the space as if seeing it for the first time ever.

"There's a gala happening after the Silk and Steel Cowgirl Stampede this coming weekend," Vivian explained. "It's a fundraiser to help with the rebuilding of the Belleridge rodeo arena that burnt."

"It's a special All-Women's rodeo," Gayle added. Her excitement clear. "A chance for our cowgirls to showcase their talents in the arena."

"And we've been struggling to locate a suitable venue for the gala," Vivian said. Until now. "But I've gotten carried away and put you on the spot, Marlena. I apologize."

"Do you think you can pull it off?" Marlena asked.

"I do." Vivian chewed on her lower lip, pulling in her excitement. "I'll need to call in some help."

"We can find you assistants," Breezy assured her.

Gayle took Marlena's hand. "What do you think? One more adventure before you sell."

"I do believe I have one more in me." Marlena chuckled and shook her head. "I have to tell you that I can't quite picture all that you've described, Vivian. It seems like quite the undertaking, but I'm rather looking forward to seeing it."

"I need to call Josh. Ask him to meet us here." Vivian pulled out her cell phone and tapped Josh's name on her recent call list.

"Maybe you should..." Breezy started.

But Josh had already answered. And Vivian's own excitement rushed through her, causing her to blurt, "Josh. We found the perfect place for the gala." Vivian turned another slow circle. "It's a hidden gem really. Unconventional, but ideal. It's really three spaces that connect. One for dancing. One for food. One for mingling and the silent auction. But it'll work. I can see it already."

"Sounds like you don't need me," he said, amusement wrapped around his words.

I think I could need you. Very much. For things like a real plus-one. Vivian stopped and blinked. If only she hadn't declared independence from love. If only she could risk her heart again. She said, "I need your expertise on a few repairs to the space. Nothing major or showstopping. At least, I don't think so. You'll have to tell me." Vivian drew in a deep breath. "Josh. You still there?"

"Vivian, where are you exactly?" Josh asked. "I think I need to see this hidden gem that is practically perfect for the gala."

"Doyle Farm," Vivian announced.

Only silence answered her across the line. It wasn't the someone-pressed-mute kind of quiet either. But rather the worrying kind. The still kind where the line was live, but the conversation had veered completely off course. Unease tightened across Vivian's shoulders.

Finally, the air shifted over the speaker, then Josh's words came flat and hollow. "Don't leave. I'm on my way."

The call disconnected. Vivian stared at her phone and tried to smile. "Josh is on his way here now."

That stopped the older women. Same as Vivian had halted her conversation with Josh. Vivian focused on the trio. Their gazes were too wide. Their mouths opened at varying degrees. Breezy plucked at her bold white hair, spiking the short strands even more. Gayle tapped her fingers against her bottom lip as if catching her words. And Marlena adjusted the collar on her denim button-down shirt.

Vivian clenched her phone. "What's wrong?"

The ball on Breezy's Santa hat collapsed toward her petite shoulders. "Did we mention that the locals have a long history with this farm?"

Vivian nodded. "You talked about your adventures."

"Yes, we were fortunate that way." The colorful bead chain attached to Gayle's eyeglasses swayed against her pale cheeks. "Lots of keepsake memories from our time up here with Marlena."

"Is it possible to have too many good memories?" Marlena's expression turned wistful. "Makes me seem greedy in light of the ones who have memories from being here that they'd like to forget."

"That's the thing about having a history, I suppose," Breezy mused. "You have to take the good with the bad."

The women were making Vivian worry. She failed to keep the urgency from her tone. "I can't make things right if I don't know what's wrong." And she definitely sensed something was wrong. Very wrong.

"Don't mind us, Vivian." Breezy fluttered her hand in the air and walked to the greenhouse door. "We tend to get lost on our own memory lanes."

"We certainly tend to do that," Gayle agreed.

They weren't lost, only being evasive. That was the thing with small towns. The locals had long memories. And if someone forgot the details, there was always another person willing to bring her up to speed quickly and succinctly. That was exactly what Vivian needed right now. To be brought up to speed.

"You made me realize tonight that sometimes all one needs is a different perspective to feel hope again." Marlena stepped over to Vivian and hooked her arm around hers. Together they walked to the exit. "Thank you for that."

Vivian wanted to hug the endearing widow. Then hang on to her until she decoded whatever message Marlena was trying to give her. But the rumble of an approaching truck filled the early evening air.

"Looks like Josh is here." Marlena released Vivian and gathered her two friends. "We'll just head to the main house and see what kinds of decorations I might have stashed away that we could use for the gala."

"You're certain to have more than you think upstairs." Gayle turned and went with Marlena toward the main house. "It could take us a while to find everything."

They were leaving Vivian alone. With Josh. Vivian locked her gaze on Breezy. "What am I supposed to do now?"

"Just keep doing what you're doing, dear." Breezy smiled, reached out and squeezed Vivian's hand. "Because sometimes a different perspective is all a heart needs if it's going to change."

With that, Breezy hurried after her sister and her friend. Vivian waited for Josh to park, then watched her cowboy climb out of his truck. Her pulse picked up.

Vivian knew one thing. Her cowboy could change her heart if she had a mind to let him. But her mind was set. And her heart was closed.

CHAPTER FOURTEEN

JOSH PARKED NEAR Marlena Doyle's greenhouses. The row of buildings was like a timeline of structural advances through the decades. It started with the two original wood-framed gabled greenhouses and ended with the newest steel-framed pair. Those, Josh had helped Marlena's late husband build. He cut the truck engine, yet nothing cut his urge to throw the truck in reverse, hightail it off the property and away from his memories.

He'd already spent yesterday with his ex-wife and his past. Fortunately, the one place Isabel and Josh had always found common ground was in the arena. Yesterday had proven no different. He and his ex-wife saw eye to eye on horses and competition strategy. Outside that, all bets were off. Still, Josh wasn't particularly in the mood for any more reminders of everything he'd long ago filed under "better off forgotten."

The door to the middle greenhouse opened. The Baker sisters swept outside, followed by Marlena. But Josh's attention skipped over the trio and stuck on Vivian. The fading sunlight surrounded her as if seeking her warmth. Or perhaps that was Josh. Drawn to the cowgirl, despite all his arguments to keep his distance.

Breezy, Gayle and Marlena gave Vivian a wave and turned for the main house. Vivian walked toward the parking area. Uncertainty washed over her face. Josh reached for his cowboy hat, dropped it on his head and collected himself.

He knew the Baker sisters and Marlena would keep his confidences. As longtime friends of his Gran Claire, they considered Josh and his brothers their own. And they were as protective of Josh as his grandparents had been. No, they would not outright reveal his pain points. Yet that wouldn't stop them from dropping hints in a misguided attempt to help him get over his past. But Josh didn't need help. There was nothing to get over if he never revisited those memories.

Still, he climbed out of his truck and kept his focus on Vivian. No sense letting his gaze wander only to find himself stumbling down memory lane. Besides, he wasn't about to take Vivian along with him.

Vivian stopped at the end of the gravel walkway. "Josh."

"Vivian," he said, matching her formal tone. Her fingers twitched and flexed at her sides, hinting at her nerves. He grinned at her. "So, Marlena's greenhouses are your hidden gem."

She blinked and studied him, opened her mouth, then seemed to catch herself. "Yeah. What do you think?"

I think I want to kiss you. Stamp a good memory over the bad. Would you consider me too selfish if I did just that? He tapped the rim of his cowboy hat up and stepped closer to her. "I think you were right. It's unconventional."

"If we had power in the greenhouses, I could really show you." She ran her hand over the back of her neck and across her cheek.

He really wanted to capture her hand and tug her into his embrace. Instead, he turned away. He might be drawn to her, but he wasn't foolish enough to believe theirs was a good pairing, like his grandfather claimed. Or that it was meant to last. After all, the only certainty about falling too fast was that the end came sooner than expected. "Come on, then."

"Where are we going?" Her boots crunched on the gravel behind him.

"To get my tools so I can give you power." He moved to his truck. "And then you can convince me greenhouses are the right venue for our gala."

"I can do that." She rubbed her hands together, standing beside him. "And I know my way around a toolbox, so feel free to put me to work."

"We're changing out your radiator after this, so you'll be working then." He grabbed his tool bag from behind the driver's seat. "Right now, it's about tracing electrical wires and replacing fuses, depending on which greenhouses you want on."

"The middle three please." She touched his arm before he stepped around her. "Did you really get me a new radiator?"

"It's in the truck bed." He tipped his head toward the truck. "We lucked out and Trey Ramsey had one at his auto shop in town. I was picking it up when you called."

Her eyebrows pulled in. "How much do I owe you?"

"Nothing." He grinned at her. "You vowed to win at the stampede. That builds Artie's competition résumé and his value better than I can. When you win, we'll call it even."

"You're selling Artie." Regret shifted across her face. Her fingers flexed on his arm.

"I already have a buyer lined up, if he likes what he sees in the arena." He moved away, let her hand slide off his arm and pretended not to notice the hint of sadness in her gaze. His business was to buy, train and sell horses. Not keep them. The only thing he kept these days were his emotions in check. "I also have buyers for Fox and my quarter horse, Rumor, who Maggie is riding in the breakaway event at the Stampede."

"Do you already have a new slate of horses selected to buy?" Vivian asked.

"I'm going in a different direction." He adjusted his hold on his tool bag and strode between the middle greenhouses. "I've been asked to partner in a new equestrian training and therapy center. I'll get input on the design, have an ownership stake and become the managing director."

"That's impressive. And it would be amazing here. There isn't anything like that in the surrounding area." Vivian seemed genuinely excited by the idea. Excited for him. She added, "I imagine you'll have clients from New Mexico to Oklahoma and even Colorado and Kansas."

He didn't correct her assumption. It was bad enough he'd revealed his plans. He wanted to blame a simple slip of the tongue. But it was all Vivian. His cowgirl was too easy to talk to. And so he kept going, "I need all three horses to sell next weekend to finalize my investment portion."

Vivian leaned against the hip-high stone

wall of the greenhouse. "Your family must be thrilled for you."

Josh's fingers stilled on the fuse box. "They don't know yet. I wanted to have the details sorted and everything confirmed first."

"I won't say anything," she assured him. "But I want to be there when you tell them. They're going to be so proud."

That was the hope. Josh unlocked the fuse box.

The bit about the relocation would likely dampen his family's enthusiasm. No one had wanted his older brother Grant to move to an orthopedic clinic in Southern California last year. Fortunately, Grant had fallen in love with Maggie and discovered sticking close to home was what he needed most.

Josh valued his family and his home. Yet he understood what he needed most was to leave if he truly wanted to step out on his own. Out of his family's influential shadow and make a name for himself on his terms. He wanted to be more than one of *those* Sloan boys. Not that he wasn't proud to be counted among his brothers. He frowned and got to work on the electrical.

At a spark from the electrical box, Vivian stepped back and pulled out her cell phone.

"I'm going to search for decorations for the gala and leave the electrical to you, if that's okay."

"I thought you wanted to help," he said, a tease in his words.

"I'm better with engines rather than power surges and wires that shock." She waved her fingers around in front of her. "You don't want me interfering."

But he liked having her close by. Near enough to reach for her if he wanted to. Within minutes, the first set of lights flickered on in the greenhouse behind him. The light spilled out of the windows around them like an invitation to step inside.

Vivian squealed into her hands. Delight flashed in her gaze. "Josh, you did it."

"Not quite, but we're getting there. We still have the other two greenhouses to get working and they're older than this one." He flipped another breaker and the heating unit powered on. "Now that the power is coming on, why don't you tell me where the idea to host a gala in the greenhouses came from."

She held out her hand toward him. "It will make more sense if I show you."

He set his hand inside hers and she guided him to the center of the still-dark older greenhouse. Her words took on an edge of wonder. "Look up. You see the sky? At night, the stars, or the rain, even snow will be falling softly against the glass panes." She turned in a slow circle. "Here, it's like standing inside your own personal snow globe."

The excitement in her words drew his gaze back to her.

"We can hang teardrop icicle lights from the rafters to look like falling snowflakes. Flocked Christmas trees along the walls. Then it's like you're dancing in the forest." Vivian splayed her fingers wide and spread her arms toward the far wall. "Fresh garland draped on the windows. Snow-white linens. Cedar greenery centerpieces with floating candles on the tables in the dining area. Luminaries everywhere. Lighting the corridors between the greenhouses. All of it warm. Inviting. Magical."

And enchanting. Vivian, just as she was now. She was so very enchanting. Her cheeks tinged pink. Her amber eyes sparkling. He couldn't help but smile too. He said, "Just like being inside a snow globe?"

"Full disclosure, I love snow globes. Always have." Her words were full of whimsy and hope. "My grandmother gave me a snow globe for Christmas when I was little. There was a white unicorn in a forest and a flurry of glittery silver snow. According to Grandma, the magic inside was only good on Christmas day."

Josh grinned. "Sounds like both our grand-mothers knew the secrets to magic and wishes and all things Christmas."

"I think they would've liked each other." Vivian stuck her hands in the pockets of her knee-length sweater jacket and seemed to settle into her memory. "Anyway, I saved up my wishes all year long. Then I woke up early on Christmas Day, shook my snow globe three times and made my wish."

"Only one wish," he teased.

"I may have made more wishes throughout the day," she admitted. "Just in case the magic hadn't run out on the first one."

"And are you still wishing on your unicorn snow globe?" he asked. He couldn't remember the last time he'd wished on anything. Or even wanted to. But something about Vivian made him wish...

"The first year my parents decided to travel to the tropics for Christmas, I packed my snow globe in my suitcase." She winced slightly, just around the edges of her eyes. "But even bundled up in my favorite blanket, it still broke."

"I'm sorry to hear that." Even more sorry for a younger Vivian who had likely been devastated.

"My parents took it and told me they'd fix it. But I never saw that snow globe again." She shrugged, but the movement was far from indifferent. She said, "It doesn't matter. I still have the memory."

He wanted to give her more than a childhood memory. He wanted to draw the hope back into her gaze. "One day you can pass the tradition on."

"Right." She brightened. "Now that Heather is pregnant, I'll have nieces or nephews to gift snow globes to."

He nodded, even though he'd meant passing the tradition on to her own family. Sharing her same wonder and love of the season with her children.

"Okay. You did not need to know all that. I obviously got carried away." She paused, pressed her fingers against her cheeks and laughed. "Let's get back to the gala. The reason we are even here. Please tell me you can at least see the potential. The space really is perfect."

There was something perfect about the moment. Something worth stepping into. He walked closer to her. "You're starting to convince me it could work."

Her smile stretched into her cheeks. "Then, we should get working on the power and heat for the other greenhouses. If we don't have that, we don't have a suitable venue and all my rambling was for nothing."

It was definitely not for nothing. "Before we get back to the electrical, there's one more thing we should test." He closed the distance between them and held out his arm. "Vivian, can I have this dance?"

"You want to dance?" Vivian considered his hand. "Here? Now?"

"We should make sure it'll work as a suitable dance floor, shouldn't we?"

She chewed on her lower lip, reached for him, then pulled back inches before their hands touched. "There's no music."

"I can fix that." He pulled his phone from his back pocket. Finding his music app, he selected a slow Christmas country song, and turned up the volume. He propped his phone on the windowsill and joined her in the center of the greenhouse. "Let's try it again. Vivian, may I please have this dance?"

Vivian dropped her hand into his and he never hesitated. He spun her once across the dusty concrete floor as the country duo sang about having a merry little Christmas. Then he guided her into his embrace. And finally, Josh could see the second things turned perfect. He could almost feel the magic of it too.

If only he hadn't stopped believing in all that. But he was no good for someone like her.

Too critical of love and too wary of relationships.

Still, he drew Vivian closer, but not *too* close. And told himself it was only one dance.

After all, it was important to set boundaries. Otherwise, his heart might start to think of his cowgirl as someone he was meant to hold on to forever.

CHAPTER FIFTEEN

VIVIAN'S HEART RACED. One of those rapid staccatos in her chest. The kind that made her simultaneously flushed and chilled. She wanted to lean into Josh, so steady and sure. And she wanted to run.

Worse, her heart wanted to take the lead.

Josh's hold shifted, tucking her closer before he spun them around. Warmth spread from her shoulders to her toes. Nerves, a heady blend of excitement and anticipation, hummed through her. Around her, the country singers crooned about all her troubles being out of sight.

Except Josh was right there. Trouble was in her arms. If Vivian had a goal of becoming a couple, this moment would've put them within reach. But they weren't even on a real dance floor. They weren't even on a date. They were no more than casual acquaintances. Cochairs. Yet Vivian felt something she hadn't in years. Something that went beyond attraction.

Awareness. Deep-seated and dangerous and all too compelling.

The song ended. They slowed and stilled. Right there in an empty greenhouse. In each other's arms. She couldn't look away from him. He watched her. Their breaths matched. One inhale. One exhale. Again.

If she only leaned forward. If he only... Vivian caught herself mid-lean and stepped out of his embrace.

She knew what followed when she blurred those relationship lines: believing in a shared connection. One-sided feelings. Messy emotions and even messier goodbyes. And suddenly dancing with Josh seemed like a very bad idea. "I think it'll work fine for dancing."

"Want to try another song?" His mouth lifted on one side.

"No." Not now. Not ever. *Because I'm terrified you could sweep me off my feet. And I might let you, although I vowed no more second-place finishes. Especially when it comes to love.* She motioned toward the doors. "We should probably get to the electrical before the daylight gets away from us."

"Vivian. Josh." The singsong warble of the Baker sisters filled the greenhouse.

Vivian turned to find the trio of women pressed up against the glass, their hands framing their faces while they peered inside.

Josh lifted his hand in greeting and called out, "We'll be right out."

No sooner had Vivian stepped outdoors than Breezy clapped and jingled the bell bracelets on her wrists. "Vivian, wait until you see what we found in Marlena's attic. It's much more than holiday jewelry."

"I daresay you won't have to buy many decorations. What with all the goodies stashed up there." Gayle declared and held up her hand. "We found not one, but five metallic Christmas trees just waiting for the dust to be shaken off and ornaments hung."

"My late husband loved decorating every holiday, but especially Christmas," Marlena explained, her words wistful. "When the farm was open to the public, he'd pick a theme and decorate every inch from the front gate to the main house to the gardens."

"When I was a kid, this was one of my favorite places," Josh admitted. "It was like visiting the North Pole. I was convinced Marlena's husband, Bobby, was related to Santa."

"I do believe Santa made quite a few appearances over the years." Marlena chuckled. "And you, Josh, were always first in line."

Vivian arched an eyebrow at Josh and tried to picture a younger Josh eager to spill his secrets to Santa.

"Of course, as everyone grew up, they would often bring their dates here," Marlena said. "Josh always helped us string lights throughout our winter gardens for the couples to stroll through."

The boy who'd loved Christmas had grown up and not lost that affection for the season. She'd caught a glimpse just now, inside the greenhouse. In his arms. For one dance.

But the cowboy met her gaze, guarded and reserved again. He said, "I'll finish up the electrical work while you go look through the attic."

"What if you need—" *...me.* Vivian cleared her throat "—help?"

"I've got this," he said and gave her a small smile. "And there shouldn't be things that spark and shock up in the attic."

No, but there was that awareness. And she feared it would be there even when her cowboy wasn't. Vivian suddenly wanted to recapture their dance. Hold on to the moment like those in a snow globe.

"Come on, Vivian." Breezy linked her arm with Vivian's. "We can sort through the attic and come up with a proper decorating action plan."

"Gotta have a good action plan." Gayle nodded and stepped to Vivian's other side. "Lead the way, Marlena. We've an attic to sort."

Vivian headed toward the main house, listening to the highlights of the goodies waiting inside. Everything from a pair of nutcrackers as tall as Gayle to dozens of waist-high, prelit, candy cane candles to oversize silver bells for the yard. Vivian glanced back once, but Josh was already gone.

AN HOUR LATER, Vivian declared a time-out and dropped onto what Marlena had called an antique settee. The trio hadn't exaggerated. If anything, they'd downplayed the collection of stuff in the walk-in attic that stretched almost the entire length of the house.

"I peeked out the dormer window. The lights are on in the greenhouses." Breezy settled beside Vivian and leaned her head against the mahogany-trimmed backrest. "Now, we're going to need younger backs and arms to carry everything downstairs."

"I'll work on that tomorrow," Vivian promised. "We've accomplished more than enough today."

"You and Josh deserve to treat yourselves to a good dinner." Breezy patted Vivian's leg. "I know just the place in Belleridge. Quiet. Private booths. Good food."

"Are you thinking of The Spiced Beehive Bistro?" Gayle leaned her arm on the top hat of a nutcracker and brushed at her forehead. "Lovely spot for a date night."

Date. With Josh. That was Vivian's cue to take her leave. She stood up and wiped her hands on her jeans. "Josh and I have a date replacing my radiator tonight."

"I used to help my husband with his projects too." Breezy waggled her eyebrows, stood up and sauntered to the door. "When I was next to him, holding the flashlight or a tool, I could always steal a kiss."

"That reminds me," Gayle announced and motioned toward Marlena. "We need mistletoe for the gala. Strategically placed, of course."

"It is now on our to-buy list." Marlena grinned and clicked her pen on the pad she'd been using for their notes. She followed Breezy into the hallway. "Anything else?"

Vivian added *mistletoe* to the list of things she needed to avoid. She followed the women downstairs, promised to look over the notes and be in touch with next steps the following day. Somehow, she'd not only secured a venue, she had also gained a committee. She was more than grateful.

Now she was seated beside Josh, headed to the bypass to repair her truck. She searched for her irritation or frustration for a day that had gone nothing like she'd expected. But all she felt was relaxed and energized. And so very content. She picked up the cookie tin on the bench seat. It was Tess's way of thanking Josh for his help with her display case, and he'd told Vivian to help herself.

Josh steered them off the Doyles' drive onto the main road and glanced at her. "Can I ask you something?"

Vivian plucked at the curly ribbon on the cookie tin cover. "Sure."

"What is this fake relationship between us?" he asked.

"An-attempt-to-convince-my-family-I-have-my-whole-life-together kind of thing." She gave in, opened the lid on the cookie tin and considered the assortment of cellophane-wrapped caramels and cookies inside.

"And a boyfriend will help convince your family that you've got it all together." He leaned over and picked up a chocolate-and-white cookie with crushed candy canes sprinkled on top.

"A boyfriend certainly helps. At least, that's my parents' perspective." Vivian selected a caramel. "I'm approaching thirty and should be settling down in their eyes. But I had a few missteps in the relationship arena that I don't care to repeat."

"Care to share what happened?"

"In college I was best friends with Kara, my roommate, and Jared, who we'd met at orientation. The three of us were inseparable after that," Vivian explained. "Then I fell hard for Jared only to discover that Kara and Jared had already fallen in love with each other."

Sympathy flickered in his gaze before he looked back at the road. His voice was reserved. "Did you ever tell him how you felt?"

"I tried. It was awkward," she confessed. Jared had thought she was kidding at first. She added, "But he was kind." So kind it had edged into pity and only magnified Vivian's own mortification. "That was when he told me about him and Kara. We never mentioned it again." Yet her feelings for Jared had lingered.

Silence stretched inside the truck cab.

Vivian rushed to fill it. "But it's fine. I was Kara's maid of honor at their wedding and threw the best shower and engagement party ever." She'd smiled through it all too, while stifling her own feelings and trying not to feel like a fool. She continued, "And that's not all. Wade happens to be Jared's older brother."

Surprise flickered across Josh's face.

"I introduced Heather and Wade with Jared's encouragement," Vivian said. "My sister and Wade hit it off immediately. They double dated with Kara and Jared." And they always tried to set up Vivian, which only ever left her feeling like the proverbial fifth wheel. She fiddled with the candy wrapper. "Now, they all live within walking distance of each other. And at our extended family gatherings, I get to see Kara, Jared and their three kids."

"That must be—" he started, then his gaze slanted toward her "—strange."

Not as strange as realizing she honestly felt nothing in the retelling. No bitterness. No twinge of regret. Or sadness for what might have been. It was part of her history, but not a defining piece. She supposed she had the cowboy seated next to her to thank for that. He always made her feel less alone. Too bad he wasn't part of her future. "I moved on and dated other people, who later moved on to other relationships."

He nodded and searched her face. "And now?"

"Now I'm good alone. Perfectly fine on my own." She unwrapped her caramel candy. "Not at odds with my single status. Not even a little bit."

He finished his cookie and brushed his fingers on his jeans. His words were pensive. "But everyone thinks you will be better off with someone special in your life."

"Exactly." Vivian bit into the soft caramel. The sea salt crunched inside the chewy candy, adding a sharpness to the flavor and her words. "And convincing my parents that I'm happy being single is…"

"Impossible," he finished for her.

"Yes," she said. He understood her better than she'd anticipated. And Vivian found herself wanting to shove aside the cookie tin and scooch across the bench seat to be right by his side. As if she wanted his arm around her. His comfort. *Him*. She shifted and scooted closer to her door. "My turn to ask you something."

"Yes, I do intend to sample everything in that cookie tin." His grin reached into his cheeks. "You better act fast if you see something you like in there."

She liked him. Just as he was now: charming. Funny. And allowing her to be herself. She scooped the caramels into her palm. "I'm calling dibs on these."

"Did you seriously just call dibs?" Josh laughed and reached for a caramel. "I haven't called dibs since grade school."

"These are mine." Vivian pushed his arm away and chuckled. "That's what *dibs* means."

"Okay. Fine." He glanced at the cookie tin then arched a brow at her. "Dibs on the peppermint bark cookies."

"But I wanted to…" she started.

"Fair is fair," he interrupted. "Or rather all is fair in love and cookies."

She broke a piece off a peppermint bark cookie.

"Hey. I saw that," he said. "You owe me a caramel."

"Fine." Vivian chuckled. "You owe me an answer to my question."

"You never asked me one," he said.

Did you really say you would marry me? And please don't tell me it was a joke. She couldn't be that. She didn't want to face being his joke. She'd felt like someone's joke before. Vivian pressed the lid back on the cookie tin and reminded herself nothing about this was supposed to feel so real. "Why did you go along with my whole fake-boyfriend scheme?"

His fingers tapped a slow, silent beat on the steering wheel as if he were running through responses and discarding one after the other. Finally, he said, "Can't it be as simple as wanting to help you out?"

No. Because that spoke to her heart. It was her career and life that were on the line instead. "Maybe if we were friends for longer than a few days. Perhaps if we hadn't just met."

He nodded and considered her. "So, what would you believe?"

"That you want your ex-wife back." That a

fake relationship was the only possibility between Vivian and him. Because Vivian had
vowed if she ever contemplated love again, she
would tiptoe into it. Yet, something about her
cowboy tempted her to jump with her whole
heart and both boots. But she couldn't trust
she'd recover from a fall like that again. And
that meant leaving the risk-taking for the arena.

His gaze returned to the road. His words
were once again reserved. "Did someone tell
you that's what I want? My ex-wife back?"

"Isabel mentioned unfinished business when
she walked into the arena the other day," Vivian explained. "I assumed..."

"That she meant us," he mused.

And if he wanted his ex-wife back, that
should be more than enough to effectively
clip Vivian's interest in him. To convince her
that whatever she was feeling between them
would go nowhere. That way her heart would
finally retreat into the background where she
wanted it to be.

"That's fair," he said.

"Am I right?" Vivian pressed. Did they have
separate goals? Ones that would keep their relationship firmly in the pretend category?

He eyed her and countered, "If you are correct, how exactly does our relationship help
me with Isabel?"

"Jealousy." Vivian searched for a convincing smile. "It's the oldest ploy in the relationship handbook."

"You sound eerily like my brothers." He rubbed his chin and studied her. "Everyone wants what they can't have."

"Exactly." *You can't ever be mine.* Vivian yanked her attention from her cowboy, unwrapped another caramel and sidestepped her disappointment. Then she reminded herself what she felt for her cowboy was no doubt temporary. Fleeting. Like salt on her tongue. "Now, with Isabel coming over to practice, you two can see…"

A stillness settled inside the truck cab despite Josh never tapping the brakes. Never slowing the vehicle. Though Vivian was suddenly backpedaling and second-guessing and wondering if she'd gotten it all completely wrong.

"So, let me see if I have this straight." His expression was guarded. Yet a hint of surprise shifted through his words. "You convinced me to give my ex-wife a horse and coach her so I could get back together with her."

"If you'll recall there's that unfinished business," Vivian rushed out. "I didn't want to be the one standing between you and your second chance. After all, this whole fake relationship is my fault."

He gave another slow nod as the silence stretched between them again. Another mile passed. More silence. Finally, he slowed the truck behind hers and put it into Park. Then he looked at Vivian. "I don't want a second chance with Isabel."

Vivian held his stare, felt that hit of a connection again. That shock of awareness. "You don't."

He shook his head and met her gaze, direct and steady. "No."

"Then, you're going along with this whole scheme for…" She stopped, wanting to press pause. To look one more time before she proceeded, as if she'd bumped into some imaginary caution sign.

"You," he said, simply and firmly.

The heat coming from the truck vent warmed her skin. But his gaze, fixed entirely on her, heated Vivian from the inside out. She worked to keep her tone casual. Unaffected. "For the record, I stopped liking Jared years ago."

His blue eyes flashed. One corner of his mouth tipped up. "For the record, that is very good to know."

Still, I need your promise. Your promise not to let me fall for you. Vivian crinkled the candy wrapper in her hand. "What do we do now?"

His gaze dropped to her mouth, held for a

beat, and another, before lifting back to hers. A lightness tinged his words. "We change out your radiator. Get dinner and put together the best Christmas gala Three Springs has ever seen. Then you have the fastest run at the stampede."

Vivian blinked, then nodded.

He opened his door and glanced back at her. "Hey, Vivian."

"Yeah," she said, unable to stop the breathless catch in her voice.

"I call dibs on your first and last dance at the gala." With that, he climbed out of the truck and left Vivian to finally catch her breath.

Less than a week. That's what she had with her cowboy. Not a lifetime. Not that it mattered. Forevers took more time to find anyway.

Everyone knew there was nothing instant about love. And getting there the fastest, only counted in the arena.

CHAPTER SIXTEEN

THE REPLACEMENT OF the radiator went well. Too well, in Josh's opinion. He always preferred to work alone. Yet Vivian had kept pace with him, even proving to be one step ahead at times. Josh had fun working with her. Too much, really. He'd even checked her engine for their next potential repair job. It was certainly inconvenient. Finding more excuses to spend time with his cowgirl only took him away from what he truly wanted. The life he intended to build on his own terms outside Houston.

He turned onto the private road leading to the farmhouse, following behind Vivian's now-running truck. What he needed was more than a car distance from his cowgirl. He'd almost kissed her in the greenhouse. Considered kissing her several times during the radiator change-out. And he was still thinking about kissing her now. One more inconvenience to add to his list.

Josh eased his foot off the gas pedal, putting more road between his truck and Vivian's. That was exactly what he needed to do. Back off. Ease a little space between himself and Vivian. Then he'd remember what mattered. Not dances in empty greenhouses, stolen kisses or his heart's happiness.

After all, he'd chased all that before. Ended up alone. And discovered love was more illusion than substance. And he had no interest in fooling himself again. Even if his car-fluent cowgirl captured his attention in a way he hadn't known was possible.

Still, love couldn't be trusted. Not like hard work and horses. The very things that would get Josh exactly what he'd been striving for the past five years. The right to call himself one of the most sought-after horse trainers in the South. Love wouldn't build his platform. Only an investment in Bellmare would get him where he wanted to be.

That meant stepping away from Vivian, fading back into their fake-relationship arrangement and getting on with his own business. His new plan in place, he parked his truck in the driveway beside Vivian's, climbed out and headed inside the farmhouse to quickly check in with his family.

"There's Josh now." Grandpa Sam's words were dipped in wry amusement. "We were beginning to wonder if you took a wrong turn and got lost on your way home."

More like lost in his own thoughts. Josh dropped his cowboy hat on a hook and entered the kitchen.

"Well, you have to hurry, Josh." Vivian's mother pressed a forest green sweatshirt into Josh's hands. Her words quick paced. "Vivian is already upstairs changing. Everyone else has already left."

"We sure don't want to be late." Sam pressed his black cowboy hat on his head. The same one his grandfather always referred to as his dressing-up hat.

Josh looked from his grandpa to Vivian's mother. And that was when he noticed the dozen comical dancing reindeers on Catherine's bold red, snowflake-adorned sweater and the words *Grandma To Be*. His fingers curled into the sweatshirt he held, just as a not-so-good feeling began to take hold inside him. He asked, "Late for what?"

"We're meeting everyone downtown." Grandpa Sam adjusted his black suede bolo tie. The one with a picture of a jolly Santa and colorful Christmas tree on the silver clasp.

The bad feeling expanded. Josh hedged, "I need to check on the horses. I could meet up with you all later." *Or not at all, perhaps.*

"Maggie and Caleb took care of the horses already," Grandpa Sam paused. One white eyebrow arched as if he knew his grandson was scrambling for an excuse to bow out. The other eyebrow arched to meet the other, signaling his grandfather was fully prepared to counter Josh. Grandpa Sam added, "I mixed the grain for Rumor and Fox myself. I know how very particular you are about their special feed ratios in the evenings. Gave them each an extralong rubdown too."

Josh knew how well prepared his grandfather could be when he wanted to get his way. Still, he'd learned from his grandfather not to back down. Josh said, "I should check over Vivian's truck for leaks."

Catherine swatted that neatly away. "Vivian mentioned her truck is running like new. Not one warning light lit up on her way home."

Oh, but how his grandfather's gaze lit up at that. As if his grandfather and Vivian's mother weren't in on this together. Still, one more excuse to avoid the outing had been rather efficiently removed. Josh said, "I still don't know what we're doing, exactly."

"We're headed to the Feisty Owl for Reindeer Games—Couples' Edition." Vivian's mother straightened the sleeves of her ugly Christmas sweater as if it was a silk blouse.

"You and Vivian are on Maggie's team with Wade and Heather."

"Caleb is emceeing the event. Vivian's father is helping him set up." Grandpa Sam watched Josh. A gleam in his shrewd gaze. "It's a fundraiser for the town's Christmas toy drive."

Josh was still stuck on the "couples' edition" of Catherine's statement. That was exactly what he was not wanting to promote—him and Vivian as a couple, in front of the entire town. His words were hesitant. "Vivian agreed to go?"

"Of course." Catherine chuckled and shook her head. "Vivian loves this kind of thing. One year, on the Carolina coast, she begged us to enter the life-size chess tournament. The next year, in the Florida Keys, she talked us into the beach-sports day. It was more fun than I ever expected." Catherine paused. Surprise flashed in her gaze. "It became a sort of family tradition, I suppose. Every year, we entered a contest together. We haven't done anything like that in ages."

"Tonight we can pick up the tradition, right, Josh?" Grandpa Sam's words were smooth yet determined. "After all, it's important to support the kids."

Josh agreed. Letting down his cowgirl didn't sit well either. Not that he'd ever admit that out loud. His cowgirl certainly was trouble.

Tomorrow he'd get back to remembering he disliked inconveniences. And had long since stopped finding trouble. He sighed. "Let me just go change."

They weren't too far behind schedule when Josh walked into the kitchen fifteen minutes later and found Vivian already there. She wore a matching forest green sweatshirt imprinted with a cartoon-y gingerbread woman plus crown. Underneath the gingerbread queen were the words: *I'm the Ginger to his Gingerbread.*

Delight lit her face and sparked in her eyes as she took him in. Her laughter spilled free. "I didn't think you would actually put your sweatshirt on."

He ran his hand over his coordinating forest green sweatshirt with a gingerbread king on it. It had the words: *I'm the Bread to her Gingerbread.* "It's not the fashion statement I usually make, but it seemed like the thing to do for the team." *Or rather, you.*

Because seeing Vivian smile with such genuine joy was becoming something of a preoccupation for him. One he'd have to get over, starting tomorrow when he focused on what he wanted again and not on his cowgirl.

"Let's get going." Catherine slipped on her

jacket. "Reindeer Games wait for no one, not even the gingerbread king and queen."

Josh's curiosity finally got the best of him at the end of the Sloans' private drive. He turned onto the main road and slanted his gaze toward his passenger. "It's time to confess, Vivian."

She shifted in the front seat toward him and sounded cautious when she spoke. "Confess… what?"

"Just how far this family-competition tradition extends." Josh shifted his gaze back to the road. "I know about chess and beach-sports day. I need to know what else have you dragged your family into over the years?"

"I prefer *persuaded*." Vivian's laughter rushed through the truck cab. "And we won several times. Remember, Mom, when we won that scavenger hunt and got free holiday desserts for the rest of our stay at the hotel? We finished second in the Jingle Bells Art Wars and received tickets to a Christmas-themed luau."

Josh smiled at her obvious joy.

"That was rather delightful," her mother said from the back seat. Amusement coated her words. "But the year we entered the boat-building regatta and our boat sank at the starting line was not as thrilling."

Yet the pleasure on Vivian's face was obvious. Josh asked, "Where did you go wrong in the boat build?"

"The plastic lining," Vivian admitted. "Heather tore it accidentally and used duct tape to repair it. Even though Mom and I told Heather we needed all new plastic."

"It's always in the details, where things go wrong," Josh offered. Like right now, Josh noticed how Vivian's amber gaze sparkled. And how he wasn't feeling the slightest bit unsociable. He was in fact looking forward to joining his cowgirl for some reindeer games after all. He wanted in on the fun with Vivian. And wasn't that a step too far.

"That's not the worst of it." Vivian frowned, but her words remained lighthearted. "Heather managed to convince Mom and me that we would be better captains than her and Dad."

Josh tried to stop his laughter.

His grandfather chuckled in the back seat and said, "Very clever of your older sister."

Josh had outmaneuvered his own brothers a time or two growing up. The same as they'd done to him over the years and still continued to do. Soon enough, he wouldn't be around to join his brothers whenever he wanted. He shifted on the bench seat.

"Ted and Heather stayed completely dry on the pool deck, laughing so hard they were buckled over, while Vivian and I disappeared under the water." Catherine's words were dry. "I don't think I've laughed that hard since then."

"But Mom and I got them back the following year, didn't we, Mom?" Vivian leaned around and peered into the back seat. "We nominated Heather and my dad for the whipped cream–pie throwing contest the next Christmas."

"Nice revenge," Josh said. Some of the most fun was in the plotting of the payback. Caleb and Josh had spent hours devising ways to get back at Ryan and Grant for pranks they'd pulled. He grinned at his collection of memories.

"By the end, Heather and Ted were covered from their heads to their flip-flops in whipped cream. All the while Vivian and I wiped our tears of laughter off our cheeks," Catherine said. "Those competitions certainly taught us how to band together. Even more, we learned how to be very good teammates."

"Those are valuable skills both personally and professionally," Sam added. "Time well spent, to be sure, even if your boat did sink."

Catherine chuckled. "And now we have many wonderful memories."

"It's always good to revisit those moments together." Sam patted Catherine's arm. "My

Claire always claimed it was in the revisiting that we tightened any loose family ties."

Loose family ties. Certainly, his family's wouldn't loosen when he relocated to Houston. Distance was rumored to make the heart grow fonder. That claim would surely be put to the test soon and with a certain cowgirl. After all, Vivian would be leaving too. And Houston wasn't her destination. Again, Josh shifted on the bench seat, as if the restored leather was the problem.

"Sam, that is a lovely sentiment," Catherine said. "Thank you for that."

Josh saw the affection and hint of sadness pass over Catherine's face. For all her stoic business demeanor, Vivian's mother loved her daughter. And if Josh wasn't mistaken, she missed Vivian deeply. He feared he already understood how she felt. Josh glanced at Vivian.

Now quiet, she faced forward and stared out the windshield as if she'd already retreated. But Vivian and Josh were together now. And wasn't that all it was ever supposed to be? Here and now. They had only committed to the fake, not a real future together. He refused to be sad about something he'd never had.

He cleared his throat and tried to sound upbeat. "Of course, Gran Claire also told my brothers and me that we obviously hadn't been gifted long memories, since, if we had, we wouldn't have always found ourselves in hot water."

"Isn't that the truth?" Sam's bark of laughter filled the truck cab. "And when Josh says always, he sure does mean it."

That brought Vivian's smile back. She leaned around her seat again. "Time to tell us, Sam. How much hot water did Josh get himself into?"

That launched another round of storytelling about Josh's childhood escapades. Like the time he talked Ryan and Caleb into climbing on the barn roof to hang Christmas lights for Santa to land more easily. And the time he organized a hockey game in the middle of the bull pasture. Then he had to defend himself when Sam shared the story of how the twins once swapped classrooms during their final exams. Josh took both math exams for the twins and Caleb took both English exams, and they passed with high grades. That one had been masterminded by his twin, with Josh's encouragement, of course. Once again, laughter and joy spread around the truck cab.

"My Claire never minded the boys' antics. Not one bit," Grandpa Sam mused. "If you asked her about her favorite Christmas memory, she always told the same one."

Josh glanced in the rearview mirror and met his grandpa's soft gaze.

"I heard so many stories the other night while we were decorating," Vivian said. "How could Claire have picked just one Christmas memory?"

"The boys made it easy." Grandpa Sam touched the corner of his eye. "Their Gran told them to write their letters to Santa. She was thinking it would get them to sit down for a spell."

Soft chuckles came from the back seat. Catherine said, "Poor dear probably wanted to close her eyes for a quick nap. I know I would've wanted that."

"There was no time for a nap." Grandpa Sam chuckled too. "The boys were quick that afternoon. They'd written one letter together. Only wanted one thing."

Vivian leaned even farther around her seat.

"They wanted to have the Sloan last name too," Grandpa Sam added, his words wistful. "Same as Claire and me."

Josh cleared his throat. "Gran Claire and Grandpa Sam chose us, and we wanted to choose them back."

Vivian pressed her hand to her mouth. Her gaze gleamed.

"We made their wish come true the very

next day," Grandpa Sam explained. "I'm not sure who was more proud, me or my grandsons, when we left the courthouse officially as the Sloan family."

His grandparents had made certain their family ties were double-knotted all those years ago. He would forever be grateful. Especially now when he would soon be testing the strength of those family bonds.

Too soon, they arrived at the Feisty Owl and Josh parked in one of the last empty spots in the almost full lot. Josh held the door open to the bar and grill and waited for Sam to escort Catherine inside.

"I want to give you a fair warning, Josh." Vivian stopped in the open doorway of the Feisty Owl and grinned at him. Her words light and playful. She chuckled and set her hand on his chest, right over his heart. "I can't seem to help myself. With these sorts of events, I always play to win."

Josh realized he couldn't seem to help himself either. Because he was beginning to think he wanted to play for keeps.

CHAPTER SEVENTEEN

RUDOLPH'S REBELS WERE currently in second place.

Vivian's team was right behind, The Noel-It-Alls, led by Maggie's older sister, Kelsey, and her fiancée, Nolan Davis. The two teams had gone to the bonus round in reindeer trivia. But Vivian's group missed the question about what magical vegetable gives Santa's reindeers the ability to fly. Chef Nolan knew the answer was corn and Kelsey's team took the lead.

They'd tied things up in the gumdrop build, thanks to Josh's impressive construction skills. Their toothpick-and-gumdrop chimney tower was not only the tallest but it was also still standing by the end of the challenge. Later, Carter edged out Grant in the final leg of the Pass the Presents Relay to secure The Noel-It-Alls the top spot again.

Now Vivian stood on the dance floor with her other teammates, wrapped from her boots to her head in colorful blinking lights for the Living Christmas Tree Challenge, where four team members needed to be lit and decorated the fastest. Wade was currently dressing up Maggie and Grant nearby. Vivian hollered and cheered and couldn't imagine anyplace else she'd want to be.

Her sister settled a sparkly headband into Vivian's hair. The tinsel slid down on Vivian's forehead. Vivian scrunched her face, but only worked the tinsel lower. She said, "Heather, who are you waving at?"

"Oh, I thought that gentleman over by the bar was Mr. Nesci." Heather pointed a candy cane in that direction and grinned. "Josh, doesn't he look just like Mr. Nesci? I swear they could be brothers."

"Are you talking about Miles Nesci?" Josh asked.

Vivian heard the frown in Josh's voice and shuffled around until she faced Josh. For a cowboy who claimed to keep his distance from holiday fun, he'd certainly jumped in with both boots this evening. He was proving to be as competitive as Vivian.

"Yes." Heather smiled at Vivian. "Mr. Nesci was quite debonair, Viv. I told him he looked like an actor from Hollywood's golden age."

"Who is Miles Nesci?" Vivian blew at the tinsel creeping toward her eyes.

"Josh's friend." Heather hooked several candy canes on Josh's tinsel-covered shoulders.

"Miles Nesci is a sixth-generation cattle rancher from northern Oklahoma," Josh explained, seemingly unconcerned about the colorful lights swinging from the brim of his cowboy hat in front of his face. "Miles wants a competition-ready horse as a Christmas present for his rodeo-bound grandson."

Miles wasn't a friend. He was a potential buyer. Vivian stopped worrying about the tinsel and swallowed her sudden unease. "Heather, how do you know this Mr. Nesci?"

"I met him this afternoon when he stopped by the farm. I was the only one there." Heather paused and eyed them as if considering her next design element. She picked up several metallic bows—another required element for the challenge. Then she continued, "Fortunately, I'd just woken up from a power nap or I would've missed seeing Miles standing outside Artie's pasture."

"Artie," Vivian said. Miles Nesci wasn't interested in just any horse. The cattle rancher wanted the best. Vivian focused on Josh, but the Christmas lights twinkled on and off, casting his face in multihued shadows.

"What did he say?" Josh's words were hesitant. And too contained for Vivian's liking.

More unease flashed through her.

"Miles told me that he wanted to buy Artie. I knew that couldn't be right." Confusion crossed her sister's face. Heather glanced from Josh to Vivian, then asked, "Viv, you aren't really thinking of selling the fastest horse around, are you?"

Vivian was not. But Josh, well, he certainly was. Vivian shook her head and tried to shake the tinsel out of her eyes. "Heather, what did you tell Mr. Nesci?"

"I apologized and told Mr. Nesci that he had the wrong horse." Heather pressed several sticky bows on Vivian's arms. "Then I explained Artie belonged to my little sister, who was riding him in the rodeo next weekend."

No. No. No. Her family still believed Artie belonged to Vivian because neither Vivian nor Josh had ever corrected them. Now Heather had unknowingly interfered with a potential sale for Josh. Vivian peered at Josh. He was as still and contained as a netted Christmas tree.

"We even went to the stables so Mr. Nesci could see the other horses," Heather went on. "Did you know there isn't another horse who looks like Artie on the property? Artie is certainly special, but you guys already knew that much."

Artie was the only Arabian currently in residence in the Sloan stables. He was unique. And no doubt required the right buyer. Vivian knew enough to know Josh wouldn't sell Artie to just anyone. Vivian scrambled for a way to right the wrong. She hopped, spinning until she faced the bar and dislodged several bows in the process. "Where is Mr. Nesci now? You thought you saw him just now, didn't you, Heather?"

"Stop it, Vivian. You need to be wearing a dozen bows." Heather smacked the bows on Vivian's back. Her words and touch irritated. "Mr. Nesci mentioned something about heading to Colorado from here."

Vivian winced and squeezed her eyes closed.

Josh's words were low. "He's headed to Fort Collins to be exact."

"Does he live there?" Vivian asked, heard both the desperate hope and tension in her own words.

"A quarter horse by the name of Hawk Eye lives there," Josh explained. "The gelding has been on an impressive winning streak recently. He'll likely be a Christmas present for Miles's rodeo-bound grandson."

That was bad. *Bad* bad. Artie was supposed to have been the Christmas present. That was what Josh hadn't said. But Vivian knew from the resignation and hint of frustration in Josh's demeanor. But Vivian's well-meaning sister had interfered. Vivian appreciated her sister's protectiveness over Artie, even if it was misplaced. Yet Heather was not to blame. This was all on Vivian for never correcting her family when they'd first arrived at the Sloan farm. For her claiming Artie when he wasn't her horse. Now Vivian had cost Josh a sale. And an important one at that.

She wiggled, struggled against the colorful lights trapping her. Why had she even agreed to a night of reindeer games anyway? As if she was in town for fun and frivolity. Nothing was merry about any of it now. Why had she dragged Josh into this? He could've been selling his horse, earning that investment money he needed. "Heather, hurry up with that star already." Impatient, she wriggled some more.

"It has to light up. That was one of the requirements for this round." Heather lifted an eyebrow at Vivian and wrinkled her nose. "You're the one always telling us not to lose on a technicality."

Vivian wanted to unplug herself and bust free of the lights. Forget the entire challenge. More impatience flickered through her like a shorted Christmas light strand.

Finally, Heather settled the star topper on Vivian's head and flipped the switch. Then she reviewed her work. Satisfied, Heather raced to hit the buzzer, landing them in first place. It still wasn't fast enough for Vivian. She shimmied and yanked on the lights. Bows and candy canes scattered around her boots. Then she spun in another quick circle, unwinding herself. Finally free, she unwrapped Josh, grabbed his hand and dragged him into the mechanical bull area.

The bull was dressed for the holidays in cute wrapping paper and covered in several layers of sparkly green-and-red tinsel. And, fortunately, it was turned off for the night. More importantly, the cordoned-off area was empty. There was a half wall that divided the dance floor from the mechanical bull. Observers could watch dancers and the dancers could watch the mechanical bull riders. Vivian kept her back to the dance floor where the other teams were finishing their living Christmas trees and concentrated on Josh.

"What's Mr. Nesci's phone number?" Vivian pulled her cell phone from her back pocket. "I can call him and explain. Get him to come back."

"He's almost to Fort Collins by now." Josh wiped his palms over his face. "Trust me, he isn't turning around now."

"Then, I'll stall him. That I can do," Vivian

countered, then considered Josh. "Unless you have a backup buyer for Artie?"

He shook his head.

How could he be so calm? Vivian felt like she was tripping over her own alarm. She flung her arms wide. "How can you not have a backup?"

He set his hands on his hips and eyed her. "You know Heather wasn't wrong. Artie is special. It has taken time to find a buyer."

Exactly what she'd feared. Exactly what she already knew. Vivian yanked the last of the tinsel from around her neck and tossed it aside. She blocked out the laughter and friendly shouts coming from the dance floor behind her. She wasn't in the mood to be merry anymore. Not until she helped Josh. "I'll fix this. I promise I'll find you a new buyer. You have my word."

"Vivian," he started. His gaze flicked over her, toward the dance floor.

"No. This is all my fault." Vivian squeezed her forehead and motioned to him. "But, first, we must call Mr. Nesci."

"I plan to call him in the morning," Josh said.

"That could be too late," Vivian argued and lifted her voice over the growing noise. "It'll only take a minute. We have to try."

Josh conceded. He took out his phone, tapped

on the screen and held the phone up to his ear. He looked at her and said, "It went straight to voice mail."

Vivian took the phone from him, left an abbreviated explanation for the rancher and a request to call Josh if Hawk Eye turned out not to be the right gelding for his grandson. She disconnected and handed the phone back to Josh. "What now?"

"We wait." Josh returned his phone to his back pocket. "See if Miles calls back tomorrow."

It was going to be a very long night. Vivian huffed out a frustrated breath. "Why is everyone being so loud?" Vivian needed to think, not cheer.

"They're calling our names," Josh said. His words were bland.

Vivian tried to block out the clapping and shouts of encouragement. She needed quiet. A few minutes to figure out who was in the market for a new horse. For a special Arabian horse. She had to know someone on the circuit. A shrill whistle cut into her concentration. Then she frowned at Josh. "Did you say they are calling our names?" At his nod, she asked, "Why?"

He lifted his arm and pointed his finger toward the ceiling.

Vivian followed the direction and tipped her

head back. Her gaze snagged on a neatly hung sprig of mistletoe directly over their heads. Apparently, there were secret sprigs of mistletoe hidden all around the bar and grill. Vivian gaped at the plant like she would a hairy spider. "They can't be serious. We're in the middle of a disaster." Trying to problem solve. It was definitely not the appropriate time to be seeking out stolen kisses under secret mistletoe.

"Rules are rules," Josh said, his words indifferent. "And I believe you were the one who ordered all of us to follow the rules earlier tonight."

That had been her, alright. And those had been her exact instructions. But that was when she'd been excited and wanting to win bragging rights. The first rule of Reindeer Games—Couples' Edition had been any couple caught under the secret mistletoe had to share a kiss or they were disqualified. That rule had been very specific and repeated more than once. Vivian returned her attention to Josh and blinked. "You can't be thinking…?"

"Our team won't be happy if we get disqualified now before the final snowball fight." Josh watched her. One corner of his mouth lifted. "We're so close to winning it all. That is what we came for, isn't it?"

Vivian couldn't remember why she was there.

What she even wanted to win. Her thoughts kept circling back around to Josh and the misplaced mistletoe. But it was only mistletoe, nothing more than an old silly tradition. Her hands fluttered in front of her. Those butterflies took flight in her stomach. The cheering grew louder.

Yet, it was all wrong. Josh had just lost a buyer because of her. Surely, he wasn't considering kissing her. Surely, she wasn't considering kissing him either.

"We'll just… We can… Make it quick. Brief." To satisfy their audience. Not Vivian. That was hardly relevant. But this was only a fake relationship. She shouldn't be blurring those lines even more. Vivian looked everywhere but at Josh. Her words sounded weak, even to her. "It doesn't have to be a real kiss, right?"

"Vivian," he said. His voice, warm and gentle, curved inside her and drew her gaze back to him.

And Vivian, suddenly, couldn't look away. The affection in his eyes captured her. Enchanted her. All she managed was a slow hum.

"I want to give you fair warning." He closed the distance between them in one step. His hands landed on her hips. His grip light yet steady.

Unlike the quick race of her pulse.

He added, "I would like to kiss you, Vivian."

Her fingers finally settled on his shoulders, as if she always reached for her cowboy this way. She felt herself falling. Into the moment. Into him.

He leaned closer, paused before his lips brushed against her mouth. His gaze collided with hers and held. "I would like to kiss you, and nothing about it is going to be pretend."

CHAPTER EIGHTEEN

NOW JOSH KNEW. Knew exactly what it was like to know something while wanting to unknow it at the very same time. Post-kiss, he took in Vivian's blush, tingeing her cheeks the prettiest pink, and heard the catch in her exhale. Wondered if her pulse raced in a similar double beat as his. He tucked her hair behind her ear and stepped back before he gave in and learned even more about his cowgirl by kissing her all over again.

Kissing Vivian was like opening a gift on Christmas morning and getting the better version of what he'd wished for. Like when he was a kid and wanted a toy race car and he'd gotten an entire fleet instead. He'd been thrilled. Delighted. Same as he was now.

But he wasn't a kid anymore. And whatever was between himself and Vivian wasn't a game. Or child's play. That made right now unsettling. And more than a little unnerving. Since he now knew one kiss with Vivian wasn't ever going to be enough.

"We should probably get ready for the snow-ball fight." Vivian touched her bottom lip.

Josh wanted to ask if she was trying to capture the kiss or forget it.

One corner of her mouth lifted. Her words were wry. "I promise not to get us caught under any more mistletoe."

Josh was not about to make that same promise. And that was certainly the problem. The quickest fix would be to stick to the crowded dance floor and avoid going anywhere else with Vivian alone. And he'd have to be hypervigilant about scanning the room for more mistletoe.

He followed Vivian into the dance area and cornered his twin at the podium. "Did you really have to point out where Vivian and I were standing to the entire bar?" Josh had noticed the glittery ribbon on the mistletoe just seconds before he heard his brother's voice booming over the microphone, declaring a secret mistletoe reveal.

"Yeah. I kind of had to." Caleb picked up the paper on the podium and tapped it, not looking or sounding the least bit remorseful. "If you'll recall the hidden mistletoe was rule number one. The first I read off tonight." Caleb paused and eyed Josh. "Don't tell me the kiss wasn't worth it."

Sure, Josh's curiosity was appeased. But he knew things now. Like he wanted to kiss Vivian again. Hold her longer. That was dangerous territory for a cowboy like him, who was never putting love and a relationship first again. He set his hands on his hips and frowned at his twin. "That's not the point."

"It was very much the point." Caleb's laughter rumbled around Josh.

"Changes nothing," Josh countered.

"Then, why are you upset with me?" Caleb mimicked Josh's stance and gestured at him. "If it was nothing, then let it go."

"I already have." But letting Vivian go. He wasn't sure how he felt about that. Other than not good. That could be just a side effect from indulging in too much holiday revelry that night. He should've bowed out of the evening entirely.

"Maybe you should get a sub for the snowball fight," Caleb suggested. "You still look dazed and distracted from that kiss you claim to have forgotten. We wouldn't want a snowball to hit you in the head because you aren't paying attention."

"I'm fine," Josh said.

"You've always been fine. That's your default." Caleb's hand landed on Josh's shoulder.

His gaze turned serious. "But with Vivian, you might be even better."

"Don't you have a snowball fight to referee?" Josh asked.

Caleb caught a soft fabric snowball from their older brother Grant and tossed it at Josh. "Just think about it."

Josh caught the snowball and grinned at Grant. "Did you come up with the winning snowball strategy?"

Grant waved his phone at Josh and frowned. "Mom has been trying to get ahold of you. Now she's decided to enlist my assistance."

Josh had already had his fill of irritating news for the night. He squeezed the snowball hard and kept silent.

It had started with Heather's unknowing interference with Miles Nesci. Josh was now left hoping Miles wouldn't see the other gelding until tomorrow. Only after Josh had had a chance to speak to the longtime rancher and plead with him not to impulse buy. But it was never wise to bank on hope in any business dealings. Josh feared he might've lost a very important sale.

Nothing he could dwell on in the moment. Otherwise, his twin would pick up on his bad mood and ask questions. Caleb could be relentless when he wanted answers. But Josh wasn't ready to talk about his future plans. Not yet anyway. Now Grant wanted to discuss their mom. That was one more conversation Josh didn't care to have.

"Well, welcome to the conversation, Dr. Buzzkill." Caleb crossed his arms over his chest. "Our brother just kissed the woman of his dreams, and you have to come over here and ruin it by bringing up Mom."

"Woman of my dreams," he muttered, as if Josh allowed himself to dwell in his dreams these days. That had been fine when he was a kid. But he'd grown up and the only way to make things happen was to get to work. He narrowed his gaze on his twin. "That's a bit much, isn't it?"

"Time will tell," Caleb assured him.

"What does Mom want anyway?" Grant tucked his phone into the pocket of his jeans and shifted his gaze from Josh to Caleb.

"Don't look at me, Grant." Caleb lifted both hands. "Fortunately, I'm not the one Mom has been calling."

"I don't know what she wants either," Josh said. "I haven't spoken to her at all." Or answered her texts. It used to be that silence sent a message. But their mother seemed intent on not acknowledging that meaning.

"You can't ignore her forever, you know?"

Grant scratched his cheek and warned, "Mom will get to you too."

His older brother would know. It was only that summer when Grant had walked into one of his exam rooms at his orthopedic clinic to find their mother pretending to be a patient. All to get to her son, who'd also been ignoring her phone calls and texts at the time. Grant and their mother were talking now. But Josh still found he had nothing he wanted to say to Lilian Sloan.

He took off his cowboy hat and rubbed his head. "Well, Mom will just have to find me first." He grinned at his older brother. "Now, boys, are we winning this snowball fight and taking our big brother down or not?"

That statement got Grant's full attention and turned the conversation away from Lilian Sloan, just as Josh had intended. He wasn't ready to face his mother, or the truth that he was becoming more like her than he wanted to ever admit. Choosing his career over family. Same as his mother had done all those years ago.

He'd been so certain he wasn't like either of his parents. He'd willingly fallen in love, given his heart and floated into marriage, certain he knew the key to a long-lasting partnership. Certain if he only put love first, he would prove he didn't take after his parents at all. But then his marriage fell apart. Much like his own parents' marriage had. And love, he realized, was nothing he could rely on.

"Carter is out first, this round." Grant rubbed his hands together. "And I know exactly how we're going to do it."

Josh strode off with Grant to plot their older brother's snowball defeat, certain not even one world-tilting kiss with his cowgirl was enough for him to give love a second chance.

But a second kiss? Well, that could be a game changer. And Josh wasn't certain how he felt about that.

CHAPTER NINETEEN

THE NEXT MORNING, Vivian slipped on her boots and ran through her priorities. *Practice. Practice. Practice.* Simple. Straightforward. Easy to remember. It was time to get back to who she was. A professional barrel racer with the career she wanted on the line. And a cowgirl who now needed to win at the stampede for more than herself. Artie's résumé was on the line now too. The Arabian needed a first-place finish as much as Vivian. Together they could get there.

But Vivian had to focus. Stick to what she knew. Concentrate on what she wanted. That wasn't getting caught up in the fun and games, leaning into knee-buckling kisses under the mistletoe or falling for a cowboy. As for that connection strengthening between her and said cowboy, well, that wasn't relevant. Nothing she couldn't sort into the not-pertinent-to-her-goals category. Time to prove she had the discipline and determination to get what she wanted.

She had one foot out the bedroom door when

her discipline faltered. And through no fault of her own. No, the blame belonged fully on her cowboy coming out of his room. Looking entirely too handsome, his hair damp and his expression just shy of disgruntled.

Instantly, Vivian was both nervous and unsure. She'd felt less awkward last night, kissing Josh with an audience, than she did now. Standing less than a doorstop away from him.

The bedroom door next to Josh's opened. Caleb walked out, yawned loudly and turned to face them. His gaze was too alert for the early morning hour. His words too cheerful. "Do you guys want me to go get some of that mistletoe Maggie and Grant insisted on bringing home with them last night?"

"It's coffee before conversation, Caleb." And there would be no more mistletoe. Fake girlfriends shouldn't steal real kisses after all. Vivian slanted her gaze toward Caleb and added, "But you should know that already. You are Josh's twin."

"But, Vivian, you should know that there's always an exception to every rule." With that, Caleb turned and headed downstairs. His laughter trailing behind him.

"Well, I need coffee." And something else to focus her attention on. And quickly. Before she misplaced her priorities and forgot her cowboy wasn't one of them. Vivian started for the stairs.

Josh touched her arm and linked their fingers together in one swift move before Vivian could pull away. Before she could disengage her hand and her heart. She lifted her gaze to his face.

He watched her. His smile barely there. His words clear, slow and sure. "Caleb isn't wrong, you know? About there being an exception."

Vivian searched his blue eyes. Waited. Wished. She supposed that was going to be the way of it with her cowboy. Because their time together was coming to an end. And no amount of wishing could stop that. His life was there. And Vivian's wasn't.

"I think perhaps we need a different start to the morning." He reached up, framed her face with his free hand. His thumb stroked across her cheek before he leaned in and brushed the softest, fleeting kiss to her mouth.

Wishes stirred along with those butterflies in her stomach.

Then he whispered, "Good morning, Vivian." With a squeeze to her fingers, he added, "Now, how about we get that coffee?"

Vivian kept her hand in Josh's all the way to the kitchen and tried to talk away their second kiss. That had been entirely too brief to qualify. To signify, really. It was more like half a kiss. She simply wouldn't count it. Nor would she count the fact that she wanted another one. Only this time she wanted to tug on his hand. And pull him into her and kiss him until he was as breathless as he had made her last night under the mistletoe.

But kissing Josh wouldn't secure her a spot on the River Forge team, or her barrel racing career. It would only tangle up her heart and make their inevitable goodbye all that much harder. Vivian released Josh's hand, opened a kitchen cabinet and reached for a mug instead of her cowboy.

Breakfast was spent discussing gala details and dividing their task list among the helpful and willing Sloan family and Vivian's family. They'd walked over to enjoy what Caleb had touted as the best omelets they'd ever taste. He hadn't been wrong.

No sooner were the breakfast dishes cleaned and put away than everyone dispersed. Caleb and Wade headed to the Doyle Farm to carry decorations from Marlena's attic to the greenhouses. Carter promised to deliver and help hang the extra icicle lights, which Tess had at the general store, after he checked in at the distillery. Tess was coordinating with the DJ and several of the local restaurants that had agreed to cater. And Vivian's parents, along with Sam and Heather, got to work on the carnival games.

That left Josh and Vivian to handle the stables. Vivian spent a good portion of her time with Artie, proving to herself she had her priorities straight. When she caught herself smiling over Josh's cheerful commentary and care with the other horses, she ordered herself to stop being so aware of her cowboy.

Still, it was hard to deny how at ease and content she was working beside Josh. How at home she felt. And how foolish was that? She was merely a guest. Soon to be gone. On her way to fulfilling her dreams, which had nothing to do with a home and a cowboy.

With Josh's guidance, Vivian and Artie found a rhythm together during their practice. They warmed up with figure eights, spirals and walking the cloverleaf pattern. The Arabian proved to be more than willing, agile and spirited. Their practice ended with Artie's quickest run around the barrels. Josh explained he wanted both Vivian and Artie to finish the session on a good note.

While Vivian praised Artie, Isabel struggled to find the same partnership with Fox. The thoroughbred was mild-tempered and reliable and fast. When the pair knocked the same barrel on the same turn for the third time, Vivian winced at what she knew would be a deep bruise on Isabel's knee.

"That was on me." Isabel brushed at the paint on her jeans from her run-in with the barrel.

"Your hands are too high, Isabel," Josh called out, then righted the tipped barrel. "Since when do you look at the barrel instead of where you are going?"

"I know." Isabel grimaced and adjusted her position in the saddle. "Beginner mistakes."

"You're hardly a beginner," Josh said, his words brisk. Yet his touch was gentle as he checked over Fox. "Isabel, you know better than anyone what being distracted for one second will cost you in competition."

A belt buckle. A jackpot. The win. Vivian stroked her hand down Artie's neck and hoped she sounded encouraging. "We all have bad days, Josh. Off days. Isabel knows what she needs to do."

"There isn't time for bad days," Josh countered. "Or off days. And if Isabel still knows what she needs to do, then she needs to start doing it."

"That's harsh," Vivian retorted.

"No. That's the truth. Josh was always good at giving it straight. No warning. No warm-up." Isabel dismounted and shook her head. "I need a minute."

"Isabel," Josh started. "You can't just…"

"I'm not quitting, but I am stopping for today." Isabel gave Fox a quick hug and rubbed between his ears. "It's not you. It's me, Fox." Then she glanced at Josh. "Make sure Fox ends on a high note, please." With that, she turned and walked outside.

Vivian dismounted and handed Artie's reins to Josh. "Let me talk to her."

Outside, Vivian found Isabel at the back pasture, closest to the indoor practice arena. Her forearms were braced on the top rail and her head was hanging down. Yet there was a stiff set to her shoulders, as if the former rodeo queen was refusing to give in.

Vivian approached, unsure if she could help, but wanting to try. "Isabel, you okay?"

"My mom always told me to be careful what I wish for." Isabel brushed her fingertips across her damp cheek. Her gaze remained fixed on the pasture. "I never really listened to her. I always thought I knew better than my mom."

Vivian propped her boot on the bottom rail of the fence and said, "I think that happens with most kids."

"But most kids don't believe themselves to be better than their mothers, like I did." Isabel pursed her lips. "I've met your mom, Vivian. I cannot imagine not wanting to be like her. Your mom is welcoming, supportive and present."

Vivian's mother was all those things. She'd been encouraging Vivian all the way from her first horse lesson through college. Her mom had even stocked Vivian's camper with food and necessities the night before Vivian headed out for her first professional rodeo. Her mother had been consistent since arriving at the Sloan ranch too. Always around and available, as she often was, in case Vivian needed her. It was Vivian who made herself unavailable. Otherwise occupied. Then and now.

That truth landed hard, like a tipped barrel in a race. Vivian curved her fingers around the wooden fence rail as if she needed the support, not Isabel.

"Meanwhile, I'm now one divorce away from matching my mother's record of three strikes at marriage," Isabel confessed and touched her finger, as if noting the absence of her wedding ring. "My second husband and I finalized our divorce right before Thanksgiving."

"I'm sorry," Vivian said.

"I'm not." Isabel tipped her head and looked at Vivian. "I wished for a fast track into a lifestyle I always fantasized living. I got it, finally, but I didn't get what you and Josh have."

Vivian stilled. "What's that?"

"You and Josh work together like a team. A true partnership." Isabel watched her. "Josh and I only ever had that in the arena, and sometimes, not even there. I thought I'd found it when I met my second husband."

Josh and Vivian's true partnership wasn't real. It'd all started on a fabrication. One created by Vivian. Yes, she wanted to be part of a great team. So very much. For her career. But for her personal life? She was fine on her own. No team required, right? Vivian concentrated on Isabel. "What happened with your second marriage?"

Isabel's smile lacked both warmth and sincerity. Her words held a bite as if she mocked herself. "Simple. I got the lifestyle I desperately wanted. It was even more than I ever dared to imagine."

And there in Isabel's gaze, Vivian saw the sadness. The pain her vibrant eyes failed to conceal. Vivian pressed, "But."

"But I didn't get the love." Isabel shrugged. "I realized my mom was right all along. She used to tell me, *Izzie-bell, listen good. Sometimes your wishes do come true, but it all turns out to be more like a nightmare. You gotta be careful what you wish for."*

Vivian reached over and touched Isabel's arm. Wanting to argue against that reasoning. Wanting to defend all dream chasers and dream catchers like herself.

"I'm done with dreaming and taking things for granted." Isabel straightened, let go of the fence and lifted her chin. "I want to prove I just might have the same resilience and courage as my mother. That I could be like her after all."

"You do have that," Vivian assured her. "You're making a comeback. Remembering your roots and who you want to be."

"But what if it's all just outside my reach?" Isabel asked. The fear was clear in her tone. "It's all I have left, Vivian. What if I'm too late?"

Dreams didn't have expiration dates. And as long as Isabel kept pushing. Kept trying. That was what mattered. Vivian's grandmother had promised her it would all be worth it. Once she found that gold at the end of the rainbow, where dreams finally came true. Vivian said, "Today was only one bad practice. My mom always tells me not to let the bad moments define my todays or my tomorrows."

"That is wise advice from a wise woman." Isabel brushed at the horsehair and dirt on her

jeans. "I think I'll head down to the Owl tonight with Kelsey. The bar is hosting country
dance lessons. Maybe I can two-step away my
bad day."

Vivian smiled, pleased to see Isabel's confidence returning, and knowing she might've
had a small part in helping Isabel feel good.
"That sounds like a really fun idea."

"You and Josh should join us. Josh is one
of the best dancers I know. He could teach
the dance lessons himself." Isabel grinned and
lifted her eyebrows at Vivian. "You should ask
him."

"Ask me what?" Josh's voice came from behind her.

Vivian turned to find Josh standing within
reach. It seemed the most natural thing to step
closer and curve her arm around his waist.
Ease into his side as if she fit there. As if that
was where she was always meant to be. Instead, she leaned into the pasture fence post.

"I think you should take Vivian to the Owl
tonight," Isabel suggested. "They are having
dance lessons there."

"I'm not teaching anyone how to dance."
Josh shook his head and shifted his gaze to
Vivian. "If they can't do a proper waltz at the
gala, then they can sit it out. And we'll have
more room on the dance floor."

Dancing. With Josh. One more thing she enjoyed doing with him. But one private dance. One breath-stealing kiss. She couldn't read more into those moments. Couldn't afford to make that mistake now. She'd done exactly that in her past friendships and was still alone. No matter how much she liked her cowboy, or how much he made her feel at home, friendship was all there was between Josh and her. Vivian confessed, "I can't waltz."

"But I can," Josh said, a promise in his words and his grin.

That made Vivian's breath catch. Made her forget her resolve. One dance—one waltz— with Josh. Surely there was no harm in that. Friends danced together all the time and nothing between them changed. It would be the same for Vivian and Josh. And if her heart raced when she was twirling around with Josh, well, that would be her own secret.

"Don't worry, Vivian. You'll pick up the waltz in no time with Josh guiding you." Isabel's smile shifted into genuinely wistful. "I can't wait to see the greenhouses decorated. Does Marlena still have her winter gardens? Those used to be Josh's favorite place up there."

"I didn't get to see the gardens." Vivian slanted her gaze toward Josh.

"Marlena doesn't have them open anymore." There was a finality to Josh's words as if he wanted to end the discussion.

"That's too bad. Each garden path had shaped topiaries and assorted potted plants and so many beautiful lights." Isabel sighed and swirled her hands in front of her as if drawing a map. "All the paths led to this wonderful private fountain tucked in the center."

It sounded lovely. Yet Josh had never mentioned anything about it. Not a word. Vivian watched him. He stuffed his hands in the pockets of his jeans. He tipped his chin, angling the brim of his cowboy hat lower as if wanting to block the sunlight. Or perhaps Isabel's words.

"The gardens are actually where Josh and I got engaged, but Josh probably told you that already," Isabel said.

No. He hadn't mentioned anything about his and Isabel's engagement. Not once. Why hadn't Josh told Vivian? It was no wonder the Baker sisters and Marlena had seemed concerned after Vivian had called Josh and then sprung her greenhouse surprise on him. Now Vivian was the surprised one.

"Josh, how many candles did you float in the fountain that night?" Isabel asked, seemingly unconcerned by Josh's rigid posture and closed-off expression.

This was not a memory Josh wanted to revisit. That was more than clear.

He crossed his arms over his chest. "I don't remember."

Oh, her cowboy knew. On that, Vivian would bet all that she owned. Vivian wanted to take his hand in hers, as if they were true partners, as if they stood by each other and shouldered the good and bad bits together, whether past or present.

"All I know is that it was too many candles to count." Isabel chuckled softly. "Josh had added red roses too."

"That must have been stunning." Vivian was even more stunned to discover her cowboy had a romantic side. He could waltz and floated roses and candles in fountains. And could, no doubt, sweep Vivian off her boots if he chose to. Her perfect cowboy, if she'd been looking for one.

"It really was. I always wondered why more couples didn't get engaged there." Isabel cleared her throat and seemed to pull herself to the present. "But who knows. Perhaps the gala will prove to be just enough of a romantic nudge to put someone in the mind to propose."

Josh looked more like he was of a mind to grind any hint of romance to dust underneath his boots. From his standoffish stance to his guarded expression, an observer would be hard-pressed to believe him any sort of romantic cowboy.

"Marlena said she was going to be sure to get mistletoe," Vivian offered and barely caught her own cringe. Mistletoe made her think of kissing. And her cowboy. All the things she wasn't supposed to be considering when it came to her friend Josh.

"That will certainly add a dash of romance to the evening. I'm looking forward to the gala." Isabel's bright, easy smile returned. She hugged Vivian, then whispered, "Thank you for earlier, Vivian. And for reminding me I'm not alone after all."

Vivian returned the hug. So many times, she had wanted the same while rushing to the next rodeo in a new town, or after a bad race or a frustrating loss. Then, there were the nights in her camper by herself. She'd will the sleepless time away. Then get up with the sunrise, determined that she was better off alone. The same as she would be when she left Josh and Three Springs behind. Better off. She clung to Isabel a beat longer and avoided looking at Josh.

Isabel released Vivian and waved to Josh. "See you both tomorrow. I'll be focused and ready and won't let Fox down."

"I know you will," Vivian assured the former rodeo queen and watched Isabel until she disappeared around the side of the stables.

Josh moved closer to Vivian and said, "You and Isabel seem to be getting close."

"I like her," Vivian said. *I understand her.* More than she cared to admit. Vivian eyed Josh. "You don't mind, do you?"

Josh shook his head. "I think it's good. You'll both be seeing more of each other out on the circuit. It's nice to have people you can rely on around you, especially out on the road."

What about you? Could I rely on you? Not just this week, but... Vivian blocked that thought and asked, "What are you doing for the rest..." *...of your life?* Again, she swatted away her misplaced thoughts. They'd shared one and a half kisses. Not a proposal. Not a future. Vivian rubbed her throat and managed to add, "For the rest of the afternoon."

"I'm glad you asked." He bumped his shoulder against hers. "I was hoping you might be free."

For the rest of my life? My calendar is open. And my heart... Vivian rolled her lips together and blamed the mistletoe talk. And the images of vibrant red roses and luminous floating candles in magical fountains inside enchanted winter gardens. And her cowboy down on one knee.

Time to deflect. Distract. Discourage. Past

time for her heart to opt out, before it misled her, and she started believing that she and Josh could be more than just friends.

"Jasper and Cashew need exercise and my afternoon riders had to cancel," Josh explained. "I was hoping you might want to ride with me."

"Sure," she said. "I'm happy to help you." As a friend, of course.

Because that was all they could be. Friends didn't break each other's hearts. And if her heart splintered a little at her decision, well, it would mend eventually. After all, a bruised heart was better than a broken one.

CHAPTER TWENTY

"VIVIAN. JOSH. WAIT UP!" Heather called out. Vivian's sister hurried down the stairs that led up to Josh's second floor apartment and bee-lined for them. "Mom told me not to interrupt your time with the horses this morning, but, Vivian, I could really use your help. We've made it to the next round for the potential contract with South Trek Enterprises."

"That's really good news." Vivian smiled, pleased everyone around her seemed to be get-ting what they wanted. No speed bumps. No setbacks. Surely that was a sign they were all on the right track. All headed in the right di-rection. Now if she would get her heart to fall in line, all would truly be well.

"But they've requested more information about our company and business," Heather hedged, not looking quite as pleased as Viv-ian felt. "And we need to respond before the close of business today."

In other words, they needed to respond im-mediately. Her sister needed Vivian now. Vivian glanced at Josh. "Will it mess up your schedule too much if we ride this afternoon instead?"

Josh shook his head.

It was at that point that Vivian realized her sister's interruption didn't bother her like she would've expected. She was more pleased about being asked to assist than annoyed. Even though she should be working on her riding skills and watching videos of her barrel races to fine tune her techniques.

"I have a few business calls to make." Josh pulled his phone from his pocket, then grinned at Vivian. "We can ride when you're ready. Just text me."

Her cowboy was accommodating too. One more reason to appreciate him. Not that she needed any more reasons to like Josh. As a friend, she reminded herself. Vivian was resolved not to complicate things with him further.

Vivian walked back to Josh's apartment with her sister. Heather had barely opened the front door when Vivian inhaled a deep breath of vanilla and cinnamon. She couldn't help herself and drew in another deep inhale. "It smells incredible in here."

"That's all Wade." Heather laughed and closed the door. "Wade made his famous layered honey cake this morning. He is swapping

CARI LYNN WEBB   277

his honey cake recipe for Tess's chocolate yule log one. Tess and Wade have been talking dessert recipes every chance they get."

"Can I have a piece and tell Wade it was for quality control purposes?" Vivian walked to the kitchen island and eyed the individual honey cake squares artfully arranged on the glass tray. "Tess is a professional after all. Wade can't be serving Tess underbaked cake."

"You know you make a very valid point." Heather handed Vivian two small plates. "I'll need to try one too, for quality control, of course."

Vivian shared one of those secret smiles with her older sister. The kind that hinted they were up to no good, but the reward was going to be well worth it. The kind that they hadn't shared in far too long. Vivian reveled in the moment and that softened her twinge of regret for all the missed moments over the years.

The two sisters settled in at the kitchen table. Laptops open and their small cakes within easy reach. It wasn't long before they hit Submit, shared a quick fist bump and matching smiles of satisfaction.

Vivian touched her empty plate and grinned. "I think we need another sample of honey cake. Two pieces is hardly a broad enough sample base."

Heather was already moving to the kitchen island and the dessert tray. "We should try these on the other side of the dish. Just to make sure everything cooked evenly."

"Good idea." Vivian laughed, accepted her second piece from her sister and bit into the honey cake. Savoring the gingerbread flavors and rich vanilla whipped filling, she finished the small cake and sighed. "We are nothing if not thorough in our quality control."

Heather leaned back in her chair and smiled. "Viv, this was fun. Working together like this."

"It really was." Vivian felt full, not from the delicious honey cakes, but rather with happiness and a sprinkle of pride. For accomplishing something with her sister. Something that mattered. "I've missed you, big sis."

"I've missed you more, little sis." Heather grabbed a clean napkin and dabbed at her eyes. "Sorry, pregnancy hormones. I promised myself I wouldn't get all mushy and emotional on you."

"It's okay." Vivian reached across the table and squeezed her sister's hand. "You're the only person I know who manages to look pretty even when you cry."

"You're the only one who's ever told me that." Heather shook her head and chuckled as if still unable to believe Vivian.

"Doesn't make it any less true." Vivian closed the laptop and considered one last honey cake. An overindulgence she didn't need. Yet she wasn't in a hurry to leave her sister. Or the moment. Not just yet.

"Well, if we are sharing truths, here is one for you." Heather paused, drew a breath, then let her words tumble out. "I know we aren't the team you want, Viv. Isabel mentioned the River Forge team when we were chatting yesterday. I have to say I would've liked to hear about the barrel racing team from you first, but it's out in the open now, so there's nothing for it."

Vivian stayed in her chair and gave up on overindulging. She had to level with her sister. Giving it to Heather straight, like Isabel had described Josh doing earlier in the practice arena. Vivian said, "I wasn't sure how to tell you guys about it. It's what I want. If I make the team, it'll mean more opportunities for me, but even more travel. Even more time on the road." Even more distance from her family.

"You will make the team," Heather said, her expression confident. She pointed to the window and the Texas countryside. "But won't you miss all this here? I know I would, and I've never considered living anywhere else than the city."

But *this* wasn't hers. Though Vivian would miss it. A lot. Just thinking of saying goodbye to the Sloans made her ache. And that goodbye for her cowboy made her throat feel too tight already. All she could manage was a small nod.

"Viv, are you truly happy?" Heather set her elbows on the table and leaned forward, studying Vivian closer. "Not just here. But out on the road."

"I am happy when I'm competing," Vivian said. In the arena. For less than twenty seconds. When it was only Vivian and her horse against the clock. And outside the arena, she was...

"But that's not enough, Viv." Heather's eyebrows pulled together. Her gaze searched Vivian's.

I'm happy with Josh. But that was only a for-now kind of thing. Nothing she could count on for the long term. Not like her career. Vivian argued, "But it should be enough, Heather. I'm following my passion."

She was taking risks and doing everything her grandmother had encouraged Vivian to do. It was supposed to be enough. More than. No regrets. No what-ifs. Only that sense of accomplishment and deep-seated gratification. And true joy. That was what her grandmother had promised her. All Vivian had to do was make her dreams come true. Simple enough. She had the passion. The vision. And the dedication. What more was there?

"But is it your passion or Grandma's you are so intent on chasing?" Heather tipped her head. Her fingers scrunched the corner of her napkin. "And, Viv, are you really fulfilled?"

I'm lonely. Vivian swatted that away. That was all part of the sacrifice. All part of the deal she'd accepted when she set out on the road. It was going to be worth it in the end. It had to be. She had come too far. No looking back. No second-guessing. "I will be when..."

"What is the 'when' now, Viv?" Heather's smile was small. Almost sad. "In case you haven't noticed, you keep changing it. First it was when you finished your rookie season in honor of Grandma. Then it was when you made the top twenty-five. Then the top fifteen. And now it's this team."

"The team gives me everything I want," Vivian argued. At least, she hoped it did. How could it not? Still, she heard the hesitation in her own words. "It's everything I've been working toward."

"Then, I hope you get it all," Heather said, sounding matter-of-fact.

"Do you?" Vivian asked. Where was the fervent push for Vivian to return to the business?

For Vivian to accept her family responsibilities and obligations. Where was the Bryant family firm for the win?

"Believe it or not, yes, I do, little sis." Heather stood and hugged Vivian tight, then she walked toward the bedroom. "Now, I'm taking a quick nap, so I'm rested for the card games Sam arranged for later tonight. Sam and I are partners and we intend to win." Heather chuckled. "Thanks again, Viv."

"You don't have to thank me," Vivian insisted. "I was glad to help."

Heather grinned and opened the bedroom door. Before she left, she turned and said, "One last question, Viv. Are you really so sure you don't already have it all?"

The bedroom door clicked shut quietly. But her sister's words blasted through Vivian as if Heather had spoken through a loudspeaker. Have it *all* already?

That was impossible. Vivian didn't have the stable job. The house. The husband. Or even the flush bank account. All the things her family measured success by.

As for everything her family thought they saw now, well, that was only Vivian misleading them. She had no boyfriend. This wasn't even her place to come back to. And it wasn't hers to have. Even if she wanted all this, Josh wasn't offering. Even he knew fake relationships weren't the foundation for a future.

Besides, Vivian's perfect life was winning a belt buckle and a jackpot, not announcing a relationship status change from single to couple. Love would come later, after she'd reached her goals.

Only the special lead extraordinary lives, Vivian. She would stand out at the stampede. In the arena. Then she would be special. And finally claim that she had it all.

Because her sister was wrong. Vivian didn't really have it all yet. *Never settle, Vivian, or regret will catch you.* But she intended to get it. And then she would be truly happy.

CHAPTER TWENTY-ONE

NINETY MINUTES INTO Jasper and Cashew's ride, to build the geldings' endurance and stamina, Josh slowed Jasper from a trot to a walk. He guided the black Appendix quarter horse beside Vivian on the wide trail. "All that's left for this pair is a cooling down."

"They deserve a long rubdown in their stalls as well." Vivian shifted in her saddle and leaned forward to praise Cashew for a job well done. "Thanks for inviting me along. I didn't realize how much I needed this."

Josh took in her relaxed smile and the soft gleam in her gaze. The high collar of her deep purple, lined riding jacket was zipped up under her chin. Her hands were well protected inside her gloves. Her cowboy hat covered her head. But the crisp breeze had gotten to her cheeks, turning them a pretty shade of pink. He asked, "When was the last time you rode for pleasure?"

"I can't remember." She chuckled and wrinkled her nose. "That's bad, isn't it?"

"That's life." He kept the pace slow and easy. Unwilling to rush the horses and his afternoon with Vivian. He couldn't recall the last time he'd been quite so relaxed either, or content, as Gran Claire would've claimed. He added, "I just happen to have a job that requires me to ride like this daily."

"You have the perfect place for it." Awe swirled around her words. "Right in your backyard."

His knee brushed against hers. "You think it's perfect?"

She nodded, then slanted her gaze at him. "Don't you?"

I think you could be perfect. For me. Fortunately, his cell phone vibrated, stalling him from detouring along some love trail that would no doubt have entirely too many ruts and potholes to ever be considered safe. Besides, now wasn't the time to drift. He needed to stick to the known trail. The one that would lead him to the life he wanted in Houston. Josh glanced at the name on his phone screen. "It's Miles Nesci."

"Please let me talk to him." Vivian stopped Cashew and extended her arm toward Josh. "I stayed up most of the night figuring out what I could say to Miles to change his mind."

And Josh had stayed up most of the night figuring out how many mistletoe kisses it would take before his interest in his cowgirl dimmed. He'd woken up to the unsettling truth. His interest in Vivian was more than casual. More than fleeting. And he had to proceed with caution. Not that he'd followed his own warning when he'd kissed Vivian good morning. But he was back on task now. He set his phone in Vivian's palm. "We have to change his mind."

Vivian tapped the phone screen, set the phone to her ear and greeted Miles Nesci. She launched into a lively and animated conversation with the longtime rancher. The call ended fairly quickly, and Vivian returned his phone to him. Her grin was triumphant. "I did it. Miles agreed to come to the stampede."

That was exactly what Josh wanted. Miles only had to see Artie compete to realize he needed the horse as his own. And that sale would put Josh one step closer to Houston. Watching Vivian now, Josh wanted to pull her closer, which was exactly what he should not want. Still, his words slipped out, unstoppable. "We make a good team."

"Isabel mentioned the same thing to me earlier." The brightness in her smile faded and her expression became guarded. As if she wasn't certain how she should feel about that. She urged Cashew back into a walk.

She shouldn't want to be on Josh's team anyway. Josh nudged Jasper even with Vivian and Cashew again. "About earlier, when Isabel mentioned our engagement." He paused, eyed Vivian's straight posture in the saddle, then continued, "I didn't tell you about that because you were so excited up at the Doyle Farm. What Isabel and I had is in the past. I didn't want to spoil anything for you."

"Still, it can't be easy to be up there." Her mouth drew in. "Even memories can hurt."

Not so much, he realized. Not with Vivian, it seemed. "Well, it'll be a winter wonderland up there soon. And it's a chance to replace the old memories with new ones." *With you.*

She set her hand on his leg. "We can do that together."

That word again. *Together.* He liked the idea too much. But couldn't see how it would work. He didn't have much to offer a cowgirl like her. And he'd learned before that his heart wasn't reason enough to stay. Besides, Vivian needed to be on the road to succeed. And he refused to stand in her way. "Not to dwell in my past, but with the mulled wine and eggnog flowing at the gala and too many guests knowing my history, there is more you should probably be aware of." He waited a beat, then added, "Isabel also handed me divorce papers at that very same fountain in the Doyles' garden."

Vivian adjusted her cowboy hat higher on her head and gaped at him. "You're not kidding."

"Not even a little bit." He should've ended the truth spilling there. He'd already revealed more than enough. Already revisited too much of his past. Yet he kept talking as if sharing with his cowgirl was all he wanted to do. "I had planned a date night for us. Reserved the entire garden for the evening. Thought if we went back to where it started, we might get back what we had in the beginning."

Vivian was still in her saddle, as if anticipating one of those potholes in the trail up ahead.

"We clearly weren't on the same page," Josh admitted. "And not going to ever get there."

She nodded and glanced quickly at him. Compassion was clear in her expression. "Can I ask what happened?"

"Tale as old as time." He shrugged, not that it dislodged his indifference. "Isabel met someone else. He suited her better. He could provide her the lifestyle she wanted."

"I can't believe she wanted more than what you have here."

"That was the problem," Josh confessed and opened up completely. His cowgirl needed to understand he had nothing to offer her either. Nothing more than himself. But he wasn't taking that kind of risk ever again. "All this belongs to my family, not me."

"But you're a big part of it." Her words were earnest and heartfelt. "Your family relies on you. Your family needs you."

His family was going to have to learn to get by without him. Just as he supposed he would have to do himself. That thought was far from welcome. Far from comfortable.

"Does it matter whose name is on the deed to the property?" She spoke quietly but was insistent. "This is your home."

Josh frowned. "It mattered to Isabel."

Vivian touched his leg again. More compassion shifted across her face. "I'm sorry being a part of this wasn't enough for Isabel."

But would it be enough for you? Would I be…? Josh shifted in his saddle and swallowed his question. "I haven't been honest with you." *I'm falling for you. But I vowed never to lose my heart, so now I must retreat.* He cleared his throat. "The equestrian center, Bellmare, that I told you about."

She nodded, slipped her gloved hand from his leg, and held on to her reins instead.

He wanted the contact. Wanted her hand in his. Wanted more than he had a right to. Knew then what he must do. It was best for them both. *Retreat.* He said, "Bellmare is outside Houston."

More than a nine-hour car drive away. Not close enough to just stop in for dinner. Or to check in. That kind of distance meant planning and coordinating schedules. Taking vacation days and time off. Then, suddenly a simple visit to see his family wasn't so simple. He'd never been farther than a tow truck ride away from his home and the place he loved. He shifted his weight in the saddle. "I won't be living here in Three Springs."

Her response was silence.

The fence of the back pasture came into view. They were back home, yet there was so much more to be said.

"It's an opportunity of a lifetime. For my career," Josh said, working any hint of uncertainty from his tone. "It won't be easy to leave home, but it's necessary." Same as it was necessary to let his cowgirl go. Even though it would likely be one of the hardest things he'd ever do.

"I get it." Her smile was close-lipped and she added, "You have to go."

"I knew you would understand," he said, wishing she would argue. For them. Knowing it wasn't to be. "When you make the River Forge team, we'll both have everything we want."

"It really is about our careers." Determination surrounded her words.

"Right. Proving to everyone around us that we're successful at what we do." And when he had that, then he'd have more to offer a partner. Something substantial. He added, "Finally showing everyone that we made it."

She nodded and guided Cashew toward the stables. "When you get to Bellmare and become a nationally recognized name in the equestrian world, will that be enough for you?"

"I'll let you know when I get there." But it had to be. If he didn't have Bellmare and the next step in his career, what did he have? His gaze slid back to Vivian, where it always seemed to want to land. "What about you? When do you say, 'I made it? That's enough. I'm good.'"

"I'm not sure," she admitted and dismounted. "I worry if I stop trying to do more and be more, I might be settling."

"Maybe we aren't the kind of people who are meant to stop." He dismounted and eyed her over Jasper's saddle. "Or to settle."

"You might be right." Reins in hand, she left Josh behind and walked Cashew inside the stables to his stall.

Josh wanted to be right. Except when he was with Vivian, all he wanted to do was stop and hold her. All he felt was settled.

CHAPTER TWENTY-TWO

JOSH WAS HUMMING. A Christmas song. One of his favorites as a kid. It was about a one-horse open sleigh, frosty air and a jingle hop. He'd woken up that morning ready for the day. It had started with another hallway kiss between him and Vivian that had left him grinning. He was smiling by the end of a very successful practice with her and Isabel. His horses were well prepared and ready to compete.

Everything was falling into place. And he was determined to stay in the moment. He hummed louder.

Fortunately, no one was around. He was at Gran Claire's property, standing on an extension ladder outside the storage barn. The stuck gears on the old barn doors had needed greasing for a while.

Vivian had joined Maggie, Tess and Heather for an afternoon antiquing spree. Everyone else was dispersed between carnival-game finishes and silent-auction-donation pickups.

Josh sang the chorus. He'd just put the

giddyup into his jingle horse when he heard a car pull into the gravel driveway. He shifted on the ladder and took in the silver compact SUV. Not one of his brothers' trucks or Vivian's. Not a car he recognized from around town either. The engine cut off. The door on the driver's side opened, and a familiar woman stepped out. Her sleek, tailored, cream-colored outfit would've been striking on a New York City sidewalk. But on a ranch in the Texas Panhandle, it was entirely too impractical.

His jingle rock lyrics faded into the wind. His Christmas cheer deflated. He whispered, "Mom."

Lilian Sloan had found him after all. His older brother had warned him the other night at the Feisty Owl. And Josh had been cavalier in his response, arrogantly claiming his mother would have to find him first. Josh frowned and silently conceded this round to his mother.

He touched the decades-old wheel on the rail attached to the barn. It still refused to budge. He added more oil to the hardware and braced himself for his first face-to-face with his mother in more than ten years.

Lilian Sloan stopped within easy conversation distance. No shouting required. "Hello, Josh. It seems you've been ignoring my texts and calls, so I came to talk to you in person instead."

What was there to say? Lilian left her five sons one summer, got divorced and never came back. On second thought, maybe there was a lot to say. No good place to start. And no real benefit from talking. Besides, he'd long since outgrown needing his mother's attention and approval.

"Funny, I seem to remember you did the same when my brothers and I were kids. Never called back." Josh wiped his hands on a towel he'd stuffed in his back pocket. "Then we stopped calling altogether."

His mother touched a finger to her eyebrow as if catching her wince. "And you were waiting for me to do the same now. To stop calling you?"

He'd been hopeful. Josh climbed down the ladder, intent on getting the conversation over with quickly. He wanted his holiday cheer back. He wanted more time with his cowgirl. He frowned. "It would've been less surprising than you standing here right now. How did you find me anyway?"

"I spoke to your grandfather earlier today." She tucked her hands into the pockets of her honey-colored wool coat. "He told me where I could find you."

"Why are you here?" Josh rubbed the grease from his fingers, but nothing rubbed the irritation from his words.

"I'm a guest speaker at Wright Well University this weekend," she said.

"Here." He pointed to the ground in front of his worn boots. "Why are you here now?"

Her elbows flared out slightly at her sides as if to steady her position. "I wanted to talk to you about Houston."

Of all the possible things she could've said—the first being: *I'm sorry*—Houston was not even on the list. Josh's fingers fisted around the towel. He studied his mother and worked to ignore the alarm ringing in his ears. "What about Houston?"

"Josh, I know about Bellmare." His mother kept to the direct approach. "Alan Whiley is a longtime patient of mine."

Alan Whiley was one of the senior vice presidents of the investment firm funding the entire Bellmare project. Alan Whiley had been the one who'd initially contacted Josh about running Bellmare and becoming a partner. Alan had hand-delivered the Bellmare business proposal, with Josh already on the organizational chart, to Josh himself.

He squeezed the towel and remained silent.

"Alan's wife's family and Gran Claire's family go way back," his mother explained. "When Alan needed a pacemaker, your Gran Claire sent him to me."

Not a coincidence. Had his mother suggested Josh for the director role? He didn't want anything from his mother. Not her handouts, her assistance or her long-overdue affection. His resentment grew. Unavoidable, he supposed. "Did you set this whole thing up?"

"I didn't even know his firm was building an equestrian center in Texas until Alan asked me if I wanted to invest several months ago." His mother didn't flinch or fidget. She simply held his gaze, her words straight-forward and genuine. "Alan has lived in New York longer than me but recently decided to reconnect with his Texas roots."

Seemed to be an affliction of late. Reconnecting with Texas roots. Yet Josh had no desire to connect with his mother.

"Alan left me with the Bellmare business proposal," she continued. "Imagine my surprise when I saw my own son's name listed as director."

Her surprise couldn't exceed his own right now. "The entire deal hasn't been finalized." He paused and considered her. "But you know that too, don't you?"

"Alan called me last week about my possible investment." Again, she held his gaze. Her expression and words candid. She added, "Alan let it slip that he was worried you might be short on your portion of the capital raise."

"I will have what I need when the time comes." Josh shoved the towel in his back pocket and set his hands on his hips. "I've got until the end of the year."

"I could—" she started.

"No," he interrupted her. "I don't want your money."

Josh hadn't asked his brothers or grandfather for financial assistance. No way would he willingly put himself in debt to his mother. Money wouldn't automatically make up for all the times he'd needed her as a kid, and she hadn't been there. Money wouldn't soothe the wounded little boy still inside him. And the man he was now understood that money would not heal an already-damaged relationship.

"Now you know why I've been trying to reach you," she explained. "I wanted to talk to you first, before I discussed it with your grandfather."

"Grandpa doesn't know about Bellmare. My job offer." Or my intentions. Josh crossed his arms over his chest. "Neither do my brothers."

"I gathered as much when I spoke to your grandfather briefly." Her smile was tight-lipped and disappeared quickly. "I won't mention anything."

Josh now shared a secret with his mother. The woman he hadn't talked to in years. The woman his heart wanted to trust. But the rest of him trusted only with his eyes wide open these days. "I will tell them soon about my investment." Regarding his mother's involvement, that was her business to discuss with whomever she chose. "So, are you going to invest in Bellmare?"

"That depends on you," she said. "Have you changed your mind? Discovered something in the business proposal that suggests it would be an unwise investment?"

She wanted his business opinion. That surprised Josh. That she looked at him like an equal caught him off guard so much so he answered honestly, "The five-year proforma is sound. Profitable. The budget realistic. The goals achievable. Bellmare is a solid investment."

She nodded and eyed him. "Can I ask you why you want to do this? Why you want to leave all that you have here?"

What he had here wasn't enough. Isabel had seen that and left. And Vivian, well, she would be leaving too. "You of all people should understand why. You did the very same thing.

Chose the career opportunity in New York over your family here."

"I did," she admitted. No hesitation and no apology followed. "Now I have the distinguished reputation and sterling career you think you want. But you have something I miss deeply."

He straightened as if to block the regret and pain he saw in her gaze. He asked, "What's that?"

"Family," she said, simply and bluntly.

She did it again. Caught him off guard. Yet sympathy wasn't his strong suit and that lingering resentment was difficult to temper. "I don't plan on losing touch with my family."

"Haven't you already started to do just that?" She watched him, her gaze assessing and clinical like the detached, unflappable doctor he believed her to be. She continued, "You haven't told your family about your choice. Nor included them in the decision."

He held her gaze. "I'm just following your lead, Mother."

"Be careful about whose lead you follow." She didn't back down. Her resolve matched his. "You may get everything you ever imagined and still have nothing you truly need."

That sounded like her problem, not his. After all, his mom had made her choices all those years ago and now had to deal with the consequences. Same as Josh would do one day. Gran Claire called that one of life's unavoidables, same as ice cream melting in the sun and working on a Sunday. Josh asked, "Are you trying to talk me out of going to Houston? Is that what this is about?"

"I wouldn't attempt that." Her laughter was short and sharp and far from amused. "We both know you wouldn't listen to me."

On that they agreed completely. He nodded.

"I know I have not earned the right, but I'm compelled to give you some advice," she said. The faintest of lines, wisdom, not laugh lines, flared out from her slightly narrowed eyes. "Here it is. Pushing people away is the easy part. But finding yourself once they are gone… That's when you discover you're more lost than ever."

Except Josh wasn't lost. All Josh was pushing away were those feelings in his heart, not people. As for Vivian, she was leaving on her own and he simply wasn't stopping her.

"I'll leave you to your work." She checked the time on her watch. "I have a business dinner with the dean of the medical college at Wright Well and the president of the university tonight."

Josh watched his mother walk away. When

she opened her car door, he called out, "Mom. Grandpa put some things aside for you. They're in the storage barn if you're interested."

"I'll come back and look through that another time." She braced her hand on the top of the car door, her expression tight. "Funny. It's just land. Just a house. The memories are as faded and dull as that old storage barn. And yet, standing here now is harder than it should be." She pressed her hand to her heart. "In here."

She was inside her car and backing out of the driveway before Josh recovered from his surprise. His mother, the renowned heart surgeon, apparently had a heart. And it wasn't as cold as he'd always suspected.

Josh climbed back up the ladder and got on with something he fully understood. Once the barn doors were gliding like he wanted them to, he headed over to the farmhouse.

He spotted the truck and trailer and realized that Ryan and Uncle Roy had returned with Dusty. Josh went to check on Vivian's horse in the stables first. He even texted Vivian a picture of Dusty in the stall next to Artie. He titled it: Dusty, home at last. But deleted the home part before he hit the send button. Soon enough, this wouldn't be Dusty's home, or hers. Or even Josh's. That thought only stirred his discontent even more.

Inside the farmhouse, Josh found only his grandfather, standing in front of the Christmas trees.

Josh joined his grandpa and frowned, realizing he was far from recovering his Christmas cheer. "You could've warned me about Mom."

"You would've hightailed it out of there." His grandfather touched a glass angel bell ornament that was one of the last Josh had gifted his Gran Claire. The bell chimed softly. His grandpa added, "Sometimes it's best to just face things head on, even when it's difficult."

Josh paced into the kitchen, away from the trees and all the reminders of his Gran Claire. His grandmother had been everything he'd wanted his mom to be and never was. His Gran Claire had never steered him wrong. She would guide him now if she was there. He admitted, "It wasn't quite as awkward as I'd expected."

"Your mother is not the villain you've made her out to be." Sam followed Josh into the kitchen and went on speaking when Josh opened his mouth to argue. "That doesn't mean Lilian hasn't made mistakes or hurt a lot of people."

Josh nodded. "Gran would say even good people are not exempt from doing that."

"The difference between the good and the bad is all in how they move forward." His grandfather opened a cookie tin on the kitchen island and slid it toward Josh. "Your mother is trying. It's up to you if you'll be open to her."

Josh ignored the caramels Vivian liked so much and picked out a chocolate cookie instead. "I don't think I can forget."

"It's not about forgetting," his grandpa urged. "It's about finding neutral ground now. A place where you meet as adults and start from there. Then maybe in time, you open your heart to forgiveness."

It seemed to always come back to his heart. The one he'd closed for so many reasons. The one he intended not to reopen.

Footsteps sounded in the laundry room. Vivian rushed inside, a burst of joy and happiness that seemed to be aimed right at his heart. Vivian exclaimed, "Josh, you're back."

Josh smiled as if Vivian was his missing Christmas cheer.

Vivian brimmed with excitement. "Josh, you have to see what we parked in your workshop. You aren't going to believe it."

Josh glanced at his grandfather.

"Don't look at me. I came on home instead of going antiquing." Grandpa Sam shook a sugar cookie at Josh. "The last time I went antiquing with Tess, she almost talked me into buying a carousel horse. Of all the things. She even tried to convince me it was a collectible and I needed one."

Josh noted the amusement and deep affection in his grandfather's gaze.

"Sam is going to think what we found is perfect. Come and see for yourselves." Vivian headed toward the back door. "Too bad you don't raise reindeer here. That would've been something."

"Reindeer," his grandpa repeated and hurried outside.

Josh moved at a more sedate pace. A clearly exasperated Vivian raced back, grabbed his hand and pulled him outside. Josh grinned wider. Now he had what he wanted. Her hand in his.

Inside his shop, Josh found a vintage sleigh. The very same kind Santa might use to deliver toys on Christmas Eve. Or in their case, the kind that would make an excellent photo opportunity outside the gala greenhouses. With a few repairs and a little paint, it would be easy to bring it back to its former glory.

Josh nodded and got to work. It wasn't very long before the sleigh was repaired. Painted. Under the stars twinkling in the clear sky, Josh sat with Vivian on the wide bench at the front of the sleigh. There were tools to put away. Paint cans to toss. Vivian's face was smudged. Josh's shirt stained. Yet it was all incredibly perfect.

Josh was not thinking about pushing away. He was content. Truly at peace.

"We should go inside and join the others." Vivian burrowed into his side and adjusted the thick blanket she'd taken from his couch in his apartment earlier.

"We probably should." Josh curved his arm tighter around her.

"I never actually thought a sleigh like this would be comfortable," Vivian mused.

"Or so roomy," he added, although his boots were stacked awkwardly on the railing. And the wooden bench was a bit stiff against his back. None of it mattered.

"It's perfect for stargazing." Vivian rested her head on his shoulder. "I can see why Santa uses one."

Josh chuckled. And he was starting to see why his Gran Claire always told him: Content *isn't a bad word, Josh. It's something we should be lucky enough to find and not ever lose.*

CHAPTER TWENTY-THREE

TWO DAYS AFTER her stargazing-sleigh time with Josh, Vivian waited in the wings at the Three Springs rodeo arena. Her barrel race finished. Her time currently the fastest of the day. But one last barrel racer waited in the alleyway. One of the best. Isabel was Vivian's last competitor for first place at the Silk and Steel Cowgirl Stampede.

Finally, Isabel and Fox charged from the alleyway. The pair rounded the first barrel. Quick. Neat. Raced toward the next. Circled it. Clean. Fast. Vivian held her breath. The last barrel complete, the talented pair raced toward the finish.

The clock stopped. The time frozen in bold red. The dust in the arena settled.

Vivian gaped. Her gaze fixed on the scoreboard. Eight one hundredths of a second.

She won. Thanks to Artie.

By eight one hundredths of a second.

She won big. The jackpot payout. The spot on the River Forge Team.

Careful what you wish for, Vivian. A tremor curved through her.

Cheers and applause echoed around her. Followed by the congratulatory pats on the back from the rodeo hands and volunteers nearby.

Vivian smiled. Accepted several quick celebratory hugs.

That tremor expanded. Tears swirled in her eyes.

The congratulations blurred around her as she was ushered by volunteers to the hospitality tent to await the award ceremony. The tears swelled more. She wanted them to be tears of joy. Desperately willed them to be. Still, she stretched her smile wider, accepted the well wishes and pretended joy was all she felt.

After all, she'd won. And finally claimed the future her grandma and she had always dreamt about. There should be nothing but elation. Satisfaction. Delight. And yet…

Inside the massive hospitality tent, her hand was clasped inside Miles Nesci's warm, all-encompassing grasp, while the elated rancher raved about Artie's talent and the Arabian's champion characteristics.

It was at that moment everything started to completely unravel like a bad dream. A very bad dream. Exactly as Isabel's mother had once predicted to her young daughter.

"I wouldn't be here without you, Vivian, buying a horse that's sure to be one of the best competitors out there." Miles gave Vivian's hand another hearty pump and rattled on, "I sure can't thank you enough for convincing me to come back."

Vivian accepted the blame. Clearly, she should've been less persuasive with the rancher. Then she wouldn't feel as if she were losing not just a horse but a piece of herself. Vivian kept her smile in place and tried to blink away her tears.

"I can't wait to bring Artie home," Miles gushed, his gaze gleamed.

No. Artie is... Vivian tugged her hand free and touched her chin, stalling the quiver and propping up her smile. "Artie is going to be a wonderful addition to your stables." *Please don't take him from me. Not the horse. Not my cowboy.* Vivian murmured, "Safe travels. And Merry Christmas, Miles."

"Certainly is going to be a fine Christmas now." Miles tipped his cowboy hat toward Vivian and laughed. "I need to find Josh and finalize our deal tonight, in fact." Miles sauntered away, whistling a jolly Christmas tune.

Vivian searched the crowded tent. Judges, competitors and their families mingled and celebrated. But Josh wasn't there. Because

Josh wasn't hers. Everything Vivian wanted—everything she'd been working for—was now hers. But not her cowboy. Still, a victory like hers was supposed to feel good. A dream come true. Vivian pressed her hand against her stomach as if she didn't feel quite so good after all.

She turned, wanting a moment to collect herself. To find her happy. Her excitement. Her joy that was supposed to be part of her victory. She'd reached the end of her rainbow. Yet she couldn't seem to find that pot of gold. Then Isabel stepped in front of her and enveloped Vivian in a tight hug.

"Congratulations, Vivian." Isabel squeezed her. "Your last ride was so inspiring. Flawless."

Vivian struggled not to apologize to Isabel. The ride of Vivian's life had cost Isabel more. And her friend's second chance was now only second place. Still, Isabel was nothing but gracious in her praise. So Vivian held on. Winners didn't apologize to other competitors. But friends, well, Vivian wanted to beg her friend to take her spot on the River Forge team. "Isabel."

"I'll be coming for you in the new year, Vivian." Isabel released Vivian and smiled. "You can count on it."

Vivian met her friend's gaze. "I can't wait."

"Now, go find Josh and get to celebrating."

Isabel gave Vivian another quick hug. "This should be the night of your life."

It would be a night to remember. Of that, she was certain. But a celebration...

"Vivian." Her mother waved and weaved around a group of rodeo judges. She swept Vivian up in an enthusiastic hug. "That was something. I was anxious, nervous, excited."

"You would've thought your mom was the one competing." Her father chuckled and hugged Vivian. "You had us on the edge of our seats for sure."

"Did you hear me in the stands?" her mother asked and laughed. "I was definitely the loudest one cheering for you."

Vivian searched her parents' beaming faces, looking for the catch or their disappointment. She'd won. She wasn't coming home. Her parents knew that. Vivian rubbed her forehead. "I wasn't sure you wanted me to win."

Her mother's eyebrows arched high. She shifted her startled gaze to Vivian's dad.

"Why wouldn't we want that for you?" Her father frowned. "You've worked so hard for this. It's what you wanted."

"But what about the business?" Vivian pressed. "That's why you came to Three Springs. To convince me to return to the business."

"You dad and I hoped if we all spent time

together, you'd want to be a part of our family again." Her mother squeezed Vivian's hand. "But your father and I agreed we wouldn't force you."

To be part of the family again? Not part of the company? Weren't they one and the same? Vivian held on to her mother's hand like it was an anchor. As if her family might've been what she was looking for after all.

"Now we see what you've got here with Josh," her dad said. Pride shifted around his words. "And now you have the team too."

But it wasn't real with Josh. And the team wasn't her family. Vivian asked, "What about that big contract? What if you get it?"

"We already got the contract with South Trek Enterprises." Pleasure lit up her mother's gaze.

"You didn't tell me." *Include me.* But she hadn't wanted to be included. Vivian had made that more than clear. She'd finally gotten what she always asked for. It was supposed to feel so much better, wasn't it? More satisfying. More rewarding. Much more gratifying.

"This is your moment," her dad said, his words earnest and heartfelt. "We don't want to take that away from you. This is too important."

"But don't you—" *...need me?* Vivian squeezed her mom's hand. "—need help at the business now?"

"We'll handle things with the company," her mom assured Vivian. "You don't have to worry about us. It's time for you to get to living your best life."

Why did it suddenly feel like her worst? "I thought you came here to talk me into coming home."

"We had every intention of doing just that." Her father chuckled and shook his head as if amazed at his own nerve. He added, "Then we saw firsthand what you have."

"With Josh," her mom stated. Delight spread across her face.

But it wasn't real. None of it was real. And yet, apparently, Vivian had sold the whole facade too well. The blame was all hers to shoulder.

"This is the happiest we've seen you in a long while," her mom said.

Vivian couldn't deny that truth. The past week with the Sloan family. With Josh, really. She'd been beyond happy. Content. Settled even. She backed away from that thought.

"We certainly don't want to take that away from you," her dad said. "You deserve all the happiness you can have."

What if her happy was already gone? On its way to Houston. Courtesy of Vivian convincing Miles Nesci to come to the stampede. Now Josh would have the funds to invest in Bellmare and have everything he wanted without her. Those tears threatened again. She focused on her parents. "What about the company?"

"We've got to have some hard conversations," her dad admitted. "Consider bringing in outside help."

Vivian gaped at her father. "You want to hire people outside the family to run the business. What about two Bryants at the helm? The tradition. The legacy."

"Being here with you and the Sloan family reminded us that family should come before business." Her dad touched Vivian's shoulder. Sincerity in his gaze. "That's the real legacy."

"Family is the most important part." Her mother released Vivian's hand and cupped Vivian's cheek. "And we're very sorry if you ever felt we lost sight of that."

"We're proud of you, Vivian," her dad offered. "And we'll always be in your corner."

Words Vivian had always wanted to hear. Words that filled her. Yet it all felt too late. Vivian had staked her course. Her future. Not with her family, but without them. Vivian embraced both her parents as if that would change the outcome.

"Vivian." A woman wearing a press badge approached with another woman holding a professional camera. "Do you have time for a few questions?"

Vivian wanted to shake her head and hold on to her parents. Pause in the moment where it was only them. No interference. Nothing that would put distance between them. Nothing that would take her away. But she'd chosen this life. Dedicated herself to having her career on her own terms. Now she'd succeeded. *Time to accept the consequences, Vivian.*

"Looks like you have important business to handle, Vivian." Her mother pressed a kiss on Vivian's cheek and took her father's hand instead. "We'll get out of your way now."

CHAPTER TWENTY-FOUR

EVENING WAS SETTLING IN. And Josh's mood was darkening with the descending night. He twisted the silk tie he'd borrowed from his brother into another mangled knot and frowned in the mirror. His brothers had already departed for the gala. Vivian too. He'd learned that from her text earlier. Vivian had wanted to see to any final touches before the guests arrived. To make sure the evening was perfect for everyone.

His tie was not perfect. His mood wasn't either. For no good reason. He'd sold his competition horses for more than expected. And now he could fund his full investment stake in Bellmare. It was all coming together just as he'd planned. The next level was everything Josh wanted. A platform to grow his name and reputation on.

Josh gave up on the tie, slipped on the borrowed black suit jacket and left his bedroom. He knocked on his grandfather's door and stepped inside when his grandpa shouted, "It's open."

"Can't seem to get this thing right." Josh held up both ends of the crushed silk tie.

His grandfather took the tie and worked it into a neat knot in several swift moves. Then patted Josh's chest and grinned. "Not too bad. Still remember everything your Gran Claire taught me about dressing up in my finer clothes."

Josh checked his image in the full-length mirror and smoothed his hands over the tie and suit he'd borrowed from his older brother Grant. This time Maggie had selected both the charcoal-and-silver-striped tie and the pale gray dress shirt, declaring the combination striking and galaworthy. "Seems I'm ready."

"For the gala, yes." His grandfather met his gaze in the full-length mirror and said, "But I'd sure like to know when you'll be ready for your move to Houston."

Josh's hands stilled on the silk tie, and he turned around to face his grandfather. "How long have you known?"

"You didn't think something like an equestrian center would be going in, even as far away as south Texas, and I wouldn't catch wind of it?" His grandfather selected a bolo tie from his collection spread out on his antique dresser. "I reckon I knew before you."

He should have guessed. His grandpa might be long since retired, but he was still well-connected and in touch. Josh stuffed his hands in the pockets of his pressed dress pants.

"And no, I didn't suggest you for the director position either. Although if I'd been asked, I certainly would have." Pride roughened his grandfather's words. "However, you earned that offer solely on your own merit and talent."

"Why didn't you say something?" Josh asked.

"Same could be asked of you." Grandpa Sam stepped over to the mirror and slipped the leather bolo tie over his head. "I've been biding my time. Figured you would talk when you were ready. But you never did. You seemed to want to carry the burden on your own."

"It wasn't a burden," Josh argued.

His grandfather set his hands on his hips and faced Josh. "Then, why do you look so defeated now?"

"It's not feeling like it should," Josh admitted. He straightened the cuff on his dress shirt and the certainty in his words. "There's still more to do before it's complete. Once the deal is finalized and the paperwork signed, then I'll celebrate." *And, finally, be truly happy.*

"You sure about that?" His grandfather smoothed his fingers through his white beard.

It took Josh longer than a minute, but he finally managed to nod.

"Then, I'm proud of you. You set out to do

things on your own and you did." His grandfather slid the silver clasp on the bolo tie up toward his neck. He smiled. "You're going to do very well in Houston too."

"You're not going to talk me out of it?" Josh asked and watched his grandfather. "Talk me out of leaving."

"You have to do what's right for you. I don't have to like it, but that's for me to deal with." His grandfather stepped forward and set his hand on Josh's shoulder. "What I have to do is respect your decision. And that's what I'll do because I love you."

"Thanks, Grandpa." Josh hugged the man who'd never let him down. Who Josh had never wanted to disappoint in return.

His grandfather gave one last pat to Josh's back. His words gruff. "One more thing." His grandpa set his palm flat on Josh's chest. "This comes from your Gran Claire, so pay attention. You make sure you're doing what's right for you in here. In your heart. You hear me?"

"Yes, sir," Josh said.

"When you do that, then it won't be a burden anymore." Grandpa Sam held Josh's gaze a beat longer and nodded as if satisfied Josh understood.

Josh understood his heart was more of a burden than anything else. It was why he'd stopped listening to it. Until he'd met Vivian. Until his cowgirl drove into his life. He resisted the urge to yank on his tie and loosen the knot at his neck.

Grandpa Sam stepped back and spread his arms wide. "Okay, we've got ourselves a fancy gala to get to. Better get to it. We certainly don't want to be late."

Late. Josh felt like he'd been late the entire day. He'd missed Vivian in the hallway that morning and he hadn't seen her other than to watch her ride in the finals. Then he'd been one step behind, trying to find Vivian to congratulate her in person at the stampede.

He'd missed her in the stalls at the rodeo grounds after her final race and instead met several new potential clients thanks to introductions from Maggie and referrals from Ryan, as well as his current clients and even Vivian. Then Vivian had already left the hospitality tent for another interview when Josh finally made it there. Finalizing the purchase agreements for his three competition horses had delayed him even longer at the rodeo grounds, and he had returned to the farmhouse later than he'd expected.

Josh dropped his grandfather at the greenhouse entrance and went to park. Now he sat alone in his truck in the full lot. And all he felt was dread, as if he'd already lost something precious at the Doyle Farm. But then, Vivian was never truly his. Not for him to truly lose.

This was Vivian's moment to shine. He'd enjoy it with her tonight. And then he'd move on and she'd go live the life that she wanted. That she deserved. He would wish her well, knowing she would soar. And if she took his heart with her, perhaps that was for the best. He didn't really need it anymore. He finally climbed out of his truck and headed inside.

The decorated gala greenhouses were more stunning than he'd imagined. A true escape into an inviting winter wonderland. Lights twinkled like stars within easy reach. Music swirled with the muted laughter and the continuous flow of easy conversations among friends. Pine and cinnamon and Christmas scented the air.

Then, there was Vivian. In a deep red, shimmery ball gown near the dance floor. Her hair spilling in the softest waves around her shoulders. All graceful movements and elegance. His cowgirl was breathtaking. Like a beacon calling him home. Drawing him to her. Always to her.

"I believe the first dance is mine." He held out his hand toward her. Held his breath. Until her palm landed softly against his. He guided her into his arms, just where he wanted her. Where he would always want her. Where she wouldn't be.

He twirled her away and led her back into his embrace. Still, his breaths wouldn't come easier. Nothing inside him calmed. And Josh found himself faking things for the first time with his cowgirl. From his stiff smile to his casual words. "You were right. This is the perfect gala location."

Her gaze lifted to the glass ceiling, then she sighed. "It really is."

He spun her out of his arms again. Her floor-length gown floated around her, the fragile fabric gliding across his dress boots. Her laughter spilled free. Then he brought her back to him. He could've danced all night with her. Instead, he held her close, until the last notes of the song, then he let her go. Preparing himself for their final dance and that final last goodbye.

Her dad requested the next dance and the pair disappeared inside the crowded dance floor. Josh retreated to the other end of the greenhouse. If his gaze tracked a deep crimson gown across the dance floor through song after song while he mingled with friends and locals, well, that was his business.

Just as he suspected, Vivian shone bright, seeming to draw everyone to her again and again. There was praise for her impressive win at the stampede. Compliments about the gala. Introductions to the locals and questions about her future. Her next rodeo. Her Christmas plans. He knew because he spent the evening fielding many of the same inquiries. But mostly there was no time for Josh to have his cowgirl all to himself.

Until the final dance. That was his. And he was simply too selfish not to have her in his arms one more time.

He set his hand on her lower back, nodded to his grandfather and Marlena Doyle, then said, "Vivian, this is our song."

"Josh." Her hesitant gaze searched his, yet her hand still found his as if she was as drawn to him as he was to her. He guided her out onto the dance floor among the last of the couples still remaining.

Her other hand settled on his shoulder. She said, "I feel like I haven't seen you all night."

But he'd seen her. Would always see her. He grinned and ignored the ache in his chest. "It was your night. Your time to celebrate your success in your own personally designed snow globe."

Her fingers flexed on his shoulder. "I would've liked to celebrate with you."

"I've been right here." Close enough. Just

outside heart-bruising range. He circled the dance floor, wanting them both breathless. Both exhausted. And ready to walk away.

"No. No, you're not here. Not with me." She stopped and stepped out of his arms. Regret and hurt shone on her face. "And I can't do this anymore. I can't keep pretending."

With that, she fled the dance floor and rushed outside. He should've walked away then. Left it alone. Left her alone. But he wasn't ready. And he followed her. Found her standing in front of their restored sleigh, her arms folded across her chest. Her shoulders rolled in. Her chin lowered. He slipped off his jacket and draped it over her, and promised himself to keep quiet before he bundled her into his embrace and promised her things he couldn't give her.

She clutched his jacket closed and rounded on him. Not with gratitude. But rather anger. "Are you about done proving you can stand alone? I think we all get it now."

"What does that mean?" He set his hands on his hips.

"Everyone who loves you and who you love, you push away," she charged. "All because you believe you have to be on your own to prove you're successful."

"What about you? You borrowed an entire

lifestyle to prove that your family is better off without you. But all you're really doing is running," he countered. "Telling yourself you don't fit anywhere. Because if you belonged, you might have to let yourself be loved. Just as you are."

"Are you saying you love me?" She straightened inside his suit jacket and tipped up her chin. "Just as I am."

Yes. The word stuck in his throat. But his love would be a burden. Hold her back. He never wanted that for her. She was too special. She deserved to fly like she had in the arena that afternoon. She had so much more to accomplish. "This was never about my heart." *But you should know it was yours from that first roadside smile you aimed my way.*

"And if I loved you? With all my heart?" she said, her words and expression open. So very unguarded. "What then?"

I would push you away. Because I can't risk my heart again. He tried to sound resolved even though he didn't feel it. "I'm not who you should want."

Her gaze narrowed on him. Her expression was one of clear frustration. "Because you refuse to love me back."

"Because love is never enough." Not his kind of love anyway. He stuffed his hands in his pants pockets and tucked his arms against his sides.

Her fingers fisted around his jacket lapels. "So, you won't even try. Won't give us a chance."

"To what end?" he said, letting his own frustration out. "I couldn't get to you today. Simply to hug you. Congratulate you. It was one afternoon."

She opened and closed her mouth. "I'm sorry. I didn't know."

"Don't apologize." He slipped his hand through his hair. "It was no one's fault. This is what we signed up for. We chose to put our careers first. We chose this." And despite one week, no matter how perfect, it wasn't going to change their choices or their futures. That would mean staking his on love. He'd been a fool once. Never again.

She huddled deeper into his jacket and searched his gaze. "What are you saying?"

"What I don't want to but know that I have to," he said, his voice low.

Her eyes closed. Her lips rolled together. A faint crease appeared between her eyebrows. The barest flinch of pain.

It wrecked Josh. Splintered his heart more precisely than anything she could have said. He found his voice, enough to whisper, "Vivian, I wish…"

"Don't." Her bottom lip trembled. Emotion fractured her words. "Don't tell me you wish you could love me. Just don't."

I love you. But I don't trust in love anymore. He scrubbed his hands over his face. Wanted to shout. Wanted to shatter the stifling silence. Wanted not to lose her. Wanted to be enough as he was now, not as the man he intended to become someday. "This is all. This is…"

"…goodbye," she finished for him. Then she turned and walked away.

It took one word to end it all. One impossibly pain-filled word. Heart-shattering. And so very final.

CHAPTER TWENTY-FIVE

THEY WERE GONE. *GONE.*

Vivian's family and the RV had left. Her mother had told her yesterday after the rodeo that they'd get out of her way. Vivian hadn't realized they'd meant to get so far out of her way.

She was free now. Free to pursue her own life on her own terms. No expectations. No obligations to the family business, to her family or even her cowboy. She was feeling like she'd lost more than she'd won.

Worse, an emptiness had opened deep inside her that left her cold. And so very alone. Vivian curved her arms around her waist.

The back door opened and closed. Sam stopped beside Vivian. "Your parents wouldn't let me wake you. Your mom claimed you were exhausted from the weekend and needed your rest."

"I should head out too," Vivian said, her words sounded empty even to her own ears. She rubbed the chill from her arms. Nothing warmed her.

"Where to?" Sam sipped his coffee and kept his gaze on the skyline.

Vivian blanched. For the first time since she had set out alone to chase her dreams, she didn't know where to go. Rodeos resumed in the new year, as did the River Forge team competition. Her family was always asking her when she was coming home. Now they weren't asking. Not expecting her. Where was she supposed to go?

She was more than unsure. She was completely lost. Tears swelled. A shiver built inside her. "I need to pick up my phone at the Doyle Farm. I forgot it last night." After she'd walked away from Josh. When she'd seemingly forgotten the simplest of things, like how to breathe. She pressed her fingers against her chest. "Then I'll be on my way. I won't be here much longer. I promise."

"Stay as long as you'd like." Sam touched her arm. His gentle words drawing Vivian's gaze to his. "And remember, you've always got an open invitation to return. Anytime. Whenever you might need us."

But she didn't belong here. She wasn't part of their family. She shouldn't need them. Not at all. Not even a little bit. And yet she did. Too much. But this was just a stopover on her way to the career and life she'd always imagined. Vivian managed only an awkward nod, felt that shiver turn into a tremor.

Sam patted her arm. His words were sympathetic. "I find talking out my troubles eases things inside me. Helps me see things more clearly."

She'd told Josh goodbye last night. There was nothing left to say. Nothing left to talk about. And nothing was clearer than the fact that Josh wanted his career more than love. Same as Vivian. Yet that truth did nothing for the deep, dull ache within her.

"My Claire always told me I had a good ear for listening," Sam added. "Just thought you should know that, in case you change your mind about sharing those troubles."

"Thank you, Sam. For everything." Vivian wrapped her arms around the older cowboy, hugged him tight and skipped over the goodbye. She wasn't ready for another one.

He patted her back and offered words meant to comfort. Those tears blurred Vivian's eyes. That tremor washed over her. But she refused to break down in front of Sam. She released him, pressed her hand to her mouth and rushed to her truck.

Her tears fell the entire drive through downtown Three Springs and all the way to the Doyle Farm. They were still falling when Vivian climbed out of her truck in front of the empty greenhouses. The bold red sleigh stood out in the early morning like a beacon of Christmas cheer. If only Santa was inside granting wishes. But wishes had led her astray. Led her to this moment. And only her will, not wishes, was going to help her move on now. Vivian shoved her sunglasses on, ignored the sleigh and willed every thought—the good and the painful—of Josh away.

"Vivian." Marlena's cheery greeting drifted across the yard. Breezy and Gayle framed the widow, and the trio waved. Marlena added, "We didn't expect to see you here so early."

"We just finished a lovely walk about the gardens." Breezy adjusted her knit hat on her head and grinned. "After a lengthy debate, we finally decided on eggs Benedict for breakfast."

"We worked up our appetites with all that dancing last night." Gayle's eyebrows lifted high above her glasses. "We need to eat up and restore our energy."

"I just came by to pick up my phone." Vivian motioned toward the greenhouse. Her breath hitched. Yet she willed her tears not to fall past the cover of her sunglasses. "It's in there somewhere." *With the pieces of my heart.*

"Oh my." Breezy was at Vivian's side faster

than Santa up a chimney. "Ladies, I think Vivian needs more than eggs Benedict this morning."

Gayle nudged her eyeglasses up her nose and blinked at Vivian. "The poor dear definitely needs chocolate chip pancakes."

"And a chocolate croissant with a peppermint-bark mimosa." Marlena slipped her arm around Vivian's waist. "Come on up to the house, Vivian. We'll see you set to rights in no time."

Vivian feared there was no setting her heart to rights. It was never supposed to be about her heart. *Never*. Still, she let the concerned and very caring trio sweep her to the main house and into Marlena's very inviting sunroom.

A peppermint mimosa was placed in front of Vivian on the quaint round table. A full-size candy cane hooked on the rim of the champagne flute. A plate of warm chocolate croissants waited for Vivian to take a sample. And Breezy bustled around the kitchen, whisking the pancake batter.

Gayle dropped into the chair across from Vivian and nudged the croissants closer to her. "Your heart might ache, but your stomach doesn't need to as well."

"I'm not usually like this." So emotional. Vivian picked up a croissant and set it on her plate. "I'm sure I'm just exhausted."

"Sleep will heal the body." Marlena walked over and stirred her candy cane in her mimosa. "But unfortunately, you can't sleep off a broken heart. Believe me, dear, I know. I've tried."

That was unfair. And quite cruel. Sleep was supposed to heal all ills. Vivian broke off a bite of croissant. "I'll be too busy soon enough to think about it."

"Back to chasing barrels in the new year, then." Breezy placed plates stacked with golden, chocolate chip pancakes on the holiday place mats around the table and took a seat next to her sister.

"That's my job," Vivian said and eyed the pancakes as if breakfast was the most important meal because it solved all life's problems. "It is my passion."

"Nothing wrong with having a passion." Gayle poured hot syrup over her pancake stack. "Only matters if that's all you've got."

"The rodeo is my career." Vivian loaded a bite of pancake onto her fork. "It's everything I've always wanted." Now she had it. And yet she still wanted...

Breezy fluffed out a fabric napkin and smoothed it over her lap. "Are you wanting a career or a lifestyle, dear?"

Vivian swallowed her mouthful of pancake

and considered her options. Considered the right answer. Came up blank.

"You always want the lifestyle, dear." Gayle aimed her fork at Vivian. "Lifestyle gives you the choice to pick and choose the parts you want."

Wasn't that what she'd been doing? Choosing the life she wanted. On the rodeo circuit.

"Your career should only be a piece, not the whole of your life." Gayle's glasses slipped down her nose. She peered over the rims at Vivian. "You know what I mean?"

The entirety of Vivian's time in Three Springs had been full. Full of more than barrel racing. She'd had great times with her friends. Her family. And mostly with Josh. Even her practices had been better, thanks to Josh and Isabel. And despite the ache in her chest, it had all been time well spent.

"My husband refused to build more greenhouses. No matter how busy we got or how often we sold out of things." Marlena's smile turned wistful. She lifted her mimosa glass toward the floor-to-ceiling windows. "He always argued, sure, we'd have the quantity, but at what cost to the quality?"

"Same goes for life, dear. Too much of one thing can be just what it looks like. Too much." Breezy swirled her fork over her pancakes and speared a chocolate chip. "Can't taste only the chocolate chips in your pancakes. That's just one flavor. The best bite has a little bit of everything."

"That's balance." Gayle grinned and sipped her mimosa. "And when you've got that, you've got your happy."

Vivian wanted that. Wanted her happy too. She said, "Is it possible to have it all, then?"

"Of course, it is, dear." Breezy lifted her champagne flute and toasted with Gayle and Marlena. "We certainly did."

"It's not always easy. It gets complicated and stressful at times," Marlena added, caution in her words but a gleam of wisdom in her gaze. "But it'll be worth it. I can promise you that."

"Just remember, dear, always enjoy the journey, not only the destination." Gayle tipped her champagne flute at Vivian. "The journey is where the richest parts of life are spent. Those moments are the ones worth remembering in your heart."

The journey. Vivian sat back in her chair and sipped her mimosa. She'd been so focused on getting to that pot of gold, she'd completely missed the rainbow. Until she'd arrived in Three Springs. Until she'd finally stopped running and stepped fully into each moment…with the Sloans, with Josh and even with her family.

Her family. Vivian found her first smile of the day. She could fix things with her family. Repair the damage and begin a new journey with them, if they agreed. She would start there. And then maybe the ache in her chest wouldn't hurt quite so much.

She set her champagne flute on the table. "This is one of the most delicious drinks I've had, but I can't drink anymore. I have a long drive ahead of me."

CHAPTER TWENTY-SIX

IT HAD TAKEN Vivian longer to leave the Sloan property than she'd anticipated yesterday. It seemed everyone from Tess and Carter to Maggie and Grant to Uncle Roy and Ryan had an argument for why Vivian needed to stay. Caleb had even taken to following her around the stables. He'd helped her load Dusty, checked tire pressure on her trailer, and all the while kept listing reasons why Vivian should spend the holidays at the farmhouse. Everyone had tried to stop her from leaving. Everyone except Josh.

But her cowboy was reason enough to leave.

Breezy, Gayle and Marlena hadn't been wrong yesterday morning in the sunroom. Balance was important. And Vivian had driven through the night to reach Phoenix and her family. To finally find some of that balance.

Though when it came to her cowboy, there was no balance. When Vivian gave her heart, she would give it fully. Risk it all. And she wanted the very same in return. No half measures. No second place. When it came to her cowboy, she wanted his heart total or nothing.

She'd boarded Dusty at her former riding instructor's stables and now parked her truck in the parking garage of the office building where Complete Milestone Insurance Company had been headquartered since her father took over. She noted her family's cars were already in their assigned parking spaces and gave thanks for her family's predictability. Their vacation had concluded, and Monday meant back to the office, back to their usual routine.

Vivian greeted their longtime receptionist and asked Leona for a favor. Then she headed into the smaller of the two conference rooms at Complete Milestone Insurance Company. The last time she'd sat at the oval table, Vivian had bargained with her parents for a different kind of future. One where she wasn't contained by a cubicle and a strict forty-hour workweek at the Bryant family business.

Now she was back to bargain again. This time for her place in her family and the business.

It wasn't long before the conference door opened. Vivian stood at the front of the room and straightened her shoulders. Her mother stopped in the doorway and gasped, preventing Vivian's father from entering.

Her mother whispered, "Vivian. You're here."

Vivian watched her mother reach behind her and clasp her father's hand. Always, her parents reached for each other. Always, they stood beside each other. That was the kind of partnership Vivian wanted. Nothing less would do. Not this time. But she wasn't there to discuss her heart. Vivian smiled. "Leona told me your calendars were clear for the next hour."

"Mom." That was Heather's voice in the hallway. "What's going on?"

Vivian's parents moved into the room and took the seats on one side of the table. Heather and Wade followed. Heather's surprise unmistakable. Along with the tears shimmering in her eyes.

"I wanted to have a meeting." Vivian clasped her hands in front of her. "With the Bryant family and the Bryant leadership team."

Wade grinned at Vivian, gave her a nod. His expression one of admiration and approval. Then he took Heather's hand and guided her over to the other set of chairs.

Vivian started with an apology. "I believed I had to chase my passion to the exclusion of everything and everyone else. Or else my passion didn't count." *I didn't count.* She knew now, she'd been wrong. She added, "If I wasn't racing at the top, then I certainly wasn't living my best life."

Her mother brushed at her eyes, then once again took her dad's hand.

"But, I've learned recently, it's about balance," Vivian continued, felt her cheeks getting damp. "And being at the top is fine, but not if I'm up there alone." Vivian accepted a tissue from her sister and met her mother's gaze. "I guess what I'm trying to tell you is that I want my family too."

Her mother's smile beamed through her tears.

Heather pressed a tissue to her eyes. "What are you saying, Viv?"

"I want it all." Vivian crumpled the tissue and found her grit. It was past time to fight for her place. "I was told I could have it all. I want Heather and Wade to have it. You and Dad. I don't know how that looks. I'm sure it's complicated, but I think I can offer something to the business and have my barrel racing career too."

Her father clasped his hands on the table and eyed Vivian. "Nothing is so complicated we can't figure it out as a family." His confidence unflinching.

"Together," Wade said. He pushed out the only other empty chair at the conference table and motioned to it. "We will figure this out together as a family. That's what we are."

And what they always would be. Vivian hurried to join her family and rolled the leather chair closer to the table. "Here are my initial thoughts."

For the next hour, the Bryant family worked together to design a remote job that would allow Vivian to contribute her skills and talents to the business, while also pursuing her barrel racing career. She would spend one week a month at the office in Phoenix, more if Heather and Wade needed her to when the twins arrived. Their parents would begin their transition into retirement over the next year. And outside professionals would be hired to fill the management gaps. It was more than Vivian expected and all she could've hoped for.

Heather knocked on Vivian's office door and held up a familiar candy box with an equally familiar purple ribbon. "Maggie claims that Tess's truffles solve any and every problem imaginable. She was kind enough to give me my own personal stash when we left."

"Maybe not every problem." Vivian tried to smile yet knew she failed.

"It's certainly worth a taste test to see if Maggie is right, don't you think?" Heather opened the box and joined Vivian at the large window that overlooked downtown. Heather continued, "White chocolate and caramel.

Used to be one of your favorite flavor combinations."

"Still is." Vivian took a truffle from the box and touched the gold design on the top. "It was Grandma's favorite, so it became mine too, even though, as a kid, I never understood the sea salt on the caramel."

"What about now?" Heather picked out a dark chocolate truffle, then set the box on the corner of Vivian's new desk.

"Now I get it." Vivian bit into the truffle. The bite of salt mixed with the sweet made her sigh. "I missed her, Heather. When Grandma passed, I felt like I had no place here."

Heather nodded and considered her truffle.

"Mom and Dad had each other. You had Wade," Vivian continued. "And I had a horse."

Heather tipped her head and considered Vivian. Understanding and a quiet hit of surprise flashed in her sister's gaze. "Your horse kept you connected to Grandma, didn't he?"

Dusty was her anchor. For so many seasons and so many reasons. Then she'd gone to Three Springs without him and found she could stand on her own. With Dusty back, Vivian felt even stronger. Vivian nodded. "Everyone had a place here, even Wade. I just didn't know where I fit anymore."

"I always envied you and your bond with

Grandma." Heather bit into her truffle and spoke around the bite as if she wanted the sweetness to soften the tinge of resentment in her words. "You and Grandma were always off plotting your next adventures and getaways for as long as I could remember. You never asked me to come along. Never included me."

"I never thought to." Vivian reached out and touched her sister's arm. "You were always with Mom and Dad. Always so excited to come here. Always ready to help. I envied you because of how close you were with them. You were always so sure of where you belonged."

"Not always," Heather admitted. "At least, not until I fell in love with Wade. Wade wanted to be included in the business and the family. I realized we could have what Mom and Dad built."

"And you felt like I didn't want to be a part of any of it." Vivian leaned her hip against the deep window ledge, the truth nudging her off balance. She'd never considered how her leaving affected her sister. She couldn't change her past choices. She could only be present going forward.

"Can you blame me?" Heather asked. "You spent more time with Grandma and your horses than with me growing up."

"There we were. Both feeling excluded from

the other one's life and instead of talking, we excluded each other more." Vivian took both of her sister's hands in hers and held her gaze. "Can we make a pact not to do that again, please?"

"Deal." Heather hugged Vivian. She laughed and motioned toward the truffle box. "I think that perhaps those do really work. Now that we've solved any future sisterly problems with a promise to talk first, how about we address the other elephant in the room?"

"What are you talking about?" Vivian had found her place with her family. Finally fit in. What more was there? Vivian glanced around the space. "I like the paint colors you picked out for this office."

"Thank you, but the decor isn't the issue." Heather arched an eyebrow at Vivian. "Your obvious heartbreak is."

"I'm just sad." Vivian traced her fingers over the window ledge and avoided looking at her sister. "Not heartbroken."

"You certain about that?" Heather challenged. "Because from where I'm standing it's looking a lot more like broken."

Vivian set her forehead against the glass window and considered the traffic on the street below. "I can't possibly have a broken heart. Nothing with Josh was even real."

"What do you mean?" Heather asked.

Vivian peered at her sister. "I mean, Josh was just the lead in my fake-relationship plot. It was all made-up."

Heather shook her head. "Viv, you are great at a lot of things."

"Is that compliment supposed to cheer me up?" Vivian asked.

"I'm not finished." Heather's mouth pulled in. "You're great at a lot of things, little sister, but feigning an attraction to Josh isn't one of them."

"Maybe that's all it was, then," Vivian said. Yet for the first time that day, her words were hesitant. Unsure. "It was just an attraction to Josh. Those fade, you know. Burn bright and fizzle out even faster."

"Are you sure that was all there was between you and Josh?" Heather pressed.

That had to be all there was. An attraction was easier to get over. Easier to dismiss than a broken heart. "I don't want there to be more, Heather." It hurt too much already.

"Why not?" Heather argued. "Josh is perfect for you."

"Just what makes Josh so very perfect?" Vivian asked. *Besides his obvious affection for horses, his loyalty, honor, sense of humor. And the way he looked at me. Like I was the only one in the room. The only one for him.* Vivian snatched a second white chocolate truffle from the box, took a big bite and pulled her wayward thoughts back in line.

"He's perfect because he loves you just as you are, Viv." Heather touched Vivian's arm. There was an insistence in her words. "And you love him the same."

Love him. Love her cowboy? Surely she hadn't gone and done something so foolish as that. Vivian shook her head.

"You can keep running from the truth," Heather continued. Her grip tightened on Vivian's arm. "But it's not going to change what's in your heart."

"It was too fast, Heather," Vivian argued. It was too quick. Too soon. Too right. Vivian had promised herself she would tiptoe into love, if she ever even fell in love again. "It can't be love."

"Why not?" Heather challenged. "Who says there needs to be a timeline on falling in love?"

Vivian opened and closed her mouth, and finally quieted her mind and listened to her heart. She loved Josh. Loved her cowboy. And she wanted him back in her life any way she could have him. Vivian whispered, "How do I ask my fake boyfriend to become my real boyfriend?"

Heather laughed and wrapped her arm around Vivian's shoulders. "I suppose just like that."

"Because that's not awkward or anything." Vivian wrinkled her nose.

"You could always take him fudge and caramel chocolates." Heather pointed at the candy box.

Vivian smiled. Candy wouldn't win over her cowboy, but suddenly she knew exactly what would. She looked at her sister. "I know what to do, but I may need help."

"Count us all in," Heather promised.

Vivian got to work. She had one more fight in her and it had to be perfect. This was the biggest one yet. This one was for her heart and her cowboy's. And Vivian intended to win.

CHAPTER TWENTY-SEVEN

DAY FIVE. And Josh was starting his morning exactly the same as he had every morning since the gala. Since he lost his cowgirl. Staring at the closed guest bedroom door in the upstairs hallway, he waited for his cowgirl to burst into the hallway. Waited for a good morning kiss that wasn't coming. Not anytime soon. Not ever.

Not everything was the same. He took his coffee to go now. No lingering in the kitchen. No sticking around for conversation. He headed straight for the stables and the horses. Ignoring Dusty's empty stall, he worked and tried to avoid acknowledging the hole inside him. More of his horses would be checking out of the Sloan stables over the weekend, heading to their new homes. Everything was going to plan. His new year would start fresh in Houston.

Josh led Fox inside the back pasture and removed the thoroughbred's halter. Fox nudged Josh's shoulder as if sensing Josh's melancholy. Josh lingered, certain more time with his horses would give him the balance it always had in the past.

"Hey, Josh," a familiar voice called out.

Not the one he wanted to hear. Josh turned and saw Isabel leaning against the fence. Fox immediately trotted over to greet her. Josh followed, his steps slower. "Hey, Isabel. Didn't know you were coming by."

"I wanted to see you." Isabel stroked her glove-covered fingers across Fox's forehead. "I wanted to thank you for letting me ride Fox. For giving me a chance when you didn't have to. And apologize for not performing better."

"Isabel, you finished second in your first competition in over three years," Josh countered. "Don't apologize for that." Not to mention, she'd helped increase Fox's value.

Gratitude framed her smile. "You're a good guy, Josh Sloan."

Josh rested his forearms against the top rail. "You could've led with that."

Isabel chuckled and met his gaze. Her expression serious. Her words sincere. "What I should've led with days ago was an apology for how it all ended between us. I could've, no, I should have handled that differently."

Josh nodded, agreed there were things he should've handled better too in his first marriage, and considered his ex-wife. "But it would've ended the same. With you and me going our separate ways."

"We were a moment. One I don't regret." Isabel watched him. "But seeing you with Vivian. Well, I want that. I hope I can find it one day."

"What's that exactly?" Vivian was gone. Josh was alone. And the hurt was nothing anyone should hope for. Not ever.

"Don't you see?" Isabel asked. "You and I fell for the images of the people we wanted each other to be, not the people we were."

Josh rubbed his chin, but nothing stopped the truth from rolling through him. He'd fallen for Isabel because she was everything he thought he'd wanted—a rodeo queen immersed in the Western lifestyle. His lifestyle. But Isabel had wanted and needed something else. And he'd been too shortsighted to allow her the space to be who she was. He said, "Isabel. Now it's me who should apologize."

"We're both to blame and it's in the past. But your future," Isabel said, then arched an eyebrow at him, "is there anything you would change about Vivian? Anything you wished was different about her?"

He wished his cowgirl was there. With him. Right now. He shook his head. "I wouldn't change a thing about Vivian."

"That's what makes it special, what you have

with Vivian," Isabel said. "It's worth holding on to, no matter what it takes."

But wasn't holding on holding Vivian back? Josh frowned.

"Just think about it." Isabel smiled and adjusted the belt on her coat. "Well, I'm off to see my mother. But when I get settled and have my finances sorted, I'll be needing a competition horse. One like Fox, preferably."

"You have my number. Call me." Josh pushed away from the fence and grinned at his ex-wife. "See you around, Isabel."

One last wave and Isabel was gone. Josh was left with a new perspective and closure on his past. Not that it helped him see his future any clearer. With his work finished in the stables, he headed inside. He was intent on silencing those wishes in his heart and finalizing his next steps.

He spread the Bellmare contract out on the kitchen table and started to review the detailed document. The legalese had his head hurting after an hour, but he kept at it. The stakes were too high to miss something important.

The back door slammed shut. Footsteps echoed across the hardwood floors. Josh flipped to the next section of the contract.

"We've called a family meeting." That announcement came from his twin. Caleb dropped into the chair beside Josh and gathered the Bell-mare paperwork into a pile.

Josh stretched his arms over his head and frowned at his brother. "I was working on that."

"We've been working on something too." Grant sat in the chair directly across from Josh.

The rest of the family filed into the other chairs around the table, including Tess and Maggie. Uncle Roy and Grandpa Sam sat together at the head of the table. His twin hadn't been kidding. It was a full-family meeting. Josh rubbed his hand over his eyes. "If this is about Vivian, I'm not in the mood to talk about it."

"We've got an agenda," Carter declared, tapping his finger on a folder he set on the table. "We'll get to Vivian in a bit."

There was no 'getting to Vivian.' Not in a bit. Not in a while. Despite what Isabel had told him earlier, Vivian was where she needed to be—pursuing the life she wanted. Josh leaned back in his chair and crossed his arms over his chest. What could be more important than his cowgirl anyway?

"First, we've got a business proposal we'd like you to consider." Ryan slid the folder across the table toward Josh. "We'll wait while you look over everything."

"Take your time." Carter slipped his hand in

Tess's. "We've all cleared our schedules for the afternoon."

Tess smiled at Josh and added, "We'll be happy to answer any questions you might have."

"What is this?" Josh glanced around the table. No one answered him.

Uncle Roy simply dipped his chin toward the folder.

Josh opened the folder, noted the thick stack of official looking paperwork and read the cover page: Sloan Equestrian Training and Rehab Center. He read the cover page two more times, then looked at his grandfather. "What is this?"

"Just what it looks like." Grandpa Sam clasped his hands together and rested them on the table. "That is a business proposal we would like you to give serious consideration to before you sign on with Bellmare." He'd never heard his grandfather sound so formal.

"This is for a training center here in Three Springs." Josh flipped through the paperwork and noted the proforma, budget, five-year outlook. It was all there, laid out in the same detail as the Bellmare business proposal had been. Josh stopped on the last page and gaped at the organization chart. His name was listed as the managing director/owner. "You want me to run it."

"And design it too," Carter offered. "You know more of what you need than we do."

"We are just your investors." Ryan grinned and motioned toward the folder "It's all there in Section Five under ownership stakes."

"You're my investors," Josh repeated, even though his hearing was just fine. It was the believing piece he was struggling with.

"You'll have the majority ownership stake," Grant explained. "And we will share equal percentages of the remainder."

Josh leaned back in his chair and still couldn't quite get his thoughts in proper order. "Why would you do this?"

"Because we know a good investment when we see one." Grandpa Sam lifted his eyebrows at Josh, pride and conviction in his open gaze. "And you, Josh, are a very good investment."

Josh ran his hands over his face. "We can't just go and build an equestrian training and therapy center."

"Why not?" Carter looked and sounded confused. "We built a distillery here."

"And that hasn't turned out half bad either," Uncle Roy chimed in and laughed at Carter's frown.

"It's more than half bad," Carter countered.

"It would be better if you let your grandfather and I distill our own whiskey," Uncle Roy argued. Laughter spilled around the table.

His brother's distillery was award-winning and gaining more national recognition every year. And it had all started with an idea and a grassroots operation. Carter had built it up from there, transforming his passion into a profitable business. Could Josh do the same with an equestrian center? His family seemed to think so.

"Can we concentrate on Josh, please?" Caleb asked. "We'll get to your distilling wishes later, Uncle Roy. Right now, we have to convince Josh not to sign on with Bellmare and sign with us instead."

Grandpa Sam smoothed his fingers through his beard and eyed Josh. "Have any other questions for us, Josh?"

"Where are we going to build this equestrian center?" He stumbled over calling it the *Sloan* equestrian center. That sounded too surreal, like a wish he hadn't known he had.

"Right here." Caleb spread his arms wide. "Well, not *here* here. But you know what I mean."

No. Josh had no idea what his twin meant.

"It only seems right to put the Sloan Equestrian and Rehab Center on Sloan property," his grandfather explained and pushed another folder across the table. "This should explain things for you."

Josh inhaled and steadied himself. He opened the second folder and found himself thankful he was sitting already. It was the deed to Gran Claire's family farmhouse, with his name listed as the property owner. "But Gran Claire's family farmhouse belongs to Mom, not me." Or it was supposed to.

"Not anymore." His grandfather beamed at him. "Lilian signed the deed over to you before she returned to New York."

"We all agreed you should have the house, Josh," Grant said, his gaze steady, his words quiet.

The rest of Josh's brothers nodded. Caleb tapped his fist against Josh's shoulder. "It only makes sense. You're the only one who can restore it properly anyway."

"And you always loved that house more than any of us," Ryan said.

Josh was stunned.

"But the land is another part of the deal," his grandfather continued. "Your mother still owns that. And she's willing to allow the equestrian center to be built on the acreage. Although, she has terms for the land lease and a contract she'll want signed."

Ryan crossed his arms over his chest. "She

was very specific about the land not being a handout. Or a gift. Or anything like that."

"And Mom expects to earn a profit," Carter warned.

"If it's a deal breaker, we can find another piece of property," Caleb offered.

"But then it wouldn't be on Sloan land," Josh said. Not a part of the family legacy they were building. Together. And wasn't that the core of it all. Vivian hadn't been wrong. It wasn't about standing alone. It was about standing together that mattered more. And Josh was better with his family. Better because of them. He grinned. "I'll meet with Mom and work out the details on the property."

"So we're doing this?" Caleb asked, excitement in his tone.

"We're doing this," Josh announced. And together his family got to work on the details and the celebrating.

A plan in place, everyone retreated to the family room. Snack foods were set out. Carter's best bourbon served. Pool table wagers were placed. Laughter flowed easily. And Christmas cheer infused the evening with hope and joy. It was one of the best nights with his family that Josh could ever remember.

And yet there was still something—some-one—missing. Josh knew nothing would ever

really be complete without that special someone in his life. His world would be just a little
bit less without her in it.

Josh walked over to the Christmas tree, took
one of Gran Claire's bell ornaments and rang
it. Gaining his family's full attention, he announced, "I think it's time to bring my cowgirl
home for Christmas."

And if things went well, he'd ask her to stay
forever.

CHAPTER TWENTY-EIGHT

JOSH PULLED INTO the driveway at Gran Claire's property, or rather, his place. Though it was several days later, it still caught him off guard, calling the old ranch house his home. He couldn't wait to begin restoring the place and finally return it to a home as inviting as the farmhouse. Yet that wasn't for today.

Right now, he was supposed to be helping his grandfather's friend, Boone, get his truck restarted. Apparently, Boone had broken down and managed to pull into the property. Odd, no one was there. And Josh couldn't see any cars on the road in either direction.

Josh cut his truck engine and called his grandfather. Grandpa Sam greeted him on the first ring and Josh said, "Boone isn't here."

"Well, Boone must've figured out how to get his truck running again." Grandpa Sam paused. Josh heard muffled voices on the other end of the line. His grandpa quickly asked, "Can you check the storage barn and make sure Roy and I locked the doors?"

"I locked those barn doors when I left this morning." After he'd returned the decorations from the gala. Eventually they'd clear out the storage barn, but that was for another time. He had more important things to do, like practicing what he was going to say to his cowgirl. Josh reached for the truck keys in the ignition and said, "It's locked."

"Just check it again." His grandfather's words were rushed and insistent. "Can't be too careful."

"There's no one around." Josh sighed. "I'm fairly sure the sleigh and snowflake Christmas lights are safe in the barn. At least, until Santa might come calling."

"It won't take but a minute or two," Grandpa Sam argued. "Besides, you're already there."

"Fine." Josh pulled the keys from the ignition, climbed out and walked along the gravel driveway.

He'd rounded the house and crossed into the back of the property when he came to a standstill. Two rocking chairs were in the backyard proper. The same ones Josh and his Gran Claire used to sit on on the back porch of her family's old ranch house while they contemplated the stars and their troubles. The same chairs Josh and his grandfather had found in the storage barn just last week.

Only now, one of the rocking chairs was occupied. *Vivian*. His cowgirl was back. *Back home*. No, he refused to jump ahead. Instead, he approached slowly, his heart hammering in his chest. "Vivian. What are you doing?"

"Returning some things you seem to have lost." She lifted her hand and motioned toward a copse of trees where Artie and Dusty stood grazing. It looked like the pair had always been companions. Always together.

He took his time taking in his cowgirl. From her boots to her cowboy hat tilted just enough to shadow her face. He moved closer. His pulse raced even faster. "Is that so?"

"I have it on good authority that you used to sneak out of the farmhouse and come over here." Vivian set the rocking chair into motion. "For some front porch sitting."

"It was back porch sitting and contemplating with Gran Claire." He grinned at the memory. "Gran Claire always used to come and find me here." And never rushed him to return home. As if she'd known he needed the space and the time. He wasn't rushing now either because he needed this time with his cowgirl.

"Any chance you might consider sitting and contemplating things with someone new?" She tipped her head toward the empty rocking chair beside her.

He closed the distance, stopped just short of the tips of his cowboy boots touching hers. He watched her. "Who's offering?"

"Your cowgirl." She pushed herself out of the rocker and right into his space. Unafraid and unapologetic. "If you'll have her?"

"Vivian…" he started.

"Let me say this first." She raised her hand and stalled him. "I thought if I stopped, I'd be settling. That I'd regret it."

He regretted that she'd lowered her arm before he'd captured her hand in his.

"But then I realized that all this time I've been running, it was to find you," Vivian continued. Her bold gaze held his. "And my biggest regret will be not settling with you." She paused, inhaled, then rushed on as if fearful he didn't quite understand all that she meant. "I'm talking roots, Josh. A family of our own. A beautiful, complicated life we settle into together."

His fingers twitched. It was all he could do to keep his arms at his sides. He wanted to hold her, draw her into his arms at last. But he refused to rush this. There were things he had to tell her. He asked, "Where exactly do you plan to do all this settling?"

"Wherever. It doesn't matter. As long as it's

with you." One corner of her mouth lifted. "If you'll have us."

He arched an eyebrow. Tipped his head. "Us?"

"Me. Dusty. Artie. We're kind of a package deal." Vivian lifted one shoulder and continued, "Then, there's also my parents. Heather and Wade. Their kids too."

Josh scratched his cheek. "Sounds crowded."

Her eyes flared slightly. The first hint of uncertainty slipped around her words. "Do you mind?"

He shook his head and held back his smile as her shoulders relaxed. "I was just thinking we might need to add a second story to the ranch house. To make sure we have enough guest rooms for everyone when they visit."

Her eyes widened. "You have a house in Houston already?"

"No." He pointed his thumb over his shoulder. "I have a house right here."

She stilled. It took only a minute for her confusion to shift to wonder. "This is yours."

"The ranch house is all mine." *Ours, if you'll have me.* He slowed himself down then said, "The land is part of a business arrangement we can talk about later."

"Yes," she said.

He searched her face. "Yes, what?"

"Yes, I want to invest in you." She held his

gaze, steady and so very sure. "Invest in us, really. In our future."

She really was all in. Really meaning to settle. With him. And build something together. His heart finally slowed. Finally settled too. Still, he countered, "You don't know any of the details."

"I don't need them." She reached up, set her hand over his heart. "I know you."

She humbled him. His cowgirl who'd believed in him from the very start. Who never expected him to be anyone but who he was. That was a gift. She was a treasure. He gave in to his desire then. Reaching up, he traced his fingers across her cheek and tucked her hair behind her ear. "That's one of the many reasons I love you."

Her gasp was softer than Santa's footsteps on a rooftop. Her words lighter than falling snowflakes. "You love me."

"Yes. Very much." He leaned in and pressed a gentle kiss against her mouth. "We'll get to all that, but I have things I need to say."

She set her hands on his shoulders, lifted onto the balls of her feet and kissed him back. Just a brush of her lips against his. Over and gone. She grinned. "Sorry. I had to do that. Go ahead. I'm listening now."

"But now I'm distracted." By the gleam in

her gaze, the flash of her dimples and the radiance in her expression. By her, simply. And his love for her.

He curved his arms around her waist and pulled her into him. She linked her hands behind his neck and met him halfway for a kiss that spoke right to his heart and a love that would only grow stronger. For a kiss that promised together. And things like lifetimes and forever.

Finally, he slowed the kiss and eased away, only far enough to meet her gaze. "I'm sorry for pushing you away, Vivian."

"Don't do it again," she ordered, then added in a softer tone, "And I won't leave again. I'll fight for us, Josh. Always."

Us. The word filled him. His cowgirl and him. Together. There was nothing more he wanted. Nothing he wouldn't do for her. For them. "You are more than I deserve, Vivian. I promise to show you how much I love you, every day."

"I love you, Josh Sloan." Vivian held him tight. "And as long as you are beside me, I'll have all I ever need."

They shared another kiss, content to linger. But it wasn't to be. Both their phones chimed at the same time, interrupting their moment.

Josh kept his arms around Vivian. "Aren't you going to answer your phone?"

Vivian chuckled, shook her head and tucked herself closer against him. "I know who it is. You don't need to answer your phone either."

Josh set his chin on the top of her head. "Who is it?"

"Your family." There was a smile in her words. Laughter on her face. "I needed a little help getting you out here."

He grinned, already guessing his grandfather had been in on things. And if Grandpa Sam knew, then his entire family did too. He released her, yet captured her hand in his, not wanting to let her go completely. "We should head back to the farmhouse and fill them in before they all drive over here."

"Can we take the long way?" Vivian motioned to Dusty and Artie.

"Definitely," Josh said. "And you can tell me how it is that Artie is back home when he's supposed to be at Miles Nesci's stables, getting acquainted with his new owners."

"Artie already has a family." Vivian squeezed Josh's hand and walked with him over to the horses. "I called Miles and explained things to him. He was very understanding."

Miles Nesci was a hardworking rancher, tough and outspoken and rarely accommodating. Josh waited while Vivian mounted Dusty bareback, then he walked over to Artie and did the same. He guided the Arabian onto the trail that led back to the farmhouse and kept their pace slow. "Well, are you going to tell me what really happened with Miles?"

"I convinced him Artie wasn't the best choice for him." Vivian lifted one shoulder, then slanted a sheepish grin at Josh. "And then I convinced Miles that you would find and train the competition horse that would be. I know I overstepped. It's just…"

"It's just perfect." Josh set his hand on her leg. "I never wanted to lose Artie."

That statement released Vivian's reserve. And Vivian recited word-for-word her conversation with Miles Nesci. The only interruptions being their shared laughter and the few times Josh paused to ask if his amazing cowgirl had really said what she'd said. Too soon, the horses were back in their stalls for the night.

Outside the stables, Vivian grabbed Josh's hand and slowed. "That looks like my parents' RV in the driveway. Josh, is that?"

"Yes." He squeezed her fingers and smiled. "They're back."

Vivian slanted her gaze toward him. "Why?"

He shrugged, tried to sound indifferent. "I invited them to spend Christmas here."

"But you didn't know I was here," she said, confusion evident on her face.

"This is where it gets a little complicated." He chuckled at her exasperated expression, pulled her into his arms and pressed a kiss on the crease between her eyebrows. "I had this whole plan to go to Phoenix. To win back my cowgirl."

She relaxed against him and linked her arms around his waist. "You were coming for me."

"Always," he said solemnly. Serious and heartfelt. "You aren't the only one who will be fighting for us."

Her smile was like standing in the full sunshine. She tipped her head and studied him. "I'm still not following how my family ended up back here."

"I called your mom," he confessed. "Like you tapped my family for help earlier, I knew I might need assistance for my win-back-my-cowgirl plan."

Vivian nodded. One side of her mouth was tipped up. "Good call. Mom must have loved being included."

"It turned out to be your entire family." Each one had an opinion and suggestion for Josh and they hadn't been shy about sharing their thoughts. Not that he'd been surprised. Her family loved Vivian as much as he did. He grinned. "They all wanted in on it."

Vivian laughed. The sound dipped in joy and delight.

That made him smile more. He continued, "Anyway, after much debate, your mom announced that they would come here instead of another Christmas spent on a beach or in a hotel. Because according to your family, Three Springs is where you belong, so that's where they should be. And I knew better than to argue with my future in-laws."

"Future in-laws," she whispered. Her gaze searched his. "Then, we are really doing this?"

"Settling in together. Building roots together. And hopefully with a family of our own." That was their future. He could see it so clearly now. A proposal. A wedding. A lifetime together. Nothing he'd been looking for but everything he needed. "Yes, we are. And it starts right now."

"With our first Christmas." She linked her hand with his and leaned into his side. "Together."

EPILOGUE

ON CHRISTMAS MORNING, Vivian opened the door of her room at the Sloan farmhouse and laughed harder than she'd ever remembered laughing before. More than a dozen bundles of mistletoe, each tied with a brilliant red velvet bow, hung from the ceiling. The bundles lined the entire length of the hallway. Vivian shifted her gaze from the surprise mistletoe to her cowboy across the hall.

Josh stood in the open doorway to his room, one shoulder leaning against the frame. His grin was one-sided. His eyebrows twitched. "Wasn't me."

Another door opened. Caleb stepped into the hallway and pointed at the ceiling above Vivian's head. "The first bunch of mistletoe was my idea." Caleb shrugged and looked sheepish, although his amusement was clear. "The rest of it was all Maggie's doing. So complain to her. I know I will be."

Vivian wasn't about to complain. But she

would thank her friend as soon as she saw her. Vivian smiled at Josh.

"Don't be too long. You guys are on breakfast duty this morning," Caleb said, then turned and headed for the stairs. "Vivian promised me as many of her buttermilk pancakes as I could eat, and I'm warning you now, it's going to be a lot."

"He sounds hungry," Vivian said, unconcerned.

"He can wait." Josh pushed away from the door frame and met Vivian under the first bundle of mistletoe. "It seems we have a tradition to uphold."

"It would be bad luck if we didn't follow through." Vivian looped her arms around Josh's neck. "That's not a good way to start our first Christmas together."

Josh bent toward her. Vivian leaned in for a sweet, gentle kiss. Then her cowboy took her hand in his and said, "This is becoming my favorite part of the morning."

"Mine too." Vivian walked down the hallway beside Josh. They stopped several more times before they finally made it downstairs and into the kitchen.

Caleb kept to his word and powered through one pancake after another. Vivian eventually stopped counting, too distracted by the Christmas hugs from her family and the Sloans as well as the lively conversations that stretched from the kitchen to the family room. Breakfast ended and Maggie declared a new family tradition.

Gifts could only be opened if everyone wore an ugly Christmas sweater. Maggie even provided new sweater options for the entire group. That started an even livelier debate about who should wear which sweater. It was close to lunch before everyone finally agreed on what sweater to wear. Vivian secretly liked her hot-pink-and-black sweater with a Christmas-bedazzled, pink-flamingo couple on the front. That no one else seemed in any rush to change out of their sweaters hinted they all secretly liked them too.

The entire day was full and happy and the evening was looking to be much more of the same. The only time the house quieted was when the doorbell rang minutes before dinner. The sound surprised even the Sloans, with Sam declaring that no one had used the front door in ages. He hadn't even recognized the sound of the doorbell.

Having been shooed from the cooking and dinner-prep area and wanting something to do, Vivian announced she'd get the door.

Vivian opened the front door and smiled at

the older woman waiting outside. She was polished and sophisticated from her precision-cut, chin-length bob to her understated pearl earrings to her tailored cashmere coat.

"You must be Vivian." The woman's smile and words were reserved. "I'm Lilian Sloan."

"My mother," Josh said. His hand landed on Vivian's lower back, and he opened the front door wider. "Come on in, Mother. Glad you could make it."

Josh's mom was there? Vivian had hoped Lilian would come when Josh had mentioned he'd talked to his brothers about extending an invitation to their mother. He'd never confirmed whether he'd actually invited Lilian or not. Only told Vivian that the brothers had all agreed. Vivian hadn't wanted to press the issue. She wanted to help Josh and his mother mend their relationship, but she also understood it was going to take time. Still, this was an important first step for both son and mother.

Vivian extended her hand. "It's a pleasure to meet you, Dr. Sloan."

"Lilian, please." Josh's mother touched her earring. "I would've been here sooner, but I got distracted going through the boxes Sam set aside for me in the storage barn."

Vivian peered at Lilian closer. Lilian's eyes were red-rimmed, and her smile strained. Vivian wasn't sure how to comfort her and said, "I'd be happy to help you in the storage barn if you need it."

"That's very kind." There was a softness in Lilian's gaze. "But I fear some walks down memory lane are best taken alone."

"Still, the offer stands, from both of us," Josh added.

Vivian saw hope on Lilian's face. Felt it inside herself. All was not lost between mother and son. And that was a Christmas gift worth celebrating.

"Before we head inside with the others, I have something I want to give you both." Lilian bent down, picked up a box on the doorstep and handed it to Josh. "I came across this today and wanted you to have it."

Vivian removed the lid and tissue paper, peered inside the box. Wonder seized her. "It's a snow globe."

"Not just any snow globe." Lilian moved beside Vivian. Her fingers drifted lightly over the top of the glass globe. "This one belonged to my grandmother. It sat on her fireplace mantel for as long as I can remember. When I was a kid, I believed there was magic inside it."

Vivian liked knowing Lilian once had a whimsical side, even if it was years ago. Vivian carefully lifted the snow globe out of the box and admired the holiday-decorated home inside, surrounded by snow-topped trees and festive garland. A horse-drawn red sleigh sat on a cobblestone bridge in front of the house. It was a perfect Christmas scene.

Josh set the box down. He looked for and flipped the switch on the snow globe base, sending the snow swirling and casting the entire scene in a warm, soft glow. "You mean the fireplace mantel at the ranch house."

"Yes." Lilian's expression turned wistful. "Now that it's your house, I thought perhaps you might want to put it back on the mantel. It was always Gran Claire's favorite."

Vivian suspected it was Lilian's favorite too. She held up the snow globe for a closer look. "It's beautiful. It should stay out all the time. To remind us of family and the magic of the season all year round."

"I couldn't agree more," Josh said.

Lilian nodded. "I'm glad to know it has found its way back to where it belongs."

Vivian hoped, in time, Lilian would find her way back with the help of her sons and family.

"Shall we head in?" Josh smiled at Vivian and his mother. "Dinner is about to be served and we definitely don't want to miss out on this family feast."

Vivian returned the snow globe to the box

for safekeeping, then linked one arm around Josh's and the other around Lilian's. "I didn't think this day could get any better, but it has."

She had her family. A place to belong. And Josh beside her. It was the best Christmas she could've asked for. Yet she knew in her heart it was only the beginning of many more Christmases to come. Together with her cowboy.

* * * * *